"Adrenaline junkies with a heart for a great story will love *The Forsaken*. Men everywhere will see themselves in these pages, which will further engross them. I don't think I've ever read fiction that speaks more directly to me as a man."

—KENNY LUCK, men's pastor at Saddleback Church
and author of *Risk* and *Every Man, God's Man*

"*The Forsaken* is a riveting story with a most compelling message. Steve Arterburn brings the truth of a healthy lifestyle together with a fictional account that is just plain and simple exciting."

—JIM BURNS, PHD, president of the daily radio broadcast
*Home-Word* and author of *The 10 Building Blocks
for a Happy Family*

### Praise for
### Every Man Fiction

"The Every Man novels thrill as well as challenge—an exhilarating, uplifting thrill ride that I know readers will enjoy!"

—JOSH MCDOWELL, best-selling author and speaker

"The Every Man fiction series creates another tidal wave of encouragement for men! You'll be strengthened as well as entertained by these cutting-edge novels!"

—SHANNON and GREG ETHRIDGE, co-authors
of *Every Woman's Marriage*

# THE FORSAKEN

**Resources for Men and Women
from the Best-Selling Every Man Series**

*Every Man's Battle*
*Every Man's Marriage*
*Every Man, God's Man*
*Preparing Your Son for Every Man's Battle*
*Every Man's Challenge*
*Every Day for Every Man*

*Every Woman's Battle*
*Every Heart Restored*
*Preparing Your Daughter for Every Woman's Battle*
*Every Woman, Every Day*
*Every Woman's Marriage*

an everyman novel

# THE FORSAKEN

# STEPHEN ARTERBURN
# AND MICHAEL MOSCOE

WaterBrook
PRESS

THE FORSAKEN
PUBLISHED BY WATERBROOK PRESS
12265 Oracle Boulevard, Suite 200
Colorado Springs, Colorado 80921
*A division of Random House Inc.*

ISBN 1-4000-7037-6

Library of Congress Cataloging-in-Publication Data
Arterburn, Stephen, 1953–
    The forsaken : an every man novel / by Stephen Arterburn and Michael
Moscoe.—1st ed
      p. cm
    ISBN 1-4000-7037-6
    1. Kidnapping—Fiction. 2. Spouses—Fiction. 3. Psychological fiction. I. Moscoe, Mike. II. Title.
    PS3601.R76F67 2006
    813'.54—dc22

                                                                    2006002835

Printed in the United States of America
2006—First Edition

10  9  8  7  6  5  4  3  2  1

**1**

**"BOSS, WE GOT A SITUATION AT THE PLANT."**

That wasn't something I wanted to hear from my secretary. She'd been with me for years, and her talent was for understatement, not dramatics.

So Bea's next words, "You better beat feet," were unnecessary. I was already up and hurrying around my desk. I grabbed the doorjamb of my office and swung myself in the direction of the main door as I picked up speed. It had been a while since I double-timed for miles in the army, but I like to think that chasing my teenagers keeps me in shape.

"Where?" I asked as I sped by my secretary.

"In milling," Bea said. "Jim Turner's got a knife at Danny Greg's throat," she added in answer to my next, unasked, question.

"Tell them I'm on my way," I said. But she was already on the phone with the news. Bea was good. Her talent at mind reading was just one of the many reasons I'd hired her to be the first face folks saw when they came into Human Resources. She knew when

1

to smile and when to answer the next question, even if it was unspoken, and when to press the panic button.

It looked like she'd decided it was panic time.

Of course, so had I.

I sprinted out of the office like the best middle-aged Olympian and headed down the hall for the back door. But I was praying even faster than I was running. *Dear God, help Jim. He was having enough problems already. Keep him together until I get there. And show me a way to help him.* I figured Danny must have shot his mouth off with poor Jim in hearing distance. But knowing why we were in a crisis didn't make the situation any better.

As usual, the good Lord didn't voice an answer to my prayer. I don't know what I'd do if He ever did. Today, my Savior was content to toss the balls my way...and I had a feeling He enjoyed watching me juggle.

I'd known Jim Turner for all of the fifteen years I'd worked at Carter Cutlery. This wasn't like him. He was nice to a fault, but quick to turn his back when those of us at the plant's picnic lunch tables said grace. "You want to find Jesus, I'll tell you where I dumped Him off my slick in the central highlands of Vietnam. If He ain't walked out, He's likely still there."

Yeah, Jim had always been very definite about standing on his own two feet, bending to no one. Until a marine officer, with a chaplain in tow, had made a visit to his house a month ago. The marine told Jim that his youngest boy would be coming home early from the war. In a casket.

2

The boy's young wife, seven months pregnant, had insisted on a church funeral. We at the plant had chipped in for more than flowers and meals. I'd been a Casualty Assistance Officer back during my four years in the service; I helped the widow find a church with a pastor who didn't mind ministering to people he'd never seen before.

I'd heard that Jim and his wife were talking to a counselor about their loss. If my secretary was right, I guess they hadn't talked enough.

Like so much of America, our employees at the plant were of several minds about the war overseas. We make the knives that a lot of the men over there count on, and every blade leaves here with a lot of prayers for the soldiers' safety attached to it. Of that, I'm absolutely sure. But above and beyond that, we all had our opinions about how we could best support the troops that carry our knives.

I wondered just what Danny had said to tip Jim off the deep end.

"God, don't let me waste time on the wrong questions. What I need just now are the words to haul my people out of that deep pit. Help me haul them both back with no blood spilled," I whispered as I ran.

Usually, I love the wide expanse of lawn that separates my office from the main plant. Today, it was an obstacle that took too long to cross. I just picked my legs up and put them down, breathing deep of the spring afternoon air so I wouldn't show up in the plant too winded to do anything.

I raced into the plant, a local landmark faced with intricate brickwork that dated from the 1920s, past the cutting and grinding machines where workers were standing around. The men and women were no longer converting steel into knives, but watching, their wide eyes fixed on the drama in the milling section.

Everyone had backed away from the two men involved in a life-or-death scuffle. They left a clear space around Jim. He was a tall, dark-haired man now going gray, with a fair complexion. But at this moment, his face was red with rage. He held a roughed-out example of one of our fine bowie knives at Danny's throat.

Danny was pale as if he'd seen a ghost. His own.

Near those two stood Jeb Shepherd, the day shift general foreman. Several section foremen had gathered around him. They were silent. Not one was making a move against Jim. I guessed they were all talked out.

I joined the group at Jeb's elbow. "Bea said you called."

"Yeah," Jeb said. "As you can see, we got a situation here."

"Maybe I can help," I said quietly.

"It's all yours," Jeb said and stepped back even farther. The foremen followed suit.

I was left standing in the open, looking at Jim and Danny.

"I'm gonna kill him," Jim shouted to me, following his promise with a stream of the kind of language I hadn't heard since my army days.

"You think Danny needs killing?" I asked. "I kind of like him better alive."

4

"I'm gonna kill him. He said my boy's dying was a waste."

"I didn't, I didn't," Danny pleaded.

"Shush," I said to Danny in a soft command. "You've said enough."

Danny shut up.

"Police?" I whispered aside to Jeb.

He shook his head. Carter Cutlery took care of its own. It wasn't in any of the personnel policies I'd written. No, this mandate had over a hundred and seventy-five years of unspoken practice behind it and didn't need to be in print to put it in full force.

But in this case, everyone else at Carter had taken their best shot and come up empty. I was the last hope. *Dear God, please show me the path for my feet.*

"If I'm not getting somewhere with this pretty fast, call the cops," I whispered to Jeb. Then I motioned Jeb and the others to step back even further. As they did, I sat down cross-legged on the concrete floor.

It still had winter cold to it, but I ignored the discomfort even as it sent a chill up my spine. *Finally*, I thought. *A reason to shiver that has nothing to do with the situation I'm in.*

I looked up at Jim, locked eyes with him. "See, I'm not coming any closer. We're just gonna talk. This making you feel better?"

The bowie knife blank, its edge dull, was pushing at the flesh of Danny's throat. It wasn't cutting anything...yet. Put enough pressure on it, and even a dull knife will cut human flesh. And there was always the point, already wickedly deadly, even on a knife blank.

The blank's point was less than an inch from Danny's carotid artery.

I prayed that Jim would listen, just listen to me long enough to let me break through his fury.

It took a while for my question to make its way past Jim's pain and rage. When it did, he shook his head. "Nothing feels good. I'm never gonna take my boy fishing. Never play football with him again. It's all gone."

"I know," I said quietly.

"But it ain't wasted," he growled, working the knife a bit deeper against Danny's throat. "It ain't a waste."

Danny whimpered, but for once he had the good sense to say nothing.

"No, Jim, it's not a waste. A good person like your boy is never wasted. I remember him when he was just a kid, coming to the Christmas parties. What was he—eight, maybe?—when he tried to walk off with Santa's whole bag?"

"Seven," Jim said. "And I whopped him for that." But the edges of his mouth turned up at the memory. The boy had gotten the huge sack halfway across the room before anyone noticed. We'd all been laughing so hard that the "whopping" hadn't been more than a gentle admonition.

"And he was always in the front at the games come the annual picnic," I said, remembering him paired with my son in the two-legged race. The two of them were only three years apart in age and they'd been such friends. The thought of my son as a soldier sent colder chills down my spine than the floor.

But Jim was nodding at my words, and I dropped that thought and gave him my full attention.

"He was always fast," he said. "And he always wanted to be a soldier. Nothing I said about Nam could change that. Nothing," Jim said slowly. "And nothing I do is going to change my boy being gone." His voice was now a shattered whisper.

"No," I said as softly as I could.

"Why? Why did it have to happen?"

I let Jim's question rise to the rafters. How could I answer when I didn't understand it myself?

"You're a Christian," Jim said. "You tell me. Why did my boy have to die?"

Not only did I not understand why, but I'd never even heard an answer to that question that a grieving man like Jim could understand.

"I don't know, Jim. It's a tragedy. But I do know that your boy wouldn't want you doing this. Didn't you say that he joined the army to help people? To save the weak from tyrants? You said he wanted to stand up to the bullies for those who couldn't."

Jim was nodding along as I repeated his words of eulogy at his son's funeral.

"Your boy wouldn't do something like this. You taught him better."

"But I'm never going to be with him again." Sobs broke through as the words broke Jim down. The knife was loose at Danny's throat. Danny looked like he was ready to bolt. I froze him with a glare.

I stood slowly as Jim sobbed. I believed that Jim would one day be with his boy again before God. Maybe a better man would have found a way to witness to Jim at that moment. Me, I just edged slowly up to the man, put one arm around him while using the other one to lower the knife from Danny's throat.

Jim let me. He let me enfold him in a hug like I prayed God would someday do. *Holy Spirit of God, You alone give the grace of salvation to all. I know You got Your work cut out for You with Jim, but I sure wish You could hurry things up here. This big guy is hurting.*

I held Jim while he sobbed. I kept holding him, feeling the cold steel painfully close to my own vulnerable belly until Jim finally dropped the rough knife. I held him as Jeb sent the crew back to work, though I noticed Danny bolt for the break room. I wondered if he had a spare set of underwear stashed there. I imagined he would need them.

I was still holding Jim as his sobs wore down to tears. I loaned him my clean handkerchief when he started sniffling. "I guess I'd better get back to work," Jim finally said, looking around at the others already back at their tools.

"No," I said, shaking my head slowly.

"You're gonna fire me," Jim said with absolute confidence and more self-loathing than I'd seen in one man since I'd accompanied a drunk-but-soon-sobered-up soldier to visit his torn-up buddy at the hospital after their car wreck. I'd almost lost that boy to suicide.

"No," I told Jim, noting how Jeb and the other foremen were looking on. "I'm not going to fire you. But we have a counseling program, Jim. You really need to spend some time talking this out. We'll save your job for you, but you're going to be on sick leave for a while."

"Who's gonna want to work with me?" Jim said, dejection heavy in his voice.

"There's a place for you in my section," said Momma Boyd, a big, round African American who ran the finishing section. She'd lost her first husband in Nam, and somehow she had survived that agony and gone on to make a life for herself with a new husband and several kids from both marriages. If there was anyone I knew who could show Jim that there was life after grief, Mamma Boyd was that person.

Of course, several of her crew were wives with husbands over there. Working with a man grieving over the loss of his son would be an ever-present reminder of what could be their future.

Momma Boyd must have read my mind. She just smiled at me the way only a person of faith can. "The courage that it takes to love the man facing the gunman is no less than the courage it takes to face the gun. Right, gals?"

Several of the women behind her nodded. There would be a job waiting for Jim when he got back. Carter Cutlery takes care of its own.

I walked Jim out of the plant and across the field to where my office was in the old building. This walk was a lot slower than my run over. There was time for the sun to heal some of the raw nerves the day had exposed. Time for my own shaking legs, quaking stomach, pounding heart, to calm down.

*Lord, I know You promised that all things work for the good to those who love You. I just wish You could make my weak flesh believe it a bit more.*

I think my Savior enjoyed a laugh at my expense.

But the soft breeze across the field brought the loving scent of the earth coming alive. There's hope in every spring. Even in the depths of Jim's dark winter, I think the sunshine and grassy smells touched him somewhere deep inside. There seemed to be less despair and self-loathing in the man who finished the walk with me than the man who began it.

Back in my office, Al, the gal who handles employee benefits, had already called to make an emergency appointment for Jim with our mental health services provider. "If you can get him there in fifteen minutes, there's an opening."

"We can make it," I said.

Jim's eyes looked like a whipped pup's. "I don't know where I'm going. I don't... I, uh, I don't think I'm fit to drive," he said, thoroughly beaten by the day.

"I'll get you there. I can drive your car," I said, then I cut off his instinctive protest by reaching into my pocket and tossing my keys at my assistant, Max.

She caught them and my unspoken request. "And I'll follow you and bring you back," she said, taking her cue from me. I run a personnel *team*, I do, and we are quite a team when the fur is flying.

As I headed out the door, I waved at Al. "Call Jeb," I whispered. "Tell him to send Danny over here. He's not going to be good for much work today, and I suspect he's got a few things to say to me. Or had best say to me," I said with a rueful smile. "I'll see him as soon as I get back."

Al nodded and reached for the phone

We got Jim to the counseling service. After making sure that things were going well there, I checked with Bea. She'd called Jim's wife and arranged for her to get off work and meet us at the plant. I drove Max back to the office and got there in time to run into Danny coming in.

Danny was understandably furious.

"He had no call to do that to me," he said. "No call. That was assault. I know the law. Assault with a deadly weapon. He could have killed me."

There was no use arguing that one with the man. Danny was right. I nodded, motioned Danny into my office and sat down, ready to listen to him as long as was needed. I hadn't been in Personnel very long before I learned there are some arguments just not worth winning.

After five minutes of running in that circle, Danny was about out of steam. That was when I leaned over and said, "But you did say that whole thing over there is a waste, didn't you?"

"I didn't know he was behind me. And it is. It is."

"I'm not going to argue that war with you. We'd be here until Christmas if we tried, and that's not what Carter pays us to do. But did you really mean to tell Jim his boy had died for nothing? For a waste?"

"As God is my witness, Ben, I'd never have done that. Never."

"But you did, didn't you?"

The man in the chair across from me deflated as he let a long breath out. "I sure did. Didn't mean to, but I did it, didn't I?"

"You sure did. Not exactly what God had in mind when he said that those who mourn would be comforted."

Danny rubbed his throat; I could barely make out a trace of red where the knife blank had been held to it. It had been a tense few minutes, but it looked like we'd gotten through the situation without even a drop of blood shed.

"I don't know how I can apologize to the man," Danny said. "I never would have done it if I'd knowed I was doing it."

"And I suspect by tomorrow, or next week, Jim will know that. Then you can apologize to him. And he can apologize to you."

Danny sat there for a while, I suspect doing a careful bit of soul-searching. Finally he shook his head.

"I can't believe I'm sayin' this, but that sounds about right. For now, though, I better get back on the line."

"I think you've had enough for today. I'll clear sick leave with your boss. You go on home, and we'll start a new slate, a clean one, tomorrow."

He slunk out of my office, past Jim's wife, who was talking to Max. Danny said not a word to her in passing. *Just as well, I suspect. Sometimes the only way out of a hole you dig yourself into is to take time to let things go. It takes time, and not digging the hole any deeper.*

I sat in on Max's session with Jim's wife. I couldn't think of anything to add to her briefing on what had happened and what the company was doing about it. I drove the woman over to the counselors. She was holding back tears as they admitted her to a couple's session with Jim.

All in all, it had been quite a day. Once I got back to my office, I put my head in my hands and let the shakes take me. We'd skinned through this disaster, but it had been a close one. I'd be reliving it in nightmares for weeks, I figured.

By the time my hands stopped shaking, I noticed that it was well past quitting time. And I'd gotten practically nothing done on today's to-do list.

Tomorrow, like I'd told Danny, was another day. The things on my list would still be waiting for me. For right now, I was going home.

It was time I turned my attention to my family.

I was supposed to pick the kids up at school. I called my wife, Annie, to see if she could fill in for me while I spun out the last few loose ends from today, and struck out. She didn't even wait for me to explain why I'd called before she told me that she'd had a long day too. So I was still on kid patrol. I took a deep breath and looked at my hands again. They were steady, even if I felt like I'd run a marathon. I could handle the school run, but I wasn't good for much more.

After another call to Annie, we agreed that neither of us was in any shape to cook, so we arranged to meet at our favorite Mexican food place.

I got the kids without incident and collapsed once I hit the restaurant. They had our usual table free for us, a secluded corner where we could debrief each other on the day. Everybody else chimed in as we put paid to another day in the life of our family. I just kept quiet and watched the kids and my wife go at it. I hoped that they wouldn't notice my withdrawal from them and tried to enjoy the slow return of normalcy.

I wondered if I should tell them what my day had been like. In the meantime I let the daily trivia of their lives roll over me. It looked like Andy would make the track team, but he needed new shoes.

Joy was having a ball in the band but believed that the girl next to her had to be dyslexic. "The bandmaster orders a right turn, and she goes left every time. If she played a clarinet like me, it wouldn't be so bad, but she's got a trombone, and that can really get in your face," my daughter said, rubbing her nose.

"Well," my wife said, "the dock handlers dropped a whole container of furniture from Romania. I don't know how much of it we can still sell...and how much of it won't be good for anything but kindling. Very expensive kindling."

Somehow that seemed funny to the kids. Annie's scowl at their humor only made it funnier for them.

"How'd your day go, Dad?" my son asked. Some time back he'd decided that his best revenge for being asked how school went every day was to ask me how things went at the office.

I wondered if they really wanted to know. Sometimes I felt a bit like I was supposed to be the rock in their storms, the person who held steady while they had tempests all around me. They were so involved in their teenage drama that I occasionally felt a bit invisible. It might be a mistake, I thought, to shake that image.

I told them anyway.

Their eyes went so wide I swear you could see brains at the edges. Then they checked me out like a bargain shopper in Filene's Basement, looking for flaws. I was pronounced, thankfully for us all, unharmed and still functional. But I think the image of me talking down a guy with a knife shook them.

It certainly put kind of a crimp in the lighthearted gossip at that table. And it put a bit of distance between me and my family that I didn't expect. They seemed to pull away a bit, maybe to give me space. I pulled away a bit, too, seeing how my words upset them. Much later I wondered if that didn't have something to do with what was about to happen to us all. But at that moment, it was enough to have made it through the day unharmed.

We ended up with Andy leading us in prayer. First, my son said a prayer of thanksgiving to God that the day and my situation at the plant had turned out so well and then a prayer of petition for

God's help for Jim and his wife in their grief and for Danny in his anger. My silent prayer was from one father to Another that my son would continue in his education through college before putting on a uniform. It was followed by a prayer that this war might be over before that time came. And that no new wars would have started.

And so, after all the excitement, the day ended, like so many others, with us going home together to do homework. The children's homework...and the parents' homework.

I didn't know then that it was the calm before the storm.

"HONEY, COULD YOU GET THE KIDS OFF TO SCHOOL TODAY?"
Annie called as I cut off the water for my morning shower. Drying
myself, I glanced at the dressing table where my wife of twenty
years seemed to be applying her makeup a bit more meticulously
than normal.

"Early meeting to straighten up that dropped container yesterday?" I asked.

She nodded ever so slightly, so as not to mess the eye shadow
she was applying around her blue eyes.

"I still say you should hire some of those out-of-work wood-
workers from North Carolina to fix that Romanian furniture shipment you broke."

"I didn't break it, the dock crane operator dropped it, and I
have your suggestion under advisement," she said, giving me the
quick glance in the mirror my suggestion deserved. It hadn't taken
me twenty years to learn where her hot buttons were, or her
mine, and now we knew just how to dance around them without
tripping.

On my way to my dresser I ran my hand over her bare shoulder. Her creamy skin begged to be caressed. Maybe my fingers did dip a bit down inside her slip.

"Mister, you trying to make this poor working girl late?" she asked with a slight shiver.

I wrapped a golden wisp of her hair back around the professional bun it had escaped from. "Seems to me you've been on time every day this week."

"Right," she said giving me the eye in the mirror. "It's Tuesday."

"If we get it over with early in the week...," I said, kissing her neck invitingly.

She shook her head. "I have to get this furniture problem fixed before noon. Roberts wants to have lunch with me."

I started getting dressed, trying to keep my face neutral. I did not like her CEO. I didn't like the way he looked at my wife. I didn't like the way he talked to her. Come to think of it, there wasn't anything I liked about Bob Roberts. Well, with his track record, I wouldn't have to worry about him for too long. He never stayed anywhere much longer than his second annual report.

"Heard anything from the riot down the hall?" I asked, accepting the job of seeing that our offspring made it to the school bus with at least three seconds to spare.

"Not a peep," Annie said, finishing her makeup and reaching for a blouse. Yep, she was going power suit today. Her taste was impeccable. After all, she'd said yes to me.

Pants on, and buttoning my shirt, I slung a tie over my shoulder and headed down the hall.

There was no sound from Joy's room. A fourteen-year-old daughter deserved some privacy; I rapped on the door and got a mumbled, "I'm up," that sounded very not. I didn't challenge Joy by opening the door. *Dear God, there is a lot worse in this sinful world than a girl saying she's up when she's still under the covers.* So far, Annie and I were pretty sure Joy was navigating the rocks and shoals of this vale of tears with no more than the usual upsets. *Please God, keep her safe in Your arms,* I prayed, as I rapped on my son's door.

"Go away. Isn't it Saturday yet?" came back at me.

"Nope, not even close to Friday, me bucko. So roll out of bed, slap some clean clothes on, and get downstairs in time to eat the nutritious breakfast I'm going to cook for you."

"Microwave," he shot back.

"Whatever," I answered to the sound of his feet, big and still growing, hitting the deck.

I listened as Andy rapped on the wall to his sister's room. "Wake up, sleeping beauty. If I'm up, you'd better be up," he said.

Her reply, "Go soak your head," was muffled by growing distance as I headed downstairs.

Reasonably sure that sibling bickering would keep them both on the road to getting presentable for the day, I went to check what was in the refrigerator. Oops.

Neither Annie nor I had found time to hit the store this weekend. *Where had the time all gone?* I blinked, trying to remember how the weekend's two "free" days had vanished: school stuff, work stuff, yard stuff, church stuff. Stuff in general. Oh, right.

Promising myself to shop tonight on the way home, or maybe call Annie before quitting time and see if she could handle a bread-and-milk run, I fished out four individual boxes of orange juice and went looking for something that might pass for protein.

I recovered a half-empty box of breakfast bars from the bottom shelf in the pantry. They'd only expired last month, so I figured they would still be safe to eat, not too stale.

Annie's progress downstairs could be followed by her rapping on doors and the response of "I'm up" or "I'm almost dressed" that came in return.

I greeted her at the foot of the stairs, swapped a kiss for orange juice and a breakfast bar, got an embarrassed little grin and an "Oh, are we that bad off?"

"It's either this or I go steal the neighbor's chickens," I said…a joke she'd started.

"Call me later and we'll see who shops. Could Andy…?"

"Track practice today."

"Joy?"

"Band practice after school."

"You'll pick them up?"

"Most likely. Maybe I can take them by Giant, and we can get groceries and pizza at the same time."

"Pizza again?"

"Ever know a teenager to turn it down?"

"No, but the tummy of a teenager's mommy has its own issues," she said, patting her own flat stomach.

I never understood why she worried so about her weight. She was a fine-looking woman. She had to know that. Certainly she saw it reflected in the eyes of the men in her life—I never looked at her without being stunned by her beauty, and even that sleaze Roberts knew a good thing when he saw it.

But that wasn't a good train of thought for this morning. My wife wanted to get to work on time. Besides, the kids were waiting.

So it was back to the kitchen to fix lunches for the three of us. Sandwich fixings were in the fridge, but they looked as old as my ancient combat boots. I considered the option of PB&J, dismissed it, then fished lunch money out of my pocket for them. Taking their breakfasts in hand, I headed back for the stairs.

"Everyone got their homework?" I hollered upstairs.

Two yeses answered me, but someone's printer was suddenly on, coughing out papers that would validate that answer. I meandered over to the window.

"I see a big yellow bus at the end of the street!" I shouted.

"You mean tumbrel," my daughter corrected me. She'd studied the French Revolution last year and decreed that the school bus must, forevermore, be known by that near-vanished name for the wagon that carried so many innocents to their execution.

Being a wise man, I chose my battles carefully and had agreed.

Being a busy man, I'd forgotten that of late. Clearly, she'd remembered this morning.

"What test do you have, honey?" I called up.

"Math and English," Andy informed me.

"Tumbrel it is," I said.

"And I have a paper due in history," Joy said, appearing at the top of the stairs and revealing a visage opposite the meaning of her name. Parents can hope all they want when they name their children, but we still can't prevent what the world does to them once they're out of our safe haven. Her blue jeans and shirt met in the middle this morning. I thanked the Lord for sparing me that battle again.

Joy added the OJ and granola bar to her backpack and swung it over her shoulder. If it was lighter than the seventy-pound pack I'd lugged in the army, the difference couldn't be much more than grams.

I shoved her out the door toward the bus stop and was saved from having to threaten bodily harm against my firstborn when Andy presented his lanky frame at the top of the stairs and did a disjointed but semicontrolled fall down them.

"You know, Dad, if you'd just let me drive Sis to school, we wouldn't have to be out for another thirty whole minutes."

"But we only have two cars," I said slowly, as if just discovering that fact. "I'd have to buy a third one for you to drive."

His eyes lit up at the novel concept. "I wouldn't mind."

"Aren't you the same fellow who, only two years ago, at the wise and dependable age of fifteen, promised me that if I'd just buy you your very own brand-new, not-hand-me-down computer that you'd never trouble me about getting you a car when you turned sixteen."

Andy paused, frowned as if deep in thought, then nodded. "Why, yes, yes, I do believe I am." But before I could pounce, he pounced first. "But that old computer is really obsolete. I really need a new one. I'll keep using it a bit longer if it'll save you enough money to get a car that I could use to chauffeur Joy and me around after school. Think of all the free time you'd have if you didn't have to be there to pick us up."

"And miss out on all that quality time with you and your smelly socks and Sis cleaning her clarinet. Never!" I assured him as I tucked his morning rations and lunch money in the side compartment of his backpack and shoved him out the front door.

The yellow peril was noisily breaking to a stop. Andy had to cut across two lawns to make it in time, but he did. He waved at me as he piled on board, but he was already talking to someone on the bus.

I watched the bus pull away, suddenly overwhelmed by how much of what I loved and treasured in this world was held hostage to fate, at risk to their own blunders and the sin in the world.

*Dear God, bless them. And Annie. And me,* I added.

I did a quick check through the kitchen, downed my own juice and granola in obedience to my decree to my family that a good breakfast was essential, and went upstairs to finish getting dressed. I pulled the covers up to make the bed, still bearing the soft scent of last night's togetherness. Shoes and coat finished up my preparations for the day. I was still a bit shaky after yesterday's adventures.

What did my old friend, the chopper pilot, say? "Any landing you could walk away from is a good one." Well, any morning that I got everyone out of the house on time and prepared to meet the day had to be a good start. God willing, I could pull myself together and the day would be blessed for us all.

Memories of yesterday's near miss hung over me like a storm cloud. I really didn't need anymore "situations." Any blessings God cared to throw my way would be very much appreciated. I felt a little disconnected and unsettled. I prayed for peace—but I didn't get it.

**3**

THE WORDS "MR. JAY WANTS TO SEE ALL THE DIVISION HEADS in his office at eight" didn't sound like a blessing for the good day to come. I hoped it wasn't something to do with yesterday's fiasco. Given he was calling in everybody, it probably wasn't, which was just as well. I wasn't sure I was ready to talk about it to "Mr. Jay" just yet.

I'd barely gotten through talking about it with my family.

But I'd managed to get back a bit of my equilibrium this morning. The air was fresh, and it made the walk from my car to the office a pleasure. Rabbits were still munching on the lawn that stretched a good hundred yards between us and the factory and the woods around us. The plant's beautiful red and yellow brick facade with large windows was another holdover from earlier years. The profits from the bayonets we turned out between 1914 and 1918 had gone into its construction. A blockish add-on shouting 1950s modern was the result of World War II. Its denizens now were the plant management group and corporate reps.

Walking farther, I turned toward my office building and took a deep breath. At least the surroundings were beautiful, even if I was a stressed-out mess. Freshly painted white, the building's front turret gleamed in the morning sun, pointing the way to heaven. Built in 1846, it had been the original home of the Carters and was now on the historical register. When Calvin Carter first decided to try his hand at knife making, they'd turned the front parlor into a small factory of lathes and saws. When the country's expansion west showed a hunger for knives, Calvin had knocked out a wall to include the front porch, then added more.

I had no right to feel the pride, but my Personnel Office was located in the original shop, and sometimes I could almost feel the soul of old Calvin looking over my shoulder, nodding happy agreement as I added yet another person to the long list of people who'd made his dream of gleaming knives a reality.

Annie tells me I'm a hopeless romantic. She's wrong on that one. I'm just a hardheaded manager with a taste for history. Really. And right now I was a tense one.

I was fifteen minutes early, but all three of my crew were at their desks. "Morning, Bea, Al, Max," I called to the girls. They were all older than me, but they'd taken me aside when my concession to modern sensibilities left me stumbling over how to address them. "We're girls, boss, and will be girls till the day we die," they'd told me. I knew when to surrender.

With a sigh this morning, I thanked my secretary for telling me that Mr. Jay, that is Mr. Jason Franklin, wanted to see all of us first thing that morning. I settled into my office with a strong hunch that the best part of today was over already.

A quick check of my desk showed nothing new in my in-basket. My Workforce Analysis sat forlornly beside it. I estimated that ten percent of our workforce would retire in the next five years. We needed to start hiring trainees, getting their skill level up to the superior craftsmanship of the men and women who'd made Carter Cutlery a proud name around the world for over a hundred and fifty years.

I'd turned it in a month ago, and I'd heard nothing from Jay. Not a good sign.

The phone rang. I had ten minutes to cross the yard. Surely time enough to take one quick phone call. "Carter Cutlery, Taylor here."

"Ben, Hanson here from Haslet Trucks. I'm putting together the agenda for tomorrow's Human Resources Directors luncheon, and I was wondering if you were willing to put on that program you did five years ago for the wage-survey people?"

Every five years the HR offices in the area did a combined wage survey to make sure that our white-collar and nonunion pay scales were not out of balance. Others used it to talk to their unions come negotiation times. Five years ago I'd led the two-day course we held for the supervisors chosen to actually perform the survey. It was a short thing, just a bit of advice on what questions to ask so you got the most information in the shortest amount of time. I'd also done it ten years ago, and fifteen years ago, I'd learned how it was done from an old geezer now long since retired.

"I'll check with my plant manager," I told Hanson. It was a mere formality. This kind of thing was good community involvement. We'd always done it before. With luck, Jason Franklin would understand that.

"Well, can you get back to me before lunch?"

"I'll try. I have a meeting with the man just now, so I have to run." And with that, I hung up and actually got ready to run.

I had one hiring request from Marketing that I needed to get Jay's approval for. I slipped it into a folder, put it on top of my copy of the Workforce Analysis, and headed out the door.

Bea was typing something as I left, possibly an e-mail to her husband who was overseas with his Guard unit. Al was preparing a retirement estimate for one of those ten percent I expected to lose, combining our small company-retirement benefits with Social Security to show him what he could expect to live on once he left us. Al had worked on the Production floor before she developed an allergy to the finishing washes she was using on our steel. We looked for a job for her inside the company, found this one, and she had fit well in my shop, discovering a strong suit in computations.

Max, my assistant and another refugee from the shop floor, was studying a new Maryland law and its impact on our unemployment insurance costs. Once Max finished her review, Bea would type up the report for me to take to Jay. Another rising expense.

I turned down the central hall of our landmark and ran into Rod Montgomery, headed in the same direction.

"How's our man of steel?" I said with a grin. Rod handled procurement. He bought everything we needed, from computers to etching tools, but steel was what we needed the most. And Rod knew steel.

"Not so good," Rod growled. "How would you like to take two tons of aircraft carrier armor off my hands?"

"Aircraft carrier armor?" I said, raising an eyebrow.

"Yeah, two-and-a-half-inch-thick steel-belt armor off the *Wasp* or *Hornet* or *Bumblebee* or whatever the last carrier was that they scrapped and didn't turn into a rusting national monument. I finagled a four-by-ten-foot slab of it. Now wouldn't that make for a great commemorative bowie knife for next December 7? A cut from the carriers that avenged the Day of Infamy."

"Old man Tom Carter would have loved it," I said, suspecting I knew what came next. "But won't that armor be a bit hard to work?"

"Yeah, that's exactly what Jay Jay the Jet Plane told me after I waltzed into his office to tell him my latest coup. Stuff was up on eBay, and the bidding was going like mad for all ten lots. I barely got the one thin enough for us to work."

"You bought it first and then asked Jason if it was a good idea?"

Jay was our boss, and I didn't envy him the job. If he wanted me to, I'd call him Mr. Franklin...even if he was ten years my junior.

"I keep forgetting I don't work for Carter Cutlery anymore. Who are we working for this week?"

That was an inside joke among us dinosaurs. Carter Cutlery had been family owned for over a hundred years. Then Old Man Tom Carter died five years back come November. His heirs decided to take the money and run, and Heritage Specialties was very happy to buy them out. Our knives matched well with their stock in trade, and we sold to some markets that they hadn't gotten into yet. Great match until they merged with PK&E Unlimited to do an IPO. At the time, it seemed like a good idea. But then Prestige Corp. grabbed all of us in a hostile takeover. I forget exactly what they were after, but I'm pretty sure no one on Prestige's board of directors had ever heard of Carter Cutlery or even Heritage Specialties. We were the black sheep of the family, the second cousin's twice-removed stepson, and that would be fine by me if they'd just ignore us.

But that didn't seem to be happening.

Meddling was going on at a brisk pace, making our jobs progressively more difficult every day. Is there a CEO on God's green Earth who has the wisdom and grace to leave well enough alone? If there is one, I haven't met him. And I was none too sure the Lord had, either.

When old Barney Wells retired after fifteen years as the plant manager, there was Will Fortier, his deputy, and three good foremen having thirty years or more with the company in the running for the top job. Any one of them could have run the factory, with us supporting him.

Fat chance of that in today's market.

Prestige Corp. selected Jason Franklin to manage Carter Cutlery *and* run the plant. He had made quite a name for himself, running several pharmaceutical plants that needed turning around. How different could knife manufacturing be from drug manufacturing?

It came as a shock to all of us that we needed the leadership of a turnaround expert. It also seemed a no-brainer that a plant that made sharp objects out of steel was a far throw from something that made drugs out of whatever it is you make drugs out of.

Jay had struck me as a fast study, but it seemed pretty clear to me that he didn't follow some of the special twists that we'd been doing for the last fifty years to make us unique in the marketplace.

"Martin," Rod said as the head of Marketing joined us. "What do you think of my idea for a Pearl Harbor Day Bowie Knife? There a market for it?"

Martin pursed his lips as he fell in step with us. "The Greatest Generation would lap your knife up, but they are getting fewer and farther between. Lately we're selling more specialty knives to Japan. Rod, I kind of doubt that market would go for that particular knife."

Rod had the good sense to wince at that.

"Battleship armor. How hard will that be to work?" Martin asked.

"Carrier armor," Rod corrected, "and that's the problem. It's tough to start with. Tough all the way through production. It would bust a lot of saw blades, need a lot of sanding and polishing." Rod's shoulders were slowly drooping.

"Battleships may be obsolete, but they're still sexy from a marketing perspective," Martin pointed out. "Production costs would eat into our profit margin, and I'm not sure the market could bear a premium price structure."

Rod sighed. "Care to buy half a ton of carrier armor? I can sell it to you cheap," he said.

We covered the distance to the corporate offices in silence. The spring sun was warming the day. I spotted a mother bunny nudging her offspring toward the woods as we went by.

Years ago, Andy and Joy were always delighted when Annie brought them down to my office on afternoons when I worked late. At ages six and three, they'd taken it as their personal duty to see that the rabbits got plenty of exercise dodging the kids in their idea of a game of tag. These days, they weren't so enthusiastic. Teenagers had other ideas of what was fun. Even though the rabbits didn't miss the kids, I did. But, except for the Christmas party, they hadn't been down to the plant in more than a year.

Which might be for the best. I wasn't sure how Jay would react to children bouncing around and shouting happily in his plant's front yard.

The plant manager's conference room had been expanded only recently so we all could sit down together. Old Tom Carter or Barney rarely got us all together, and when they did, they kept us standing to make sure the meeting went quickly. Now a wall had been knocked out, and the former deputy plant manager's office provided plenty of room for a long wooden table and comfortable chairs, bought the first time Jay hosted higher-ups from Prestige Corp. headquarters.

I knew old Will Fortier hadn't planned on retiring for several more years, but I'd personally helped him review his retirement plans after Jay got the top job. Again, I knew more than most because I'd counseled Will about his feelings of frustration as assignments dried up under Jay. In fact, I'd been deputized by Will to see if there was any way for him to improve his situation.

Will knew he was asking a lot of me. An old hunter, he knew the risk people ran when they came between the hunter and the target. I'd taken on the job of emissary because, well, the cattle that tread the grain are worth their hire, so to speak…and my reading of Jason wasn't all that bad.

"I was hoping someone would come talk to me," Jason said after I explained my mission. "I'm glad it's you, Ben. You're the youngest manager I've got, and you look to be the only one who's not at that hardening-of-the-arteries stage." He gave me a smile that I suspect was supposed to make me feel he viewed me as his ally in this battle. I smiled back, wanting to be a peacemaker but knowing full well that while God might call such as me a son of

God, in *this* world it usually meant I was dodging bricks from both sides.

"You're also the only one here with an MBA," Jason went on. I knew we shared that credential, but mine had been earned from night school at the University of Maryland. His was far more prestigious.

"So maybe you can explain some things to me," Jason said, leaning back in his chair. "It looks to me like Barney and Mr. Carter left the running of the plant to Will. What did they do with their time? I mean, I'm running the plant pretty much by myself, and it's not taking anywhere near my full time."

I nodded, trying to look helpful, and decided to lay a lot of cards on the table...face up. "Mr. Carter spent most of his time with the customers, Mr. Franklin."

"Call me Jay,"

"Yes sir."

"And don't 'sir' me. With men under me old enough to be my grandfather, 'sir' me makes me wonder what they're really thinking."

I forced a friendly chuckle and said, "You bet," and made a note to pass the word that this northerner didn't understand the southern way of showing respect. "Well, as I was saying, Old Man Tom was really three-quarters of our marketing effort. He considered each of our customers his personal friend. And Barney, well, he did run the plant, but he was a hands-on type of guy, wanted to know everyone by name, or nickname, know their kids, and what the missis was doing. He did a lot of work with the community.

Tom Carter liked that, considered it good for us to give back to the place that bred us. Anyway, they needed Will to see that all the details got done." I paused, then added slowly, "You're not leaving him a lot of details to pick up."

"It's not my style to leave loose ends hanging," Jason said, coming forward in his seat. "Sloppy work costs money," he said, glancing at the profit-and-loss chart he'd had installed on the wall next to his desk. We'd worried about end-of-year reports. He worried about end-of-month balances.

"What can I tell Will?"

Jason shook his head. "Mr. Fortier had better start scrambling to make himself useful. His salary is a mighty big chunk of overhead, and I can't keep letting it go for nothing. He's been here forty years. He must have some idea of what he can do that will contribute to improving the bottom line."

Two weeks later we threw a nice retirement party for Will. A month later his old office had been gobbled up as part of the conference room that Jason used to seat the bigwigs and outline his expectations for the coming year. The exercise had left the rest of us worried about being the next one to go if Jason wanted to expand the conference room again.

Now we waited for Jason to come through the door from the front office to the conference room, having all entered from the hall to avoid tromping through his front office. The conference room was modern, with gray carpets, gray walls, windows on one side overlooking the woods beyond. Charts were on one wall, and photographs of the high-muck-a-mucks at Prestige were on another. The last wall, at the foot of the table, had one of those new arrangements that was a combination screen and whiteboard. For years I'd suggested to Old Man Tom that he get one of those.

Now we had one. I also noticed that we had a new laptop computer in front of Jason's leather chair, with a projector rigged to it, aimed at that screen on the far wall. I'd been known to bring my personal portable to meetings once in a while to take notes and had been ribbed unmercifully for the innovation.

Oh, the times they were achangin'. I was worrying already that I might not be up to those changes.

Beside the three of us from the old house in attendance, there was Jeb, the day-shift foreman at the plant, and Greg Coxon, "Doc," the head of our tiny Product Development lab. Most everyone thinks a knife is a knife, but new products made of new materials were coming on the market every day. We hadn't made any carbon-fiber knives yet; they'd require a whole new set of tools. But you could fill a book with all the different kinds of steel there were these days. I know—Rod has shown me his copy.

Mary Oppie handled accounting, both accounts receivable and payroll. She'd gotten her degree thirty-five years ago from a business school and was now pulling her hair out trying to keep up with Jason's demands that she computerize her domain—yesterday. Seated across the table, as far from her as possible, was Mark Attlee, the only hire Jason had made in the last year. Fresh out of Carnegie Mellon, Mark knew computers and was having the time of his young life bringing Carter Cutlery from the nineteenth century to the twenty-first century at what appeared to be lightning speed to the rest of us.

Assuming he and Mary and the rest of us survived the trip.

But for now, we waited. And according to our various beliefs and temperaments, we endured, we prayed, and we hoped. And it was a good thing—because it turned out we needed all the help from prayer that we could get.

# 4

"THANK YOU FOR COMING SO EARLY THIS MORNING," JASON said as he entered the room. Young, athletic, tall, and with an unruly bush of brown hair he was always brushing back out of his face, he looked like the kind of guy most parents hoped their kids would grow up to be.

Me, I wondered where, or if, he attended church. That was one topic that never came up in conversation with Jason. I'd also want my son to have a bit more sympathy for his aging elders than Jason exhibited.

I suppressed the urge to jump to attention. I'd done my four years in the army, but that was a long time passing. Still, there was something about the energy in Jason's step that brought to mind my old battalion commander. Jason, who made no bones about his lack of use for the armed forces—though he now made knives for them—would not have been amused.

Taking his chair, Jason started without preamble. "Normally I would have covered this in the Monday morning staff meeting, but

Prestige didn't drop this particular bomb in my lap until close of business yesterday. I don't think we can afford to wait until next week to discuss it. As you know, I've been tracking our financials on a monthly basis and want to get on a weekly basis with projections as soon as Mary and Mark can get the necessary systems up and running."

We nodded understanding. Mary kept us up to date on progress in the battle during our lunch hour get-together, usually leaving us laughing or fuming, depending on how the effort was going.

"I've been passing the monthlies along to corporate, and it seems that Prestige is not happy," Jason said, flipping on the projector and casting what was showing on his computer against the far wall. "I promised them three months ago that we would meet their twenty percent profit goal for this year. We are now three months into the year and hardly managing eighteen percent."

"But it's the best year we've ever had," Rod pointed out.

Jason paused to glance at Rod. "I don't need you, or anyone else, to tell me how poorly this company has underperformed throughout its history."

I made my face bland. Very bland. When my opinion was needed, I was pretty sure Jason would give me one. Smart people should need only one warning, and my mom didn't raise any dumb kids. Well, maybe my kid brother.

Around me, people shuffled in their chairs but said nothing more. Jason went on.

"We have been holding at eighteen percent for the last two months. If we continue to underperform my forecast, the only prospects we will have for making the target will be to get our profit margin above twenty-two, maybe twenty-three percent for the entire second half of the year." Jason looked around the table.

"Do any of you have any suggestions for how we can do that?" he said.

Even as my stomach went into free fall, I was careful to force my face to neutral. I tightened every muscle in my neck to keep my head from so much as quivering.

But around me, others were shaking their heads and muttering.

"That's impossible," seemed to be the main mutter.

Jason waited for the rumbling to run down to silence, then fixed us with a glare that again reminded me of my old battalion commander. Jason might come from a totally different background, but he did know how to face down a mutiny. "So, since we are agreed that jumping our profits from eighteen percent to twenty-two percent at midyear is rather unlikely, it is agreed that we will just have to work ourselves up to twenty percent right now."

"But how?" Rod kind of squeaked.

"I believe the usual answer to that is increasing sales while decreasing costs," Jason said with a smile that could have etched one of our anniversary knife sets, it was so bright.

"You have any suggestions?" Martin asked, letting his glance stray to the folder in front of me containing his request for a new salesman.

"Why don't I let you take the first cut at suggestions? With any luck, I'll just approve your ideas and we can all take it from there. I want them on my desk by noon today. Suggestions for immediate implementation, plus any long-range ones you might have in mind."

And with that, he stood. We followed his lead and stood…and did him one better by heading for the door.

"Ben, could you stay behind for a moment?" Jason said.

I stepped aside and let the others go ahead of me. Rod gave me a sad shake of the head. Martin gave me a thumbs-up sign, but it wasn't at all jaunty.

"Yes, Jay?" I said when we had the room to ourselves.

"I see you brought your Workforce Analysis with you."

I shuffled it to the top and nodded.

"It's a good piece of work. In normal times I'd say run with it."

"But…," I added for him.

"We are overstaffed. We need to be more productive with the people we have. I hope Jeb will come up with some suggestions for how the plant can make more product. I'm betting that Doc can come up with some cheaper product lines for us. I can't believe that they weren't falling all over themselves the second I laid out the problem." He shook his head slowly.

It felt good that Jason was taking me into his confidence. That he considered me one of his "us" against the "them." But those "thems" had been my friends for the last fifteen years.

It felt nice to be on the inside, but what use was it if I couldn't speak honestly to this man? *Lord, this is not one of my better days. Please help me find the right words,* I prayed as I took a deep breath.

"Jason, have you read the testimonial file?" Before he'd put up the corporate rogues' gallery of pictures, on the walls of the smaller conference room had hung letters, some dated back to the Civil War. Letters from soldiers and workmen, hunters and fishermen whose lives had been saved by the quality we put into each Carter knife. There wasn't a man or woman in the company who couldn't quote several of them word for word.

"I've leafed through the pages," he admitted.

"People count on our knives, Jason. Sometimes their lives depend on our knives." Years of being the fellow who spread oil on the troubled waters between people came to my aid at that moment. I didn't say what I'd intended. My Father softened my words into a question. "Maybe I misunderstood you. Do you really want us to cheapen our knives, lower our quality?"

"No, blast it," Jason exploded. "You, Ben, of all people must understand me. I say we need a less expensive line of knives that maybe we can make a better profit margin on. Everyone looks at me as if I've suggested we turn out tin knives that will bend in a kid's hand. That's not what I'm saying. Not what I want."

*Thank you God for not making me eat the words that were on the tip of my tongue. The ones I did say will need some ketchup and salt, though,* I thought to myself while saying, "Then help me understand what you do want, Jason, because I'm confused and I'm pretty sure everyone else in the plant is."

For a moment, Jason just stared at me like I had two heads, or maybe none at all. Then he nodded and took his seat at the head of the table, waving me to the one next to him.

"Ben, maybe you can translate what I'm saying to the rest of them. I thought I'd pretty much gotten rid of my Boston accent, but it's clear that my words just are not translating into Maryland-ese. Or is it that my drug industry lingo isn't making it in a steel world?"

I just shrugged. My gut was all knotted. My mouth was way too dry. *Lord, I really don't need anymore days like these, thank You very much. First yesterday, now this...* But if I could be a bridge between this man and a lot of my friends who were in line for a world of hurt, maybe God had me where He wanted me, despite my wishes.

Jason leaned back in his chair. "Back around the turn of the century, the last one, nineteenth to twentieth, three percent profit was considered fine. As long as the Carter family made enough money to live on, pay its employees and suppliers, and bank the rest, they called it a good year. Carter made its mark. But the times changed, and yet Carter kept on doing the same old same old, Ben."

I nodded. Even I could see that. And if I was honest with myself, I had grown to like it. But for everything, there is a season, and it looked like Carter Cutlery was headed for a season of change. *Dear Lord, make me a peacemaker between my friends' world and this man's world.*

"I don't want us to make cheap knives. Do you think I want to read in the paper where some soldier died with one of our knives broken in his hand? God forbid it.

"But there are new steels on the market, easier to work, that can be hardened at the final stage. There are new tools that last longer. I need for Doc to look at all of this, not just how we can cut up tough-as-nails carrier armor into a knife no one will ever take off their mantle. I say these things, but no one seems to hear me. Can you hear me, Ben?"

I felt like someone whose ears had been stopped up with paper and wax…and was having them cleaned out with acid. "Yes, I'm hearing you. And, yes, I wasn't hearing you before."

"Thank God, Ben, because we're in a fight for this company's life. I get a kick out of watching the rabbits running around on the lawn when I walk in from the parking lot each morning. I like listening to the wind in the trees when I leave late at night. You know what corporate thought of that?"

I shook my head.

"They said, 'Wow, the real-estate value of this place alone would be worth a half a million stock options. How soon do you think you can close this plant down and ship the jobs to Pakistan?'"

"They didn't," was all I could get out.

"Yeah. They did. That's their way of thinking."

And most of us old-timers had assumed that Jason was just another one of those corporate hoods, out to mug us. Kind of strange to find an ally in the front office.

But he didn't need to be fighting us when he was fighting them. "Boss, I think I'm starting to understand better what you're up against."

"Think you can help?"

"No question about that."

"Good," he said, but he didn't stand up. Instead, he fished an envelope out of his pocket. "I'm really sorry about this, Ben. I went to bat for you. Told them that they couldn't find a better man to handle the Pay and Benefits program for Prestige, but they went outside to fill the job."

I'd been wondering how my application for a job at corporate had been going. It was kind of Jason to do this personally, not just let the letter drop into my in-box. Still, it hurt. But it was not unexpected.

I tried to shake off the pain for the moment. Yesterday had me enough off balance as it was. Today was going to be way too busy for me to let things keep me down. "Thank you," I managed to say as I slipped the letter, unopened, into the file folder that held Martin's unaddressed vacancy paperwork.

"I'll get Jeb and Doc together and see what I can do for you," I said, standing. "Oh, one thing. I've been asked to do the training for supervisors and managers who will be involved with the wage survey we do in the area every five years. It will only take two days.

I can do the wage-survey analysis at night. You mind me volunteering to do it?"

"Anyone else who could do it?"

"I did it the last few times, and they say I'm good at it."

He chuckled. "Yes, you're good. Help me out here, and with luck, we'll all be working here when the time comes to do this wage survey again. Besides, you may need that data the next time we talk to the folks on the plant floor. Unless you can come up with a miracle, we're going to need wage concessions."

I winced. "I'll start praying for that miracle, boss. I really don't want to be in on those kinds of talks."

The words were yet another lance to my armor. I was beginning to feel like Atlas, holding the world on my back. I shouldered the new load and struggled back to my office. *Dear Lord,* I prayed, *I could use some help here.*

## 5

DETERMINED NOT TO LET MY TROUBLES AT THE OFFICE IMPACT
my family, I picked the kids up, almost on time. At least, Andy
insisted they hadn't been waiting more than five minutes. We drove
home with them telling me about their day and my mind still held
hostage by mine.

It had been a day of meetings, bloody meetings, and then more
meetings. It had not been fun.

Jeb Shepherd had not been hard to talk to. "I've been thinking
we might need a less expensive line of knives for some time," he
nodded when I told him about my talk with Jay. "Can't say I dis-
agree with him. Lot of my hunting friends are kind of crimped in
the wallet. Some of their young uns would be glad to sport a Carter
knife if it didn't cost them an arm and a leg."

"I see the advertising," Martin put in. "Lots of folks claiming
their steel is as good as a Carter. I guess we could market a line of
knives that have Carter strength, Carter reliability, but don't cost
as much. Assuming they were just as good, I mean," he finished,
maybe not as sure as he'd been when he started.

"There are new steels," Rob admitted. "Less expensive. Easier to work. You have to make sure you get the finishing process done right." He glanced at Jeb.

"My machinists will do it right. We always do," Jeb assured us.

"We'll need Doc to run quality assurance," I pointed out.

Greg Coxon brushed a wisp of white hair across his bald pate and shook his head. "Quality control is a waste of time. It's either in there, or it ain't." Doc would rather skip a round of drinks at the pub tonight than spend his day running tests on finished steel. "My job is to find prettier, shinier, tougher steel for our customers, not make sure Jeb's crew remember how to do what they're hired for."

We spent about an hour talking him around to Jay's point of view. Two hours later we had an action plan for developing a smaller, less expensive line of knives. If we didn't run into any problems with the new metalworking processes, we could have them out for Christmas this year.

Jeb and I took the plan back to Jason. As I walked him through the development steps, he listened, offered some improvements, and seemed satisfied with our work. "I suspected if I got the right person talking to my crew, that the guys had what it took to get some new stuff moving," he said to me as Jeb and I stood to leave.

"One more thing, Ben. I forgot to mention this to you after this morning's meeting." I paused at the door of Jay's office. "Not only will the company put a freeze on hiring anyone for the next year or two, you also need to cut back on your staff. I'd like a suggestion from you on which positions you can afford to cut."

"None of them," I said, my stomach going back into free fall.

"Just the answer I'd expected from you, but not the one I can accept. Think it over, Ben. You've got a very good plan here. With a few changes, it's one I can run with, take it up with our VP at Prestige. It might buy us some time. But we still need to show that we're paying attention to their concerns, Ben. And it's logical that the cuts need to come from Personnel. Cutting a slot out of Marketing may not be a good long-term approach, what with our launching a new line that I think will be popular in more markets than we've got at the moment. And production may need to ramp up to supply inventory for the new line. That leaves your department. Cutting straight administrative overhead shows solid attention to detail. You've shown me you're a team player today, Ben. Don't disappoint me now."

That's how Jason had left it. I needed to let somebody in my department go. These were people I'd worked with for years. Most of them were just a few years away from retirement—it wasn't going to be easy for any one of them to find a new job.

Needless to say, his words still held me hostage. But the kids were so full of their own concerns that they didn't even notice my distraction. Until it became so evident that even they couldn't miss it.

"Dad, we are going home, aren't we?" my son asked from beside me. I realized I'd nearly driven past our house in my haze of work worries. I braked hard and made the turn into the driveway.

"Man," Andy said. "What's wrong with you?"

"Just checking to see if you were on your toes," I said lightly. But my kids were no dummies. I needed to shake off the problems at work and pay attention or they were going to worry.

Annie's blue Camry was already parked there. I brought my older green Taurus to a stop beside it. I hadn't found the time to call Annie; unless she had made a stop at the grocery store, the house was just as famine-stricken as it was this morning.

Joy announced a race to the front door...when she was already halfway there. Andy, laden with his spring track bag and books, managed to tie her. Joy had a full load of books, too, but only a clarinet to add to her load. They nearly demolished the front door in the process of getting through it as I plodded up the front walk.

I arrived at the house to find my wife bubbling with joy in the foyer. She was so full of good cheer that my lack of it didn't even make a dent in her mood. In fact, I'm pretty sure she didn't even notice.

"You kids get to your homework," she said. "I've ordered pizza in for you. Your dad and I are going out to eat."

"Can't we come too?" came in two-part harmony, with little harmony in it.

"No, your dad and I need to talk."

I eyed my wife. "We need to talk?" Those words, especially coming from a much-loved woman, strike fear into the hearts of men everywhere. They form an ambiguous phrase that can cover a whole range of options, from "Whoopee, I'm pregnant," to…well, the less said about those times the better. From the grin on my wife's face, though, and the tendency for her to bounce on her toes, it looked to be one of those "Whoopee" moments. Maybe I didn't need to brace myself.

"Should I get some kite string before I risk taking you out where the wind might blow you away?" I asked.

It was an old joke between us.

Today, Annie tossed me a spool off Joy's last kite. "I thought you might say that," she smiled.

I made an act of studying my wife. She worked out at the health club two or three times a week. Annie was indeed a pleasant woman to look at.

At five foot six, there was a lot of her to enjoy. Despite whatever the day had brought her, her blond hair was still tight in her professional bun. Three-inch heels showed her calves to good effect. Her trim, A-line skirt did the rest, even as it ended below the knee. The white blouse and blazer finished her ensemble, topped off with a gold chain I'd given her last Christmas.

But it was her flashing eyes and spreading grin that held my attention.

"You're either pregnant, or you just got a promotion," I said after a studied pause. "No, from the look of that grin, I'd say you're both."

"Dear God, protect me from such a fate," Annie laughed, letting her eyes follow the noise of our offspring as they thundered up the stairs. "Two kids are quite enough to keep up with. No, my loving and supportive husband. It's the latter. I have a promotion. And what a promotion! Supper tonight is on me."

"I take it Bob wasn't too upset about that dropped container of furniture?" I said, backtracking toward Annie's car.

"It didn't even come up," she said, heading for the driver's seat as I went around to the passenger's. "You might like to know that Bob Roberts very much approves of your choice in a wife," she added. "The profits from my section of the Baltimore office have been way out ahead of anything on the East Coast."

She glanced my way after she backed out of the driveway. "He said that I really know how to get a man's attention."

"Or a man...ager's," I added.

"That's what he meant, Benjamin."

"Yeah, right." I couldn't keep the sarcasm out of my voice. But my wife was flying too high to pay attention.

Annie bubbled about her day for the short drive to Mason's Steakhouse, a surprisingly good independent restaurant tucked away in our neighborhood. I nodded along to Annie's gushing about her day, trying my best to look happy for her. But I felt separated from her joy, set apart from her by the weight of all the stress I was carrying from my job. My day, I kept locked down in my gut. I tried to look enthusiastic—no need, I told myself, to let my problems seep out to sap the joy of my wife's moment. There would be time enough for me once she had celebrated her day.

At the restaurant, we settled down in a dimly lit booth in the quiet back of a steakhouse that took its western decor seriously: knotty pine walls, cowboy boots that looked well worn, branding irons that showed signs of the many fires they'd known. It brought back good memories of when we'd been out West during my army tour, before coming home to be near our folks and start my career.

Annie ordered from the top of the menu. It was a day of celebration. I did likewise, adding a lobster tail to my Kansas City cut. And then, with our waitress gone, I leaned back in my side of the booth to listen to more of Annie's day.

She reached across for my hands, and I offered them to her. For a moment she just caressed them. Then Annie let go of my hands, took a deep breath, and said, "Bob has offered me my own shop."

It should have been great news. But even as distracted as I was, I could tell by the look in Annie's eyes that there was catch in there somewhere.

## 6

## SO SHE'D HAVE HER OWN SHOP.

I'd used those same words when Carter Cutlery offered me the position as head of Human Resources. "Annie, they're offering me my own shop. I'm still thirty, and I'll be getting my own personnel program to run," I'd crowed.

"I'm glad for you," I said now, echoing Annie's joy at the time of my promotion. "So they're not just stringing you along with nice words. They're ready to put their money where their mouth is. Great, honey."

"Yes," she answered. "I'm so excited."

But there was something around the edge of her words that was still out of tune with the rest. I gauge the honesty of people every day. That's my stock in trade. My wife wasn't being totally up-front with me.

"Is Wilson getting a promotion too?" I asked. Wilson ran the Baltimore office of Triton Imports. If half of what Annie said was true, he didn't deserve a promotion. Was my wife about to replace him?

"No, he's going to stay put," Annie said, fiddling with her napkin.

"Are you being promoted over him?"

"No."

I swallowed a lump suddenly rising in my throat. Enough of twenty questions. I sat, face carefully neutral, and waited for Annie to let me in on her secret.

The quiet stretched long and started to bow in the middle.

"They've offered me the Portland, Oregon, office," Annie said.

I blinked twice, running her sentence twice through my brain as I tried to fully parse all the meanings in her words. Portland. Oregon. As in Left Coast. Wrong Coast! Long, long way from this coast.

"Oh," I finally said, glancing around at the western decor and taking in its full meaning. "Now I know why we're celebrating here tonight."

"You've always said that our days out West were the best years of our life together," Annie said, reaching for my hands again.

I let her take them. "But we were just married, hon. Andy was a little bundle that we could carry anywhere we happened to wander off to."

"You think he and Joy will have some problems with moving?" Her hands were holding mine, not quite as desperately as a drowning man might.

"High school is a tough time for kids to pick up sticks, leave all their friends behind," I pointed out, knowing I was saying the obvious. Also knowing I was hiding behind the kids.

*Dearest Lord above, won't this day ever end? I know You promised that we'd never face more than we could handle, Father, but it would be nice to have a bit more of a safety margin, don't You think?*

My prayer must have gotten filed for a later reply. I hoped the Lord's angel in charge of filing was as good as Bea.

"Benjamin, I can't say no. They're offering me my own import section. I'll be the first woman in the company to head up a section. I've got to do this. No. I want to do this more than anything I've ever done. Benjamin, help me make it work."

I stared at the ceiling, then closed my eyes. Annie and I were two of a kind. I'd known her since elementary school and Sunday school. In all that time, we'd never been seriously at loggerheads. We'd always wanted the same things, or close enough, or what she wanted I wanted to give to her...and vice versa.

That didn't mean our life together was easy. It had been rough helping Annie get her MBA when she decided that, when the kids were old enough, she wanted to go back to work. I'd spent a lot of time taking care of the kids while she went to class and did homework. Of course, upon review, it hadn't been such a bad thing. I got to know Andy and Joy when they were still short and the world hadn't done its best to steal them away from me. We had bonds like few fathers and kids had, from what I heard at the office and at church.

Back then, I'd prayed to God for the patience to help my wife through grad school...and He gave me my children in a way I'd never have thought to pray for.

What was God trying to get at today? No, let's focus down to just what was going on at supper; the entire day was way too much of a muddle for this mere mortal to figure out.

"You really want this," I said to Annie, letting my fingers wander the palm of her hand.

"As much as you wanted your own personnel shop. Benjamin, this is a chance for me to show them what I've got. No," she shook her head, "to show myself what I've got. Isn't that what you said when you got the offer from Carter? A chance to run a program, to have the full responsibility for it all in your own hands."

Which was exactly what I'd said. Back then, my wife had been listening to me, really listening. Now it was my turn.

"We moved back here to be close to our folks," I said.

"And your mom has moved to Florida." She didn't mention my dad's passing two years ago. "My folks are as likely to be in Greece as across town. Would we see them any less if they had to get on an airplane to visit us?"

I couldn't argue with that. That was one of the things that drew us back to Maryland fifteen years ago that didn't seem to apply anymore.

"And Triton has a program to help you find a job if you move with me," Annie rushed on.

I knew about spouse placement programs. I regularly got phone calls from larger corporations in the area asking me if I had a vacancy for the wife of a man they'd just transferred into the area. I'd even gotten one or two about placing a husband.

Those programs usually worked best when the spouse had clerical skills. How it would work for a chief of HR was something I really didn't want to think about. I'd shared my opinions of spouse placement programs before with Annie. If she was choosing to not remember those words just now, I wouldn't repeat myself...for a while.

Our dinner arrived, and Annie talked about her memories of the Pacific Northwest through the meal. I tried to listen, but I kept thinking about what these changes would mean to me. No question, we'd really loved our time there, even if I was in the army and Annie had been throwing up her toenails for a couple of months when Andy was on the way.

I smiled along with her reminiscences, letting her assume I was smiling with her at the fond memories and not at how selective she was in pulling them out.

Toward the end of the meal, Annie played her last card. "Benjamin, I've prayed over this decision. It wasn't as if I didn't see it coming."

I bit down on a slice of steak and choked back the words I wanted to say, "It would've been nice to share that with me as well as with the Lord." I didn't need a boot from my Maker to know that such words would not be a good idea just now. I was supposed to be a peacemaker, not the guy lobbing grenades into the conversation.

"You've been saying for years that you've been at Carter Cutlery too long. I can tell you aren't happy there anymore. You've been saying that you wanted to reach out, try something new. This isn't just a chance for me. It's also a chance for you. I know the kids will be a pain, but if you're behind me, Benjamin, I know we can bring them around. Joy thinks you're the greatest. She'll do anything for you."

"And I thought I was the one wrapped around her little finger," got out before I had a moment to reflect.

"Then both of you would do anything for the other," my wife pointed out.

"Just like I'll do anything for you, love," was such a natural comeback that it also escaped my lips without reflection. That was the way we'd lived our lives. Her laying down her life for me and the kids. Me laying down mine for them as well.

Paul had told the Corinthian church that that was the way we should live, oh so many years ago. Annie and I had done our best, with the grace of God, to live in that light. But somehow I doubted that any Corinthian husband had a wife who got promoted to Portland, Oregon. But then, the Holy Spirit must've used a problem just as difficult to prod Paul to say to us what he said.

*Dear God, help me,* I prayed when the check arrived and Annie paid it. *I don't know what Your intention is, but I know that You never test us beyond our ability to grow in Your love. In Your Son's name, amen.* That sounded like a very firm prayer. Why did I also hear this timid little voice inside me adding a trembling, *Please?*

## 7

AS I EXPECTED, THE PIZZA WAS GONE, AND BETTER THAN half the homework with it, before we got home.

"So, what's so big that you need to talk about it between the two of you before you can share it with us junior partners?" Andy greeted as we passed his door. His computer was on. A school paper filled part of the screen with a Google search for civic duties taking up the rest.

Andy and I had a standing agreement. I could call up his "history" file anytime to see where he'd been on the Internet. He'd made the offer originally with some strings attached. "You'll let me know, Dad, when you want to check." I'd insisted on "no notice" inspections. I knew he could erase an entry in his history file any time he felt like it. Andy had grinned and agreed. Annie had the same agreement with Joy. There were some things done father-son, mother-daughter. It made for better talks while you were doing it.

Now Annie glanced at me. This looked to be a family conference she wanted led by the head of the family. Organizing my thoughts, I leaned against my son's door as Joy came to her door and her mother wrapped an arm around her.

"Triton's giving your mother a promotion," I announced.

"Great," Andy said. "You deserve it, Mom," had a squeal attached to it from Joy as the two women in my life exchanged a hug.

"She's going to run her own import shop," I added when things quieted down to a dull roar.

"Now you'll show them, Mom," Andy said, throwing himself into that hug. I joined in too, trying not to let my misgivings and the effects of my difficult day drain any of the happiness this moment deserved. Somehow, the problems of my own day had never become a topic of conversation at dinner. I could live with that.

"You going to boot old man Wilson into retirement or something?" Joy asked.

"Or something," Annie answered.

We aren't raising dumb kids. Andy craned his neck backward, something only a teenage track star could manage, and lowered his eyebrows at his mom. "What kind of something?"

"You remember all the stories we've told you about the Pacific Northwest?" I said.

"Yeah. You make it sound like it's right next door to heaven," Joy said.

"Well, Triton is offering Mom the chance to run their import center in Portland, Oregon."

The group hug ended abruptly as the kids dropped their arms to their sides and took two or three steps back.

"Portland?" Joy said.

"Oregon!" Andy finished.

"Yes. I'll be handling about a quarter of all Triton's imports from Asia. It'll mean a nice raise. Maybe I can get you that new game platform you've been eying," Annie said to Andy, hitting him far below the belt in the one true addiction we allowed him—his video gaming.

He let that pitch go right by him.

"We'd be moving in my senior year!"

"Well, the summer before it. Or we could move right now," I offered, knowing that was not a viable alternative for Andy.

"Right now?" Joy gasped.

"Not for two weeks," Annie corrected, as if two weeks made a big difference. Somehow that short deadline for the relocation had-n't come up during our dinner conversation. Annie did not need me adding to the kids' freak-out, but I did raise an eyebrow her way.

"They want me out there in two weeks, but you guys can come along later. At the end of the school year if you have to," Annie added quickly.

"Two weeks?" Joy exploded.

"To move across the country? Away from all our friends?" Andy added. "I just made the track team!"

"Okay, folks," I cut in. "This is turning into a full-fledged family council. Let's move it downstairs where we can all sit down and talk it over." I was a personnel manager. I knew how to arrange a meeting. A negotiating session. Clearly, we needed some time to get everything out on the table and into the open.

Just as clearly, I'd let my concern for Annie's needs dictate what we talked about over dinner. The kids were hitting on things I should have asked about then. I hadn't, but there was no question in my mind that we were all going to get everything out in the open now.

Not a bad pair of souls God had granted Annie and me to shepherd for the few years we would have them. And I was constantly surprised by what the good Lord taught me through them.

Andy led the way downstairs, his hands in his sweat-suit pockets. "I need a beer for this talk," he muttered.

"There's a root beer in the fridge," Annie said.

"Get me one too," Joy added.

Andy did the favor, producing bottles of root beer for them, cans of diet colas for his parents who no longer could count on a teenage metabolism to burn off the carbs. I settled into my overstuffed dad chair. Annie took the rocker across from me. The two kids filled up the couch between us. At least we had them surrounded.

Ha. It was more like they had the internal lines and could switch their center of gravity in either of our directions as their axis of attack changed. After four years as an infantry lieutenant, I never would get that kind of thinking out of my head.

*We aren't going to war tonight,* I reminded myself. *Dear heavenly Father, help us find Your will for all of us. And find the grace to submit to it as You would have us, with a joyful heart, not a rebellious one.*

"Annie, you want to fill the kids in on what you've told me?" I said to start things off.

She repeated for them what she'd told me, how important this promotion was to her and how much she wanted it. Now she added that they wanted her in place in the new job in just two weeks. "The previous manager left suddenly. He didn't give them a lot of notice, so they can't give me any time before I take over."

"Why'd he go?" Joy asked.

"Where'd he go?" was Andy's take on it.

"With one of our competitors. It happens. Dealing with the Pacific Rim is a high-stakes business," she added.

I was proud of our kids. Many people their age might need to look at a map to know what their mom was talking about. Not ours. I also noted that neither of them had to look for an atlas to find Oregon or Portland. Good kids.

"Do you really want us to move in two weeks?" Joy asked. "Have you thought about what it would take? The house? Packing? School? Are you out of your mind?"

"Not really," Annie said, grinning. She knew that was a fair shot. "I don't think we could pull a move off that fast, even if we all thought it was a great idea. I'm going to have a hard enough time getting my job here closed down and me ready to go. But don't worry. You won't have to pack up the house when we move.

Triton has a contract with a moving company. They come in, pack everything up, and even arrange to have our cars moved. 'No hassle moving,' they promise."

I was glad to hear that, since it looked like I'd be doing the job of the stay-behind spouse, managing things at this end while she took off for her new fiefdom.

"Will you be taking your car, Mom?" Andy asked.

I gave him a scowl, but it was clear the devil was in the details, and Andy was looking for any devil that turned a detail in his favor.

"If you are going to wait until school's over to join me in Portland, I may need to buy a car out there," Annie nodded. "I guess that might mean adding a third car to the family."

*Might, my eye,* I muttered to myself. But it was clear my teenage son was selling his senior year for a pot of porridge. How quickly people grab for the immediate good. I sighed, seeing my son switching sides.

Joy elbowed him in the ribs...hard. "You'd do anything for a car."

"Mom will still insist I pay the insurance," Andy said, deflecting the next jab. "Besides, you've got that friend who moved to Portland a while back. I don't have such an easy reason to move."

Joy glared at him.

"Well, maybe not," Annie said. "They are doubling my salary and adding stock options based on performance." That was something else she hadn't mentioned at dinner. Her last performance evaluation had edged her ahead of me in salary. We'd laughed about her now being the main breadwinner. Doubling her salary meant...

My stomach took a sour turn. I'd be making less than half of what my wife did...and that was assuming I got a job in Portland that matched my present one. I blinked and swallowed hard. My esophagus was really getting a workout today. And the roller-coaster ride I was on just kept getting wilder and wilder. No, a roller coaster had ups and downs. There only seemed to be downs and more downs on this ride I was on.

The kids rambled on about cars and friends and what it would feel like to leave everyone they'd known since kindergarten and have to make new friends in Portland. It didn't take long for me to sniff the direction this was going. They were talking themselves around to what Annie wanted. It was a painful process; change always is. We gave them the time they needed to talk it out.

In the end, we were back in a group hug, kneeling on the living room floor together. As Andy led us in a prayer of thanksgiving for the gifts God gave us, and asked God's grace in our new journey across the country, I thanked God for the gift of my family. I had no idea what I'd be without them, and I never wanted to know.

It seemed that we were going to Portland.

Eventually.

## 8

THE NEXT MORNING I DROVE TO WORK, STILL STRUGGLING with my problems from the day before. Maryland, however, had on her springtime smile, and my lingering depression lightened as I took in the glory of God's creation. The morning was clear, with just enough wind to keep it that way. The smell of spring was so strong I rolled down the windows and let the fresh air fill the car, driving out the musty winter smell. Even the cherry trees along the road were showing signs of budding, promising a gorgeous burst of flowers soon.

Maryland can be cold and damp and miserable. It can be hot and humid and miserable. But in between, there's spring and autumn, and you remember why you love living there.

The liveliness outside was a major contrast to the ugliness inside me. No, not ugly, just confused. Mixed up about the changes hurtling at me with so little warning. No, that wasn't fair. I had no right to say that I hadn't seen all of this coming. I had. I just didn't want to acknowledge it.

Take my job. Anyone with an ounce of foresight knew that we at Carter Cutlery were way too close to the head of the line for out-sourcing. The land our plant was on might once have been sur-rounded by pastures, but now it was prime for development.

And the work we did was being done very competitively by a dozen different factories overseas. Our reputation, the cachet of a Carter knife, had protected us for a long while. But every new day's newspaper hummed its little warning of another American busi-ness that had to go overseas to keep its prices down where the American consumer wanted them.

Even if I skipped reading the paper, I always had Annie telling me about her latest coup in Romania or Pakistan or China or wherever. Sooner or later I had to know this would happen to the people I worked with and loved. But I'd believed I could stave it off as long as I was free to do anything about it. And maybe I was right.

Yesterday I'd done my bit to help Carter and its employees stay here in Maryland. And today I'd do more. That was something I could feel good about. So why did I feel so uneasy this fine spring day? It couldn't be the thought of picking up stakes and moving the whole family all the way across country. *Nah.* It couldn't be the thought of having to break in a whole new job with people I'd never met and in a business community I had no connections to. Who didn't know me and what I could do. *Nah.* It couldn't be that I was having trouble thinking of my wonderful wife as the one who put the bread on the table for our family. The one who paid the mortgage. *Nah.*

She *was* the one putting away the bulk of the money for the kids' education. For our retirement. For the extra things we wanted.

*Yeah, right. Face it, fellow, she's passed you up. And you saw it coming.*

That probably hurt more than any of the other barbs I was throwing my way. Back when I was a young and eager fellow counseling others on how to have a hotshot career, I'd known that four or five years at a small factory like Carter was good for an up-and-rising Human Resources Director. What I hadn't expected was to get myself into what I knew was a steppingstone job, then discover I really liked it. The job and the people. And I learned that Old Man Tom really liked me. It was mutual.

Carter Cutlery was a mighty fine place to be. It was a business where people respected your work and you could see the results of it every day in their smiling faces.

I'd set up a minority recruitment effort that doubled the number of African Americans on our shop floor and got Tom an award from the Urban League. He'd put that letter up on the wall right next to the letters from our customers whose lives our knives had saved.

Yes, it was good working with the people at Carter.

So I didn't start job-hunting on my fifth anniversary at Carters, like I'd planned to. I was happy where I was. Besides, I'd told myself,

Annie had started grad school and we didn't want to move until she finished. Then I turned down a job offer from an electronics firm outside Boston because she was just getting settled in her first job. I passed on good offers in Richmond and Pittsburgh, too, because moving just didn't fit into Annie's needs and the kids' desires.

When the job offers quit coming, I didn't much mind. I was happy where I was, doing what I was comfortable doing. Yes, I'd tell Annie that I needed to do something different every now and then, but I'd never pushed for that different something.

And then Annie's career took off.

She was the one getting promoted, moving from one import office to another here in Baltimore. We're a major port, and she had a lot of opportunities, and she made the best of them. So now all those chickens were coming home to roost. She was getting the big promotion, and I was... I didn't want to think about where I was.

I turned into the plant parking lot and sighed. Ready or not, it was time to start thinking about the day. I gritted my teeth and prayed for the strength to handle it.

The next two weeks went by in a blazing flash, the kind that can devour your life if you aren't careful. I got a lot done—including prodding everybody into producing the new knife line that we needed if we were to survive as a company. Carter Cutlery designed and produced a set of solid, less-expensive knives in time for the next trade show. And we got plenty of orders for them. The new line might be eating into our more traditional offerings, but not by that much. Certainly not by as much as it added to the bottom line.

That twenty-percent profit goal for the year was looking quite doable.

Jason was even observed to smile.

Annie closed down her job, giving us nightly reports on her progress. Me, I got leave for the first week Annie would be in Portland. That way I could go with her, support her on her new job, and also do some job-hunting. Her spouse-support contractor had sent me a list of opportunities that I probably could have put together out of the local newspaper and yellow pages, but still, they did arrange several interviews, saving me that time. Annie called her folks; they quickly agreed to house- and, no, not baby-sit our kids. They agreed to teen-sit. A much tougher job.

I put Andy on the car insurance for my old car, planning on moving myself up to Annie's Camry. After all, if the kids missed the school bus, it would be a bit much to ask the grandparents to be up and running in time to get ready and drive them to school.

Andy thanked me by arranging the airline tickets over the Internet and corralling his sister into helping him clean up the clutter the day before the maid service came. That saved Annie and me from the battle royal it usually took to get the kids to clean up...or doing it ourselves.

Deciding when to fly out turned into more of a decision than

I'd remembered from our previous few airplane trips. But then, sometime in the last ten years, air travel had gone from being fun to being a shock to the system any way you looked at it. Do we leave right after work on Friday, arrive late, and check into our hotel tired? Yes, we were gaining three hours on the flight out, but... Or do we give up much of Saturday to travel?

I suggested Saturday. Annie wanted Friday, "So we'll have all of Saturday to do things like pick up my company car, house hunt, that kind of stuff."

Company car! Another perk that hadn't been mentioned. "I just found out about it this week," Annie said, looking at me through lowered eyelashes.

"Any other surprises?" I asked.

"Not at the moment, but I'll let you know about the next one as soon as I find out about it. Okay, honey?"

I shrugged in acquiescence to the inevitable. Change. The new. The different. None of those changes came with advanced warning of the surprises ahead...other than the vague "hold on to your hat, it's going to be a wild ride."

Andy and Joy drove us to Baltimore-Washington International Airport. It had been agreed that they'd just drop us off at the curb, but the security folks were giving us the eye as the hugs and good-byes stretched into family-reunion proportions. We finally broke up with calls to each other to "Drive carefully," "Fly carefully," and "Call; that's what cell phones are for." The kids drove off, and I lugged four large suitcases full of the necessities of life for Annie and the bare essentials for me up to the counter. Security was a hassle, just as I'd been warned, but nobody had to be strip-searched, and we were on our plane and away from the gate right on time.

Annie leaned over close to me after we were settled in our seats. "It's been a long time since it's just been the two of us."

I kissed her; no question she'd been fishing for one. "Before the kids."

"Let's treat this like a honeymoon. What do you say?"

"Think we could find Thunder Ridge?" I asked, trying to look young and lusty and on my honeymoon.

Annie blushed very nicely.

I decided then that things were looking up.

## 9

WE FLEW INTO A LOVELY SUNSET. WHILE MOST OF THE TREE-covered hills and mountains were deep in shadow as we descended alongside Mount Hood, the setting sun blazed off the snowcapped tip of the mountain to reflect pink and gold on the clouds above us. Angels must congregate at moments and places like these to see the glory of the Lord reflected, for just a moment, in His creation.

It was dark in Portland as we made our weary way off the plane, but there was a cheerful-looking young woman, a petite blonde in a light blue business suit holding a sign saying Anne Taylor. She greeted Annie and me with a broad smile and said, "Welcome to Portland. Have you ever been here?"

"Not since my husband, Benjamin, here was in the army," Annie said. "What was that, fifteen, sixteen years ago?" She turned to me.

"About that," I agreed.

"Well, I'm Heather Jordan, and I'll be your relocation specialist this week. I've got your new car waiting for you in the close-in parking, Ms. Taylor, and as soon as we can collect your baggage, I'll take you to your hotel."

"Call me Annie" led to Heather and Annie getting on friendly terms. Annie did not introduce me as Ben, so I figured she wanted me to stay Mr. Taylor for a while longer. We collected our luggage, but Heather had a skycap waiting to help and a cart to roll it along behind us as she led us across the bridge to parking.

"I don't remember that," Annie said, looking up at an immense expanse of glass stretching hundreds of feet above our heads.

"That's new," Heather provided. "It keeps the rain off travelers. I'll warn you. We're in a drought. It hasn't rained for three whole days."

We laughed at the joke. The winter rains in this neck of the woods I well remembered from my Fort Lewis days. As a young infantry lieutenant, I was expected to live outdoors for weeks in that rain.

Yes, I remembered the rain.

Heather produced a set of keys, pressed a button on the remote, and a golden car at the front of the line flashed its headlights and beeped friendly-like.

"A brand-new Lexus," Heather said proudly. "I hope you like the color."

"I love it," Annie said.

*Fancy,* says I, but to myself. *Clearly, this is girl-talk fun. My fun will come later.*

Heather offered Annie the keys, but my girl declined. "You know where we're going. Why don't you drive us?"

"I'm happy to do it, but the GPS navigation system on the

dash will show you where you're going. You'll never get lost with that beauty on board."

Heather took the driver's seat, Annie the passenger front, and I settled comfortably into a spacious back that left me plenty of legroom. While the skycap loaded our luggage, Heather explained how the car's navigation system worked. "I just point my PDA at it and send it my itinerary for the day," she said, producing her slim Palm Pilot from the inside pocket of her suit coat and doing the transfer.

"The navigator checks for your next appointment and, look, it's already highlighted the Harrison's location." A building was blinking on the map. Then it automatically zoomed out to a larger picture and drew a line from the airport to the hotel, and instructions started appearing below the map.

"Exit Parking Garage" sounded good for a starter.

"Andy will just love this," Annie said with a quick laugh that bordered on the giggle I remembered from before the world demanded we become grownups.

"Heaven only knows what he'll have it doing," I agreed.

"He'll rig it to play Outback Racing if he can," Annie added.

"Well, if the system gets too confusing," Heather said, "you can always change it back to the factory presets by holding this button down for a few extra seconds."

The trunk closed; apparently Heather had already settled up with the skycap, because he just ambled away. The drive from the airport to interstate to downtown was interesting to watch. I balanced gawking out the window at a city that I didn't remember with glances at the navigator. The GPS was a neat trick. Too bad Annie would be driving this car next week. That navigator thing was a gizmo I could use to find all my job interviews.

Oh, well.

Heather had us already checked into the Harrison, complete with key cards. The bellhop took care of our luggage and Lexus without much more than a nod from Heather. I suspected she was well known among them. She concentrated on leading us to our suite.

According to the plaque on the door, it wasn't the honeymoon suite, though it sure could have passed for it. It was named after a former president, and by the look of the place, he might actually have slept here.

A huge king-size bed had its own room with an adjoining spa bath featuring both a steam shower and a Jacuzzi tub. A separate sitting room was centered around a grand piano near a picture window, with the great view now diluted by silk sheers, and a fireplace on the opposite wall flanked by designer sofas. The formal dining room had a tiny kitchen off to one side that I doubt anyone had ever cooked in.

No, it wasn't a honeymoon suite. No honeymoon suite would have wasted money on the giant plasma television hanging over the fireplace. Excuse me, not a television, an entertainment center, as Heather was quick point out. Too many satellite channels to count, one hundred channels of music—everything from traditional gospel to teenage cool rock to hip-hop to classical. Yep, an entertainment center.

I wondered how long Heather would stay with us, but women seem to have some telepathic ability when it comes to the essentials of life, like men, and what to do with us. The young woman made quick work of her exit, saying she'd call us around nine to arrange breakfast and outline some options for our day.

I stood in the middle of the sitting room, wondering how tired Annie was. She lowered the lights with an easy flick of her wrist. With another, the sheer curtains opened, letting in a dark night that sparkled from the lights of Portland that lay below us.

As Annie came to me, she was pulling the pins from the bun that held her hair. It fell free with a quick shake of her head.

She put her arms around me and looked up, her eyes gleaming in the reflected lights of the city. "I thought she'd never leave," she whispered.

I kissed my wife.

Not the quick pecks that had become so familiar of late in our busy lives. No, this was a kiss like I might have given her after a week in the woods with my platoon. Like I'd offered her the day I asked her to marry me. A kiss like you might give your wife of twenty years when you have her all to yourself, know her so well... and there's no chance that a kid or two will interrupt to ask where a clean shirt is.

And Annie kissed me back—long, slow, lovingly. Why not turn a week in the lap of luxury into a second honeymoon? I couldn't think of a single reason not to. So I picked up Annie and carried her into that decadent bedroom. It was time to test-drive the plush accommodations.

## 10

"**ANSWER THE PHONE**," MY BELOVED SPOUSE SAID.

"You answer the phone," I countered.

"It's on your side," she pointed out, sounding not so much like a bride but more like a practical wife of twenty years.

"It's a half mile away," I tossed back. We'd agreed sometime during the night that the bed was way too big. A guy could get lost in it. Worse, a woman could get lost in it and never be found by the guy. King size it was not. Someone had to have invented something larger than that—and then topped it with this behemoth of a bed.

"Answer the phone," Annie said, raising herself up on one elbow and giving me a view of herself in a wisp of lingerie that she must have had imported from France or Italy or somewhere sinful.

"You owe me," I said, rolling over and reaching for the annoying noisemaker on the bedside table. There was also a phone in the bathroom's steam shower, one beside the tub, and a pair of them in the sitting room. In fact, there were phones all over the place. Why they couldn't put a phone on both sides of the bed defied my logic.

Maybe not my wife's. She stroked my back. "I'm oh so going to enjoy paying you for this service," she cooed.

"Yes," I said into the phone while rolling back over to look *oh, so yes* at my bride of twenty years.

"Mr. Taylor," said that Helpful Heather voice, "I hope I didn't wake you."

"Not much, Heather," I said, raising an eyebrow toward Annie. She gave me a frown of indeterminate meaning…but didn't slow what she was doing.

"Ms. Taylor said she wanted to view some potential homes today. I've arranged for a real-estate broker to meet you at the hotel over breakfast and lay out some possibilities for you. I hope that won't be a problem. I've scheduled your breakfast with her for 9:30. That's, ah, forty-five minutes from now."

"Okay, doing breakfast in forty-five minutes won't be a problem," I said for the benefit of my wife and hung up.

"So, we've got forty-five minutes," Annie said, a sly smile on her face. "A bit more, if you don't mind being fashionably late."

---

I was showered, shaved, and dressed for the day…and only two minutes late for breakfast. Amber Lopez already had a table reserved for us. As we were seated, she introduced herself and told us about her real-estate brokerage firm. Something in the name—and the expensive cut of the tasteful blue business suit she wore this early Saturday morning—told me her firm didn't deal in two-bedroom fixer-upper bungalows.

After we all ordered, she pulled a slim personal computer from her briefcase and proved that I was right. I was tempted to whistle at the first home...no, mansion...that Amber brought up for us to look at, but Annie didn't bat an eyelash, and I matched my response to hers.

"I was told that entertaining will be a major requirement for your job," Amber said, as a dining room with a glowing chandelier filled her screen. "That room can easily seat a dozen dinner guests, and the kitchen is large enough to support any caterer."

More things about this new job that hadn't been mentioned in the rush.

No, I had no right to be surprised. Wilson regularly invited us to his home when Annie had foreign business connections in town. Actually, I liked it when he entertained. It was much better than when Annie and her colleagues went out on the town. A home set boundaries that some people, far from home, tended to forget.

So we'd be entertaining bigwigs. And I'd better get used to the idea that the next mortgage was going to be sized not on my salary but on Annie's.

I swallowed hard. Got over the problem I was having breathing, and kept a smile on my face. *Annie is playing in the major leagues, fellow. You had better get used to being a major league spouse,* I lectured myself.

Still, it was none too easy to go through the day, looking at house after house I would never have given a second thought to if I'd driven by them a week ago. What does a good husband contribute to these kinds of talks?

So I listened to Amber and Annie, nodded when it sounded like I should, and remarked upon lawn care for a house on a hill with a huge expanse of lawn, and then talked about boat maintenance when we saw a house on a lake with its own boat dock.

These were all things Annie and I had dreamed about having in our home when we were looking for our first place, me fresh out of the army. But they were all things we'd known we couldn't buy on the salary of a freshly hired management-track intern. Then Annie had gone back to school, and money had been tight for a long time. And once she started zooming up the career ladder, we'd been too busy to think about upgrading.

"I saved this house for last," Amber said, driving up to a sprawling two-story brick place overlooking the Willamette River. Portland's lights were just starting to come on as the daylight dimmed.

"When it's not raining," Amber said, "you'll have a gorgeous view of Mount Hood." It was no longer raining, but the low gray clouds meant we would have to take her word for the better view.

The lights were already on in the house as we came up the

short walk from the turnaround driveway that ended in four garage doors. "One for each of you and a couple for the kids," Amber added slyly.

"I am so not looking forward to sharing the road with Joy," I muttered, then dodged an elbow from my wife.

"As if Andy's all that better," she said in an aside.

"You're the one offering him a car as a bribe to move," I pointed out.

"A spoon full of honey makes the inevitable go down easier." She had a point. I was just looking for my spoonful in the mix.

"Notice the two bay windows in the front here," Amber said. "They're matched by two more in the back." Like cheerful eyes, the bay windows smiled us into the house. To the left of the grand entry hall was a study to end all studies. Carved wooden bookshelves reached to the ceiling. I mentally claimed the room the instant I saw it. *A bay window of my own,* I thought. There was plenty of room for a huge desk and computer.

"The house is fully wired for computer networking and has integrated computer controls for lighting, entertainment, and communications," Amber noted.

"Just the study you've always dreamed of," Annie said.

*Yes,* I thought, *even more than I'd dared to dream of.*

To the left was the sitting room for formal entertainment. The cream-colored wallpaper and two big beveled-glass mirrors inset into custom frames on the wall facing the window made the room feel bigger than it was, and it was already plenty big. Cheerful flowers were blooming in planters on the window seat.

"This room is lit by the large bay window, so it's always bright, no matter how gloomy the weather." Amber pushed a button on the far wall, and it began to recede on quiet electric motors. "And when you are entertaining, you just open this up to the game room."

I managed not to say that the game room looked to be about the size of our whole house in Maryland.

"The pool table and the wet bar stay," Amber said. "They want to take all the other furniture with them."

"They can certainly take that moose head over the fireplace," Annie said. She had no truck with guns, hunting, and animal trophies. It was an old joke between us that if she didn't love her steak so much, she'd have made a great vegan.

One set of french doors opened onto the formal dining room, complete with sparkling chandelier. The second opened onto the patio. Correction—"garden," Amber called it. It was huge and well organized around trees and budding rhododendrons and azaleas that looked about ready to explode into bloom. Flower boxes full of other sprouts promised more color than I'd ever seen outside the National Arboretum. Daytime shade would be provided by a latticed wooden arbor that would still let light shine through to the patio.

"I'll arrange for you to meet the current homeowner's gardening service if you choose this home," Amber let drop softly when the two women started laughing at my comment about how intimidating it would be for me and Andy to keep up this yard.

"Right, the gardening service," I muttered and headed for the pool. "Won't I get kind of wet in the rain?" I asked.

"You certainly would," Amber said, "if the builder hadn't taken our liquid sunshine into account." She pushed a switch on the outside wall. A clear plastic building began to unfold onto the arbor's structure.

"During the long, lovely summer, you can swim under the open sky. When the winter rains return, you can cover up the pool and patio area and still use it.

"They've thought of everything," I muttered.

The kitchen was as large as promised, with a pantry that included a large walk-in cooler. "Good for keeping the bodies," I whispered to Annie...and managed to dodge her elbow again.

Upstairs included a rec room for the kids at the opposite end of the house from the master bedroom. Four spacious bedrooms for offspring and visitors. And a master bedroom suite that took up most of the area over the game room below. A Jacuzzi tub big enough for two—or four if they were real friendly—got my rib cage another hit. The current owner's bed looked even bigger than the one in the hotel room. And off to a side was a nursery or sewing room or something that Annie smiled at and announced would be her office.

I was none too sure about the idea of sharing my bedroom

with my wife's home office, but then, with my book-lined study on the first floor, I wasn't sure I could throw any stones.

I sighed, but from the look my wife was giving the layout, I strongly suspected she'd found what she was looking for. A large picture window was aimed at the rumored location of Mount Hood. Next to it was a set of french doors that opened onto our own balcony.

"Perfect for evening drinks," Amber said, then when we didn't rise to that bait, she switched to, "or breakfast as you watch the sun rise over the mountains."

"Better than breakfast in bed?" I asked my wife.

"I'll think about that," Annie said with a wifely smile.

We went downstairs, me keeping quiet as Annie did the same. It had been a long time since we bought our home, but I still remembered the basic rules. You don't gush over the place you want to buy. Gushing only adds to the price.

"As you suggested, Ms. Taylor, I saved the best for last." The words left me not knowing whether to frown at Amber…or Annie.

Past the kitchen was a door I assumed led to the garage and maybe a food delivery area by the pantry. Nothing so gauche as unloading their own car trunk after trips to the local Piggly Wiggly for the folks who lived in this place.

*Note to self: How do you turn a place this big and fancy into a home?*

*Second note to self: Share above question with Annie…later. Maybe much later.*

But there was no garage on the other side of that door. Nope, there was a workshop. The walls were hung with tools for just about every kind of work a man could dream of doing with his hands. Woodworking, metalworking, car repair—you could field-strip and restore an engine with everything I saw gleaming in its own place here.

The counters and floor were clean enough to eat off of, but that didn't steal the hint of wood from the air. I took in a deep breath.

"The owner liked to make furniture. I believe he did all the built-in bookcases in the study himself."

I smiled at the well-used planer and miter box and knew I stood in the shop of a dedicated man. "Yep, I bet he did."

"Want to make the bookcases for my home office?" Annie said, coming up to take my arm.

"You did tell her to save the best for last, didn't you?"

"I kind of thought you'd like it."

"What's their asking price for a place like this?"

I did whistle when Amber said a number. Clearly, the mortgage would have to be based on Annie's income. Right now, I wasn't sure I'd have any income once we moved. Even with all the equity on our current home, we were looking at financing a chunk of change.

We turned without a word and headed for Amber's car. On the drive out of the neighborhood, we passed a church, not four blocks from the house. I noted the address and, holding Annie in my arms in the backseat, did my best to follow the route Amber took back to the hotel.

The next morning, Annie and I were up early and in a rear pew at that church. I didn't even need to use the Lexus's navigation system. I hadn't lost my gift. Take me someplace once, let me watch the way back home, and I could go there again on the first try.

The minister was a kindly old man. But his sermon that dreary Sunday was anything but a kindly feel-good affair. "Indolent living," he intoned, "is the sin of the comfortable."

I listened as he pretty much nailed my soul to the Scriptures and left me no wiggle room. I was comfortable, happy in my own life. But did God call us to be comfortable? When we were smug and content, could we even hear the quiet voice of our Savior calling us to repent of our sins and follow Him?

"Like the rich young man, will you turn away from your Lord and Savior when the time comes to choose between comfort and calling?" the preacher asked.

I looked at Annie and found her looking at me. We nodded together. If God was calling us to accept the new level of affluence and change our life, He certainly had drawn us to a church with a shepherd who knew how to light up the shadows in just that kind of life.

We stayed late after the services, waiting until we could shake the pastor's hand and introduce ourselves to Minister Baldwin. "Call me Stan," he insisted and invited us to join their Sunday school, which was meeting right now, after the early morning service.

"But we don't want to interrupt anything if the class is in the middle of studying a topic," I said. "We don't want them to have to backtrack on our account."

"I know," he said with a knowing smile. "Most people are too polite to want to interrupt things. That's why we have an open course. All they do in the class I'm offering you today is talk about my sermon. Share where the Holy Spirit maybe nudged the words He gave me. It's usually pretty lively."

So we sat around a table with steaming cups of coffee before us while other church members dissected the good preacher's words. And they weren't bashful about what they said, either. Some of the people in the room were college professors; others were business-men and businesswomen. One guy drove a big-rig truck. It was quite a mixture.

But what got me the most was, as they shared what the Scrip-tures and the sermon had said to them, Stan sat on the floor next to the door. He listened, his eyes closed, his head nodding now and then. It was as if Stan, having shared the Word of God for his flock, was now given a chance to receive it back from the class.

"Very nice church," I told Annie, as we stopped at a unique hamburger place that Amber had pointed out to us.

"Very nice church," she repeated. "I was afraid that moving would take us away from, well, God's safe harbor for us."

"When we get comfortable with one safe port, we tend to forget that God has plenty of other ones."

Annie nodded. And I tried to keep that thought with me as I went into the new week. But even I didn't know just how badly I was going to need a safe harbor.

## 11

MONDAY MORNING, HEATHER ARRIVED AT THE HOTEL AT 7:00 a.m. sharp to keep us company for breakfast. She then showed Annie how to program her car's navigation system to get her to work. With a hug and a grin for me, Annie took off for her first day running her own office, looking for all the world as happy as Joy was on her first day boarding the school bus for kindergarten.

I didn't feel anywhere near so gleeful at the prospects for my day.

"Do you have a personal data assistant?" Heather asked me after I'd waved Annie out of the hotel's underground garage.

"A Palm Pilot?" I asked. "Sort of," I said, matching my ancient electronic gizmo against a slim one in Heather's hand that couldn't have been more than five minutes out of the box.

"Let's see if yours will talk to mine," she said, punching a button with a manicured finger. My old helper did nothing for a long moment.

"I guess they can't talk," I said.

"Check your to-do list for today," she said with a confident smile.

A few clicks and I found that my day was full, as was my next day. Indeed, suddenly the entire week was booked solid from nine to five.

"And I used to consider myself on the bleeding edge of the new tech in computers."

"Snooze, you lose," this slip of a young woman lectured me. "Now let me show you a few things about your rental car."

Parked next to the space made vacant by Annie's departure was a silver version of her Lexus. "You might as well get used to driving it," Heather said, going around to the passenger side.

I settled into the driver's seat, doing the usual series of mirror adjustments. Heather sat patiently until I finished, then said, "Why don't you program the navigator?"

I'd just watched her teach my wife how to do that, but not all that closely, nor all that attentively. Heather was wearing a tan business suit today, but the blouse under it was very thin, and her bra beneath that was very skimpy and very transparent.

I'd spent a lot of time looking other places when Heather leaned forward to show Annie something and her blazer fell open. Practicing my covenant with my eyes was turning out to be a whole lot harder around young businesswomen out here than it was back home.

"I'll figure out how to navigate when I need to," I said, trying to cover for myself.

"Mr. Taylor, pull out your Palm Pilot."

I did.

"Aim it at the navigator."

I did. She leaned over and punched a button, throwing her coat open. I concentrated on the dashboard.

Surprise, surprise, the screen of the navigation system came to life as each location where I had an appointment flowed across it.

"Neat," I said. "Any more tricks?"

"I'm full of them. But you've got appointments this morning, and so do I." Leaving me wondering just exactly what she meant by that. "Why don't you drop me by my office, and we'll call ourselves even."

She tapped her digital assistant, and a new address appeared on the navigator. Guided to her office by the car, I did drop her off, and, despite traffic being terribly slow as I went up the hill by the zoo, I managed to make it to my first interview early.

I had a pleasant time. So did the fellow interviewing me. He said he didn't normally do interviews, leaving them to the younger members of his staff, but then, they were usually interviewing kids their own age. Yes, we had a good talk, the kind of thing I usually had over lunch with my fellow professionals in Maryland. A good talk among peers was a fine way to spend a lunch but hardly what I needed in my job search.

I knew that. He knew that. So did most of the other Human Resources people I talked to the rest of the week. We all knew I needed more than a discussion of how rough the job market was.

How hard it was to train people coming out of high school and college with minimal basic skills. How high salary expectations were among new hires and how tight the market actually was.

These were all fine things to talk about when you had a job to go back to after lunch. But it wasn't all that helpful when you were looking for a job and only had a week to find one.

I finished my last interview on Friday feeling no more optimistic than I had before my first one on Monday. As I headed back to the hotel, my cell beeped.

"Taylor here," I said.

"Taylor here, too," my wife said.

"Any thoughts about supper?" I asked, hoping for time now to talk about how my week had gone. We'd spent supper every night so far talking about how Annie's days had gone. I think I was doing a good job of supporting her.

I hoped tonight there might be a few moments to talk about my situation. The last interviewer, a young kid hardly much older than Andy, had tried to be helpful. He'd asked me if I would be willing to take an internship position. "I know it's a major cut in pay, but unless you found something earlier in the week, this might be your best bet."

Help like that left my stomach in knots. I needed to put some food into the twisted wreckage of my digestive tract.

"Let me think a bit about supper," Annie answered. "You remember that church we went to Sunday?"

I said I did.

"I saw a place near there I'd like to check out. We could ditch one of the cars in their lot for a while."

"That would be great. I'm stuck in traffic. If I can survive to the next exit, I'll take off for it. Otherwise, you'll just have to find someone else for supper company."

"I'll wait for you no matter how long it takes," my wife answered and added what sounded like a kiss before clicking off.

I did make it to the exit and to the church. In fact, I made it before Annie did. Portland's famous rain showers had taken a break, so I took advantage of the lull to stretch my legs.

Sea gulls buzzed overhead, but they didn't leave their mark on the rental. The air felt fresh. It even held a hint of salt from the ocean not far beyond the hills to the west. I decided I could get to like this kind of life, dodging raindrops to smell the sea.

At least maybe. If I had a job.

Annie pulled up.

"I want to show you something," she said the moment I opened the door to her car. "Get in."

"What?" I answered, climbing into the passenger side.

"A surprise."

"What kind of surprise?" I answered, getting into her mode of play. "Animal, vegetable, mineral?"

"Not one of those."

"None? It has to be one of those."

"Nope, it's not one of those. It's all of those. You're not thinking outside the box enough."

"All of the above," I muttered.

"Yep. All of the above."

"Animal, vegetable, *and* mineral," I mused as Annie pulled to a stop in the driveway of the last house we'd looked at. "I see vegetable and minerals," I said. "I don't see any animals."

"There's got to be some earthworms keeping that grass so green."

"That's cheating," I said, taking the place in with a glance. "And you brought me here and stooped to cheating to defeat me for what purpose, my dear woman?"

She produced a house key. "Want to take a second look?"

"It certainly deserves one," I said, taking the key and getting out quickly so I could skip around to open Annie's door for her.

"Married twenty years and you are still a gentleman," she smiled.

"Probably explains why you've kept me around."

I eyed the house as we walked up to it. "Lighting's better this afternoon," I said.

"Looking for peeling paint?" Annie asked.

"Something like that. It's too perfect. There's got to be some problem with it somewhere. Maybe the roof leaks?"

Annie glanced at the low clouds. "Now that would be a problem," she agreed.

I opened the door. "Oops," I said. "I think someone's cleaned them out."

Today the place was empty; every stick of furniture was gone.

"Whoever did it, did a nice job," Annie observed, walking into the study. "They even dusted the bookcases."

"I think it's that automatic air filter or something they have on the air-conditioning heat pump. Sucks the dust right out of the air," I said, quoting Amber.

We moseyed through the now empty parlor, only slight dents in the thick carpet showing where the couch, chairs, and tables had been. The flowers were still blooming, cheerfully scenting the vacant room.

"Hey, somebody left papers on the pool table," I announced.

"You don't say," Annie said, a big grin starting to take over her face faster than she could swallow it.

"I do say," I said, more interested in the way the grin was bringing out a dimple I hadn't seen on Annie's face in a long time than I was in the papers.

"Wonder what's on the papers?" Annie said with so little curiosity that I knew beyond question what they were. "Don't you want to look at them?" she said.

"I'm more fascinated by the look on your face, my bride."

"Aw, come on, you've got to wonder what would be left in an empty house."

I was, but all I could take in for a second was the parade of delight and pride and sheer joy on Annie's face playing with the light from the window. The sun must have broken through the clouds for a moment, because beams of light were streaming through the window, turning Annie's hair to gold and adding a sparkle to her eyes that only a poet could praise properly.

"Don't you want to see the papers?" she wheedled.

"They can't be all that important," I said, but I did pry my eyes away from Annie long enough to take them in. A deed was closest to me on the table. Beside it were mortgage documents.

"Someone's getting ready to buy this place," I said.

"I bought it," Annie said, in a husky voice.

"You bought it." I tried to keep the surprise out of my voice. "Don't I need to sign something?"

"There are a couple of places you'll need to sign, but Oregon is a community-property state. What I own, you own, and vice versa."

"Oh," was all I managed to get out. I was having trouble breathing again. That was happening to me a lot lately.

"The bed's gone from upstairs," Annie said, her eyes still glowing. "But they left the pool table."

"Ah, yes, ah, I'm kind of hungry just now," I said, trying to cover for the hole that was suddenly yawning in my gut. "Didn't I see a steak-and-seafood restaurant just down from the church?" I could see where Annie was going with this, and I wasn't quite ready to follow.

"Yes, it has been a long day," she said. "And I skipped lunch to get things done at the Realtor's office." Annie followed my lead. It was a tragedy to watch the light go out of her eyes, and I felt so guilty for that crime. Still, I turned from the pool table.

In a few moments, I was closing her door, and she sat very still in the driver's seat. As I came around the car to my side, I eyed the house. What was it that suddenly made me feel so sick about it?

I had to think only a moment before I knew exactly what had given me that sinking feeling in my gut. Annie bought this house. Some bank qualified her for the house, no questions asked, no need for any second income. No need for a husband's paycheck. I didn't have a job out here, and the bank didn't even care if I ever had a job. Annie's paycheck alone was enough to pay the bill for this mansion.

I was superfluous.

Rain started to fall again. That must have been the reason I shivered as I settled into my seat. Still, I forced a smile Annie's way as she started the car and we headed down the street for dinner.

"That's a big house," I managed to get out finally as Annie stopped at a stop sign to let two kids, a boy and a girl, maybe nine, race their skateboards through the crosswalk ahead of us, as impervious to the gentle rain as ducks. "Our furniture will hardly fill it up."

"Our old furniture is looking kind of shabby," Annie said. "I was thinking we'd use most of our living room stuff in the kid's rec room upstairs and buy new for the sitting room. Your office, too. And I want to get a whole new bedroom suite. I'm starting to like the size of that bed at the hotel. Be nice to have a bed that size in my very own bedroom. And I'll keep a set of flares on the bedside table so you won't have trouble finding me."

"That's good to hear," I said, glad to know that she wasn't planning on getting rid of her old shabby husband along with the old shabby furniture.

There were a million words on the tip of my tongue, most of them sharp at the edge. Way too many of them were tipped with the poison of my own wounded pride. My own miserable week.

I let the pain-filled refrains run around the back of my mouth, hating the taste of them, wishing they were anywhere but inside me, but they were mine. And if I ever let them free, they would do things to me and Annie and our life that I would never be able to undo.

*Dear Lord,* I prayed, *help me find the right words. Help me find the ones that will bless this moment rather than plunge us into a hell worse than Lucifer's.*

I held my tongue as we were seated in a darkened restaurant that smelled of hickory smoke and money. It was only after we'd ordered that I finally risked something more than a nod or yes to Annie's excitement.

"You know, honey, in the bad old days, if a husband bought a house without his wife's approval, any woman worth her salt would have keelhauled him."

Annie blinked twice as honest surprise dropped her jaw. "But I wanted to surprise you." The words came across very much like a guy line. I was finding that I didn't like playing the traditional "little lady" role.

"And you looked at the house," she went on, "and you had nothing but nice things to say about it. I could see you were just as excited about it as I was." She was right, that was all correct, but I raised her an eyebrow. Didn't she hear how much she was parroting some guy in a bad sitcom?

"And you took us to church just down the street from it. We agreed that Stan would make a great minister for us. For the kids."

There she had me. I most certainly had sent her that signal. I swallowed a big chunk of the nasties that had been stomping around in the back of my mouth. "You're right. I did, didn't I?"

"And it sure would be a long drive to church if we bought any of those other houses," Annie pointed out. "Fess up. You love the place."

"Yeah." I swallowed my pride—even though it took a big gulp. "It's beautiful. Just like you."

She smiled and blushed at that, and we went on to talk more about Annie's day. Her office was shuttling containers from as far away as Singapore to as far inland as the Dakotas. Keeping track of all that stuff was a full-time job and more. The problem of how she'd add to the present level of trade in the face of fluctuating currencies left deep furrows on my wife's forehead.

I wanted to kiss them away, solve all her problems. But this was the job she had chosen for herself, the challenge she had sought.

Me, I just needed a job.

So I listened, offered a thought here, an extra option there, and enjoyed my steak when it came.

It tasted far better than the bitter words I'd left unsaid. Later, when things went very wrong, I was so grateful that we'd spent that time together in harmony.

# 12

**"HOW'D THE WEEK GO?" WAS THE PERENNIAL QUESTION WHEN** I got back to the office on Monday.

"Great," was my perennial answer. That and a smile were what most people wanted to get from me. I gave them what they wanted and got on with the work.

"That 'great' sounded awful weak," Jeb Shepherd said, shaking his head, as we discussed our lunch options. "The wife gets a huge promotion on the wrong side of the country. You spend a week cold job-hunting in her neighborhood. Everyone else may take your brush-off, but, buddy, you are gonna have to talk it out with me."

Lunch was something I normally ate at my desk, or when the weather was pleasant, I bought something from a caterer's truck that stopped by the plant and ate it on the picnic tables outside on the lawn.

It was raining today, a gray drizzle that would have stripped off all the cherry blossoms if they'd budded early, but they hadn't. For the moment, spring seemed to be holding its breath, waiting for the winter to get out of my heart.

It might have a long wait.

Jeb and I took off for a sandwich place that warmed their subs. Warmth was something I needed. In fits and starts I told him the story of the last week. Jeb has this gift from the Holy Spirit. He can spot bunk a mile away, and he has no patience for it.

"So you did a lot of listening to what was happening to the missis and didn't do much talking about what was going on inside your skull," he summed up for me.

"Yeah. She was really occupied with her new job. Jeb, it was so much like when I got my shop fifteen years ago that I just wanted to enjoy her joy." I shrugged. "Wasn't a lot happening on my side of the dinner table worth enjoying. In fact, I was so upset with my end of the world I'm not sure I did much of a job of listening to hers. And I didn't share." I glanced outside. "Who wants to be around someone who's just raining on your parade?"

Jeb shook his head. "What happened to 'for better or worse'?" he said.

"When you're enjoying the richer side, it gets kind of hard to see," I shrugged, feeling a bit pinned to the mat with my own theology. I could already hear what came next.

"Ain't you the one always telling me that to walk with the Lord is to share? To share the good and the bad. Your sins and God's gifts. Seems to me you're not shooting as straight just now as you usually do."

"Maybe with all the twists and turns in the new situation coming down on me, I'm not doing as good a job as I usually do."

"I remember someone saying to me a while back that walking with the Lord can be easy or hard. That we can only really know we have the walk down when we can do the walk when it ain't all that easy."

"Anyone ever tell you that quoting someone's words of wisdom back at them when they don't want to hear them is not one of your most endearing qualities?" I managed to get a smile around those words.

Jeb just grinned back. "Yep. My wife. Regularly. But she still puts up with me. And you're gonna have to put up with me doing it until you get your head screwed back on right. Thus saith the Lord," he finished like some Old Testament prophet.

"Yeah. Now I just have to get into the mood to listen." I tried to put a joking tone into the words to soften them, but they were the hard truth of my life lately.

"For what it's worth," Jeb said, "when I find it hard to shoot straight in my walk with God, I find it good to go down to the firing range and put some lead into the bull's-eye. Kind of knowing I can do it, in the flesh, makes it easier for me to do it in the spirit. Or at least I can laugh at myself *before* I do something stupid. This Saturday, why don't you and the kids come out to the range with me?"

"You know how the wife feels about guns." Annie was death on having weapons in the house. There'd been an incident when we were at Fort Lewis. A soldier shot his wife and then himself. I only had to suggest having a weapon in the house to get Annie to relive that all over again. But when Jeb invited the kids and me out to shoot, which happened about every annual picnic, with the kids saying "Yes," "Oh, yeah, man," or the like, Annie would just shake her head and it wouldn't happen.

"Yes, but you mentioned that the wife is on the wrong coast. In Portland, working in a dream job and living in luxury. So why don't you and the kids come out with me? I'll let you get off a few rounds on the M-1." He knew my weakness for that World War II relic of his. "And I just finished a black-powder replica of a Kentucky Long Rifle. Kids ought to get the feel and smell of the rifle that built this country. Didn't you say one of them loved history?"

"Both of them," I said. Jeb had quite a collection of historic pieces. And it would be fun to show the kids how to sight in a weapon. Put holes in a target. Learn how to shoot straight...and do it right.

I sighed. Yes, I needed to do some straight shooting, myself.

"I'll put it to the kids tonight. Tell you what they say tomorrow."

"That's a yes, then." He laughed. "I have no doubt that they'll love it. I'll see you Saturday."

His words gave me plenty to think about, enough so that I tried to call Annie that night. But she wasn't at the hotel, and her cell phone just kicked me over to voice mail. I wondered what she was doing out there on the West Coast without me.

It was early yet out there—maybe she was having dinner with her smiling rat of a boss. I'd call her in the morning, I thought.

When morning came, I noticed that Andy hadn't given me back the keys to my old car; he'd kind of slid out of the house and into the car without saying anything. And I hadn't called him on it. The problem with learning to keep your mouth shut is, if you get into the habit, it can get hard to break.

Speaking of shut mouths, Annie wasn't answering her phone again. She was probably hard at work, showing all those Left Coast folks why they'd promoted her. I knew she'd have them whipped into shape in no time.

She wasn't the only one with a shop to run. I worked late, trying to catch up on what had piled up while I was gone. The counseling service reported Jim Turner was doing well and might be expected back to work in the next week. Not a lot of meat in the report, but I liked the way they respected Jim's confidentiality. I stopped by the plant long enough to let Mamma Boyd know she'd have a new hand. She'd been cross-training one of her employees on Jim's old job in milling and was working him half time in both slots.

"With the new line of knives we have coming along, we'll be more than glad to have Jim back. But tell him not to rush. Heaven knows it's hard getting those dark dogs to leave you alone once they've laid down with you."

That was something we could agree on.

I called Andy to make sure he and Joy were okay. He promised me they'd go straight home and hit their homework. I promised them to be home in time to pay for the pizza. He said he'd rather have Chinese. We "compromised" on Chinese.

I found that the work suddenly petered out an hour after the crew left. On my way home, I noticed that my gym bag was still in the back, along with Annie's. We hadn't worked out since, well, before she'd announced her promotion. Normally, we worked out twice during the week and on Saturday. I still had an hour before the kids needed feeding. I decided that I sure could use some stress-reduction time on the stair stepper. I headed for the athletic club.

Normally Annie and I took machines right next to each other and talked about the day, the kids, whatever needed talking about, with the air we had leftover from our workout. I'd brought a couple of magazines from the office to read at home tonight. Homework for Dad while the kids did theirs.

I took one in to read during my workout.

All the machines were free when I came in, so I took one at the end and started a slow workout; it wasn't long before I realized I'd skipped way too many sessions. It also wasn't long before two young women I didn't recognize appeared on the machines next to me. Clearly, neither of them had any idea how to program the stair steppers.

"This guy must know how to make the thing go. Look at what he's got his machine doing."

I looked up from my magazine and offered some suggestions. It might sound like a blonde joke, but the two gals only managed to klutz their machines up worse. I finally put mine on pause and showed them what to do.

They giggled and did it.

And I noticed smiles from several of the regulars as I got back on my stair stepper. Why hadn't they helped? Then it dawned on me that I'd been looking down some very skimpy tops as I talked to the young women.

And enjoying it.

I clenched my teeth. While being Helpful Harry, I'd totally forgotten to keep my covenant with my eyes. *What's the matter, Ben, can't you walk and chew gum at the same time?*

Once again, I'd been yanked out of my "same old same old," and forgotten to take the rest of me with me. *Lord, You've got to help me get better at this,* I begged.

As I finished, the young woman next to me asked cheerfully, "Want to go out for drinks?"

"And waste the good this exercise is doing me?" I shot back. "Not on your life. Besides, I already have a date."

"Oh. Someone better than us?" The question had a sashay to Lycra-clad hips with it.

"Yep. My kids," I said, wrapping a towel around my shoulders, "and their homework."

And with that, I beat a quick retreat. Or, as the marines have been known to say, I attacked in a different direction.

I was home in time to pay for the Chinese food delivery. After most of supper was eaten and our separate days had been shared, I mentioned that I'd had lunch with Jeb.

"He's just finished making a replica of a Kentucky Long Rifle. He wondered if you kids might be interested in shooting it."

"Man, would we," Andy yelled.

"You so bet," Joy jumped up and hugged me.

"If it doesn't rain Saturday, what do you say that we do just that? Assuming all your homework is done and your reports are finished, of course."

There was a small stampede up the stairs as they rushed to get back to work. I settled into my chair in the living room, three unread magazines beside me, and smiled.

People who went out for drinks at night had no idea what they were missing back home.

# 13

THE NEXT MORNING, IN A DAZZLING DISPLAY OF COLOR,
Maryland showed just how little my mood affected the weather.
The day dawned warm and lovely, and flowers once again began
threatening to bloom. Come lunchtime, my crew refused to let me
eat at my desk and just about dragged me out to a table. I got a
salad and lemonade from the lunch truck and settled down to
munching.

The midday sun warmed air that smelled of a rainbow of
bright colors. People all around me talked. Me, I leaned back and
closed my eyes. If I filtered out all the words, I could just make out
the birds chirping in the trees. A squadron of pigeons and sparrows
were making noise, demanding the leavings of our lunch. I could
almost forget the cold confusion in my soul.

"You ought to talk to Ben about that," brought my eyes open
and my attention back to the peopled world. Ready to don my Personnel hat, I turned to Max, saw who she was talking to, and realized I'd put on the wrong hat.

"Ben, how do you keep a teenage boy in line?" Max said, with Bernice Pozig from Finance at her elbow.

I smiled. Bernice had a son Andy's age. The two were good friends, or had been the last time I checked. Come to think of it, Andy hadn't mentioned Rich lately in his daily debriefs.

"Cattle prods. Electrically charged cattle prods. Works every time," I said with the best grin I could muster.

"If only Child Protection would let us," Bernice said with a sigh. "When Larry died, everybody warned me I could expect trouble from Rich, but he was such a good boy, and, well, things seemed to be going great."

Annie and I had known Bernice through Larry's work in imports. His cancer had taken a long time to do its killing thing, and we'd stood by them, holding trembling hands when they were offered and in the process becoming real friends. Bernice had not been prepared to reenter the job market nearly as well as Annie, but I'd found her a job where she could put some fresh shine on her financial training from back before she became a mother. Everything seemed to be going as well as could be hoped for.

"What's happening?" usually left people plenty of openings to say what they wanted...or not. I offered it to her.

Bernice began talking, words pouring out of her like a dam had broken. Rich had taken to coming home late, to missing school assignments, to hanging with friends that didn't seem to have parents, or at least not parents Rich wanted Bernice to meet.

"He told me he was too busy with schoolwork when he dropped

out of church group. Now he's too busy for much of anything but his friends," she said, her hands absently shredding a paper napkin.

I wanted to ask about drugs, but if she wasn't offering me that information, I doubted she knew it or wanted to know it. How much of the problem was Rich, and how much was Bernice?

"A boy that age needs a man to ride herd on him," Max observed. I nodded, so did Bernice.

"What do you say I ask Andy what he thinks is going on with Rich?" I said, thinking I needed a whole lot more input on this than I had.

"That would be good," Bernice said. "All I'm hearing from is teachers. And Rich says they don't like him." She went on about that until the buzzer at the plant announced the end of our lunch hour, and we headed back in for the afternoon.

Over seafood takeout that evening, after I'd finished work and gone to the gym, I asked Andy about Rich. He just shook his head. "I hardly see him anymore, Dad. He has a whole new set of friends."

"The type I don't want you to have?"

Andy snorted. "The type *I* don't want me to have. Remember those groups you warned me to look out for in high school?" I'd described the groups that I remembered from my time there: nerds, Christians, stoners, jocks, preppies, and "ins." I nodded.

"Well, now they've got the 'lions' opposite the Christians. Whatever we're for, they're against. They aren't stoned, at least not usually, but they're just against anything we're for. Like they show up at the Bible study we have before class each morning. Make rude noises. Ask questions you know they don't want answered. Some even pick fights to see if we're gonna turn the other cheek."

"And Rich is one of them now?"

"Well, he's running with them," Andy said, then worried his lower lip for a moment. "Dad, I don't think Rich hates God. Not really. But he's hurting real bad about his dad dying. He keeps asking why God would let something like that happen. He wants to know how a loving God could let something like that happen. Dad, I really don't have an answer."

"None of us have any easy answers, Andy," I said. I could imagine what it would be like to be sixteen, seventeen, and trying to juggle all those feelings of loneliness, hurt, anger. Having just recently buried my father after he lived a long life, I still missed him.

"Thanks, Son," I continued. "His mom was asking me how I kept you in line."

"Barbed-wire whips," his sister said.

"And if you don't behave, he'll take away your Barbies," Andy shot back.

"I don't play with Barbies anymore."

I left my kids to their argument about what kept them in line, knowing full well that it was God's love and their love for each other, for themselves, and for Annie and me that did the real work.

It was so much easier to keep people on the right path with love than with negative emotions. How did you help someone filled with pain and anger and isolation to find a way back from that road that spirals downward to fire and brimstone?

I said a quick prayer, knowing that Bernice needed wisdom I didn't have. And after the long day's work and workout, I fell asleep, exhausted, as soon as my head hit the pillow.

Lunch the next day was rained out, so I didn't see Bernice. The last two days of the week the clouds were gone, and Maryland put her best face on again. We all gathered at the picnic tables for the midday meal. Bernice joined Max and Al and Bea and me. Max and Al and I had already walked our kids through those painful years, so we shared while Bea just thanked God that her kids were still small enough that a kiss could make most of their scrapes and hurts go away.

I found myself admiring Bernice and her struggle. Many mothers would just give up, resign themselves to watching their child get seduced away by the world. Bernice was praying for Rich. And she was seeking help from the rest of us, seeking any idea that might help her reclaim her and Larry's son. It took real guts to share problems like that. I was glad that my team was there to listen to her, to support her, and yes, maybe to help her and Rich find a way back to the Lord's path.

It left me feeling good about something.

It also made me look back over what I'd come to call my

wasted fifteen years at Carter Cutlery. They might be considered a waste for some personnel types, eying them against what was now the expected norm for smart careers. But I don't think God would consider them a waste.

As I looked back, I could remember a lot of people like Bernice and Larry that Annie and I had stood by. Jim Turner wasn't the first man I'd helped through counseling so he and his family could weather a tough time.

I thought of the long list of men and women I'd done the intervention for and walked into that first AA meeting, that first anger-management class, or Family Dynamics Without Violence session. Now that I started counting, it was a lot longer list than I'd remembered of late. For some, those sessions had been a first step that led them toward Jesus. For others, well, it's up to the Holy Spirit. It's my job to be there to help in any way that God grants me...and in His time.

It was a nice thought to warm my soul for the rest of the workday.

I kept that thought with me when I went to workout at the health club. What is it about a middle-aged man working out alone that seems to attract women? The woman beside me didn't draw my attention by doing anything so obvious as the last pair, but she wanted to talk, so I ended up listening. And it seemed that she was only too willing to continue the talk over dinner. When I told her I already had scheduled dinner with my kids, she smiled softly and left the stair stepper for the treadmills…and another man doing his miles. Maybe that was God's plan for the both of them. This side of the grave I doubted I'd know the ending of her search.

Dinner conversation that night at home was almost totally devoted to discussing tomorrow's trip to the rifle range. Joy had downloaded some articles from the Internet, and I found myself explaining sight pictures, slow-squeezing triggers, measured breathing, and how you put all those together to hit what you were aiming for.

"So that's what you've always been talking about," Andy said, a light bulb all but lighting up above his head. "All the time, when the news shows some dude with an AK-47 just spraying off rounds, you always say nasty things about him. Now I get it. You think he should be sighting down his barrel and aiming for what he's shooting at."

" 'One target, one shot, that's it,' is what my sergeant taught me in boot camp. He always said, 'Anything else is a waste of good ammo.' I thought I taught you that already," I said, reaching out to tousle my son's hair.

"Well, I remember you saying all those things, but until Baby Ducks here downloaded all those pictures and you started talking just now, I didn't really put it all together."

Which reminded me that you can do a lot of preaching, but until the Holy Spirit turns on the lights, folks find it hard to see.

While I was having this moment of self-revelation—again—Joy was doing her usual reminder to Andy that she didn't want to be called Baby Ducks ever again.

Only this time my girl took a different approach.

"Okay, see, if I outshoot you tomorrow, you never call me Baby Ducks again. Ever. Or, who knows, maybe I'll borrow Uncle Jeb's Long Rifle and make an extra hole in your head."

"It's a deal," Andy said. "No squirt in the band's gonna outscore me."

I let the two of them run down that line until they fell quiet, then put my own oar in that water. "Joy, we don't ever joke about using a weapon to hurt someone."

"But he *needs* another hole in his head."

"Maybe, with your sense of metaphor, Andy does. But never joke about putting it there with a loaded weapon. Never, ever point a weapon at anyone. People have a right to assume if you're talking nasty and waving a weapon their way that it's loaded and you intend to kill them. And they have a right to act on that assumption, and what they do may very likely not be very nice from your perspective."

Both my kids were nodding; I had their attention. "A loaded weapon is serious business. Never treat it as anything else." I'd made my point; now it was time to lighten up.

"The one time I got excited, forgot the rules, and stood up with my weapon not pointed downrange, my sarge just about made a new hole in me, and all he used was the English language."

"Probably a whole lot of the school words we don't use at our house," Andy said under his breath to Joy.

"No." I put on a serious display of remembering. Actually, it wasn't all that hard to remember that day. Some things you just don't forget. "Sarge only used the words I use around the house. He just made very good use of them."

My kids laughed, and I joined them. But before our talk was over, I made it a point to warn them that if there was any horsing around tomorrow, we'd never do it again. "Any failure to show full respect for the weapons you're using, it will be Uncle Jeb, not me, who locks the weapons up in his trunk. And trust me. You'll never forget what he'll have to say about that."

Full of thoughts about tomorrow's day at the range, and sure of what my wife would think of my plans, I decided not to call Annie that night. Of course, I justified it with the thought that she'd been too busy at her new job to call me, either. In fact, I was feeling a bit neglected and resentful. *All the more reason to enjoy my day with the kids tomorrow,* I thought as I fell asleep.

Next morning Jeb came by to pick us up. As we drove out to the range, he gave the kids a safety lecture not all that different from the one I'd given them last night. My kids had the good manners to nod their heads and say, "Yes, Uncle Jeb."

The range was a plain wooden building, low and in need of paint. Even from the grassy parking lot, I could clearly see the dirt embankments that stretched away at fifty, one hundred, and two hundred meters.

Jeb opened his trunk, and there, laid out for all to see, was a full historical collection of the development of modern weaponry. His AR-15 was a civilian version that didn't look all that different from my old M-16A2. But then it had been almost fifteen years since I'd racked my rifle for the last time. He also had a semiautomatic M-14 as well as the M-1 Garand I couldn't wait to get my hands on. For Andy, he'd brought a British SMLE, the gun they used in both World War I and II. Joy picked up the Kentucky Long Rifle with all the glee and care she usually showed a new puppy at the pet store.

"It's beautiful," she whispered. "You built it yourself?"

"I put the pieces together from the kit. Ben, I've already test fired it, so you can trust that I put all the pieces together right."

I laughed as he read my mind. I trusted Jeb to run every corner of the knife factory with complete safety. But that was my baby girl holding that black-powder weapon. I'd sure hate to see it blow up in her pretty face.

I whistled as I spotted the next thing in Jeb's trunk. He had an 1847 Colt Walker revolver. Still cuddling the M-1, I reached for that. "Original?"

"Nope, another one I built. Andy, you fire that puppy just once, and you'll know just how much those westerns are faking it."

"Can I?"

"I think you're right in line behind your papa," Jeb said with a grin.

"Yeah," I nodded. "Me first."

"Aw, that's age discrimination," my son said. One of the disadvantages of being a personnel type and raising kids is that they pick up a lot of your work. And try to apply the terms and lingo to their benefit.

"You're under forty, son, so those rules don't apply," I repeated for about the forty-eleventh time.

"Well, you aren't forty yet," he pointed out, something he wouldn't be able to use against me for much longer.

"Okay, how about possession being nine-tenths of the law?" I said, hefting the revolver.

"Lady and gentlemen, we are around weapons," Jeb pointed out. "Please show them respect by canning your usual bickering. As a rule, I never party or argue when the ammo is within six feet of the weapons. Today, we live by Uncle Jeb's rules."

I winked at Andy and Joy. "Dad told us that last night," Joy said. And I handed Andy the revolver.

"Wow," he said, bringing up his other hand quickly to hold it. "This sucker is heavy." He hefted it for a moment, then handed it back to me.

"Age before beauty." His words were accompanied by an evil grin.

"In that case, brother, you'll never get to fire the gun." Joy said with an even more evil grin, though, coming from her, it only seemed cute to me. Yes, I know what little finger I'm wrapped around.

Jeb rolled his eyes heavenward. Joy spotted his reaction, and her face went dead level. "I didn't mean to argue, Uncle Jeb."

He failed to suppress a chuckle that shook his whole body. "Me and Ethel only had boys, but I did have a sister, and I do recall how she survived her brothers. And, missy, we'll declare that sort of stuff just normal sister-brother conversation."

Andy sighed. "She always gets away with mur...uh, anything," he said, now his eyes cast heavenward. "There is no justice in this world."

"I told you, brother, girls rule."

And so went our time at the rifle range. The Kentucky Long Rifle collected a crowd. Jeb fired it first, showing all around him how to load it. "You don't have to pour powder from a horn anymore," he said, ramming a gray powder tablet down the barrel. The ball went in next, wrapped in a bit of silk to help it make a seal. "You also don't use a flash in the pan anymore," he said, placing a percussion cap in its place. "This puppy is a lot safer to use than the original." With the weapon ready, he aimed it at a target fifty meters downrange and gently pulled the trigger. There was a lot of white smoke billowing from the barrel. Suddenly the range took on a definite Fourth-of-July kind of smell.

"Imagine a couple thousand of these going off," Jeb said. "Kind of explains why they maneuvered in lines and fired in huge volleys. They couldn't see well enough to aim for anyone specific. By firing volleys in the general direction of the enemy, they were betting they'd hit something. And they did. Course, it wasn't always the enemy," Jeb grinned. "There was so much lead flying around a Revolutionary or Civil War battlefield that they chopped down trees that had the misfortune of being in the general line of fire. Totally splintered them. But they couldn't see the end of their own weapons, much less the soldiers they were aiming for."

That was just the first of several history lessons, or observations from the history books, that finally made sense to my kids. Joy got to fire the Long Rifle next and nearly swore off of shooting anything else after that.

"Ow," she said, rubbing her shoulder. "I've heard weapons kick back at you, but I didn't know the kick was that bad. Feels like I've been on the wrong side of a mule."

"Better put her on the M-16 next, Jeb, or my daughter's never going to fire another rifle again."

So began a long list of comparative weapon studies. And then firing them for effect. Joy actually did beat Andy at one hundred meters firing a full thirty-round clip from the M-16. Single shot.

As the brass flew, I remembered my platoon's ammunition budget. Cartridges don't come cheap even at army prices; we had to be shooting off a fortune's worth of Jeb's ammo. "How much do I owe you?" I asked.

"Nothing. Just you kids be sure to police up your brass. I'll reload it."

"Can I help?" Andy beamed from where he lay prone, shooting the M-1.

"Son, loading ammunition is not a high-school chemistry class.

It's a dangerous job doing it, and even if you survive doing it wrong, you could take it in the face or blow up a rifle barrel. I never let my kids reload with me until they were out of high school."

"But we'll be gone by then," Andy didn't quite whine.

"Looks that way," I said.

"I don't think Mom will ever let us do this again," Joy sighed. She was probably right.

The kids went on shooting. Andy reclaimed his pride on the M-1, scoring higher than his sister. She complained the kick of that one tended to throw her off.

They tied on the British SMLE. And did just about as well with the Colt Walker revolver. Those bullets left holes in the targets so big it was hard to figure out exactly how to score them.

I think Jeb cheated, once he realized the competitiveness of sister and brother. He started using a smaller target. At least, the other folks firing pistols around us had man-sized targets. My kids were aiming at two-inch-wide circles.

I don't think the kids minded. At least when they went off with their own money to buy more targets, it was circles, not human figures, that they came back with. I suspect Annie would be proud of them.

Assuming Annie ever heard about today. Neither kid said anything about wanting to tell Mom about their shooting. I think they realized this was something between the three of us and that Mom would probably never know what they'd been up to today.

I watched my kids, making sure they were no danger to themselves or to the other shooters around them, but my dark mood was coming back, despite the nearly cloudless sky we were enjoying.

It was obvious the kids loved this. It was just as obvious that they wanted to do this again. Annie wouldn't like that. So what was I going to do about that?

I must have known that I was walling myself in when I let this whole thing happen. Well, it wasn't like I was the first one to give the kids something extra special during this moving time. Annie had let Andy have the car keys. Course, I'd made no effort to get them back once my week out there was over.

In fact, I was pretty sure Annie had knowingly bribed Andy with the keys. What was I trying to get out of the kids with a day at the shooting range?

Not a fair question, I told myself. Jeb was the one who brought it up; I'd just gone along. I needed to get some time shooting straight, wasn't that what Jeb had said? Maybe he was right. But why had I brought the kids?

And why was I standing back here, letting them do all the shooting?

Annie and I had laughed at a couple who started bribing their kids. It was Annie who first voiced the obvious. "You can always tell a family headed into a divorce. First thing they do is start sucking up to the kids to take one parent's side or the other."

I shivered, even though the sun was nearly noon high and plenty warm. I wasn't doing something so...

Or was I?

Suddenly my gut was in free fall, my knees were just as weak as when I'd faced Jim Turner. But it wasn't a knife at my gut I feared. No, this was a dagger held at the throat of everything I held dear. Everything I *had* held dear, something inside me said.

Everything was changing. It could change one way. Or it could change another way. No way could I have things back the way they'd been. That was gone. But I didn't have to leave my job, uproot my kids. I didn't have to move away from all my friends like Jeb and the office crew.

It would be lonely without Annie.

But she'd already shown what she wanted most. And Bernice's boy needed a father. I wouldn't have to be lonely for long. And I'd be freeing Annie for the life she wanted, probably on Bob Robert's arm. And I'd be doing good for a lot of people here.

Now I did shiver. *Dear God, where did all that come from?* I asked, shocked and appalled by my line of thought…and by how logical and rational it seemed at that moment.

*Lord, I can't be thinking thoughts like these. I can't,* I pleaded even as I knew that, yes, deep down, in some hidden place, I had been thinking all of them. I might want to run from the scantily clad babes at the health club. But Bernice, in her modest work clothes, talking to me with her eyes wide with hope that I might be the knight in shining armor who would ride over the hill and rescue her from her son's troubles—that, too, was attractive to something deep inside me. To that part of me that always wanted to do good.

But doing that good for Bernice was wrong. I knew it. Annie was the one I'd promised to be there for. Annie and the kids. Well, the kids would be happy staying here with me. The house might be a bit crowded, but...

*Get thee behind me, Satan!*

*Oh Lord, this makes me feel sick, and, yet, at the same time it makes me want to run out and do it. How can something so wrong be so appealing? Seem so good?*

For the first time in my life, I realized just how nicely the road to hell was paved with good intentions. Just how easy it was to mistake the path up for the freeway down.

Last night Andy had finally understood what I meant by gun control. This noon I was getting hit full in the face with how hard it can be to find right in the midst of wrong—something I'd never understood before.

No, that wasn't true. Annie was the right. Everything else might be open to question, but that I knew. Annie was the wife of my life. It was to her I'd pledged my troth. I might have to hunt around for a lot of things but not for where Annie belonged in my life. Annie and no other. That was something I didn't need to wonder about.

"Ben, you want to do some shooting?" brought me back to the range.

I shook my head at Jeb. "No, I think I've figured out some straight shooting from back here behind the firing line."

"You have?" he said.

The firing line was quiet. The kids were headed downrange to check their targets. Even from a hundred yards I could hear them debating whether that shot should count as a six or a seven and agreeing, before they got anywhere close to their usual high level of sibling rivalry, to let Uncle Jeb settle the matter.

I nodded at my friend. "I think some parts of me have been pointing in the wrong direction for some time now. I've been jerking at the trigger and breathing all wrong."

Jeb nodded, maybe understanding what I was saying or maybe just understanding that I was understanding me for a change.

"I think I know now what I have to aim myself at. And, sad to say, it means that there won't be time for a whole lot more trips to this range with you."

Jeb nodded. "'Wherever thou goest, I goeth,' was said a long time ago, but even then, you could really make a mess of your life if you didn't know how to aim your bow in the right direction," he said and slugged me gently on the shoulder.

Jeb sat as judge for the kids, now back from downrange, and managed to persuade them that they had shot to a tie. He had them police up his brass before bringing out his pride and joy, a nickel-plated 1911 Browning .45 automatic. He showed them how to load it and warned them about the way you could chamber a round, take the magazine out, and still have a loaded gun. "This ain't like a revolver where you can see what you got. This puppy can surprise you," he said, giving me a knowing wink.

*Dear God, Your world can be a place full of so many surprises too,* I prayed. *Let my aim be true.*

Andy got the first go at the automatic and, true to some action-hero picture he'd seen, turned it sideways and fired it. And just about lost it on the recoil.

"Hey, that's not the way it works in the movies," he said, frowning at the still unholed target.

"You go to the movies to learn how to shoot a weapon?" Jeb asked from where he stood beside me.

"I guess not," Andy said.

"Trust me, fellow, the movies, or television for that matter, is no place to go to learn how to shoot a weapon...or impress a woman. Most of them are just somebody's idea of fantasy, and most of it's bad. But I have to admit," Jeb went on, "that I'm kind of glad to see them demonstrating all kinds of wrong ways to use a weapon. With luck, the nutcases dumb enough to shoot the way a movie taught them will be harmless—or in a world of hurt if they go up against someone who learned how to use a gun out here at the range from folks like your dad and me."

Andy and Joy seemed to think learning the right way was a good idea, so Jeb showed them the proper stance and way to hold a gun, first two handed, then one handed. Jeb shot off the rest of that magazine, showing them how to handle the heavy recoil from the automatic—not to fight it, but to use it to bring their hand back down and the pistol's sights back to where they wanted it.

Then he gave Andy a new magazine to shoot. Joy muttered that it wasn't fair, but she kept it down. And the two of them shot near enough to let Jeb declare it a tie.

When the kids had made the full rounds of his armory and had shot off enough ammo to stage a revolution in any one of several small countries, I asked Jeb where I could take him for lunch, seeing that he wouldn't let me pay for the rounds expended. He deferred the decision to the kids, and we ended up eating hamburgers and topping them off with ice cream. A thoroughly fun day for all.

And a very thoughtful one for me.

Next morning at services our minister chose to preach on how a man cannot serve two masters. I think he was more motivated by the news of the week; nothing he said actually hit close to me. Still, it left me with a lot to think about. It was time for me to figure out which master I served.

Actually, pared down to that simplicity, there was no question where my heart lay.

Monday noon, Bernice was full of what had happened at her home that weekend. Rich had come home late Friday night, and not come home at all Saturday night. Sunday morning, he'd stumbled home, covered with his own vomit and smelling of stale alcohol.

"He was really hurting," Bernice said.

"Sounds like a good time for an intervention," Max said.

I nodded and pulled a slip of paper from my pocket and slid it across to Bernice. "That's the number of my church's office and the name of the pastor's wife." .

"The wife?" Bernice said, her brown eyes getting wide.

She was so beautiful…and she'd make some other man a good wife.

"Yep," I went on, trying not to get lost in those eyes. "She's had a lot of experience with kids. A lot of wives raising kids almost alone because of busy husbands come to her. After all, she's raising her kids with her husband busy helping others much of the time."

"I hadn't thought of that," Bernice said.

"There's a reason why preacher's kids have their reputation," Max said with a chuckle. "The cobbler's kids have no shoes, and the preacher's never around when his kids are acting up. Any woman having a problem raising a kid alone, you want to talk to the preacher's wife. She'll know what you're going through."

"I'll call her right now," Bernice said, getting up from the picnic table and heading back to the office. Carter Cutlery didn't mind employees making private local calls on their lunch hour. I'd helped revise that rule.

I could have loaned her my cell phone. Maybe I should have. Max gave me the eye; maybe she thought I should have. But those big brown eyes held powerful attraction for me. And I could not let them draw me back into a problem if I wasn't prepared to go as far as the solution might demand.

Not and be true to Annie.

For a moment, I watched Bernice go. She had a spring in her step, as if she already saw the hope at the end of her search. And the wife of our minister was just the woman to help her or to get her into a support group of other women who were where she was or had been there. Far better she follow that path than any one that involved me.

*Lord, it's not the choosing between what's right and what's wrong that's the hard part but the choosing between the so many goods that You pour out upon us,* I prayed.

There was just one more thing to do, and I'd do it tonight over supper with the kids. I could hardly wait to get started.

## 14

MY DESIRE TO WORK PETERED OUT RIGHT AROUND QUITTING
time. Any willingness I had to put in an extra hour vanished when
I opened an e-mail from Jason. It was a reminder that he wanted a
name on his desk by the end of the week of the person I was willing
to fire from my staff.

I didn't want to think about that. I left as soon as the clock
allowed.

It was too soon to meet the kids; they had practice and,
besides, Andy had a car. I ended up at the health club, in my swimsuit and pounding the water as I did laps. You can hit the water
hard—instead of hitting your boss.

Normally I can work out a whole lot of stress and "fight or
flight" in a swim. Today, the exercise didn't seem to be all that effec-
tive. I finished a half mile still jumpy enough to chop a couple of
cords of firewood.

I dried off, switched to shorts and a T-shirt, and headed for the
stair stepper. I'd left my magazines in the car; I figured I'd just

concentrate on stomping each step, like it was a bug with my boss's face on it. Or maybe my own. Just why was I so jumpy?

I was planning to tell Andy and Joy tonight that we should move to Oregon *right now.* Not wait until school was out. Just get on the other side and burn that bridge. Bring marshmallows and have a party.

Annie had at least given them time to get used to the idea, and now I was going to tell my kids that time was not what we needed. Moving now was the ticket.

It really wasn't fair for this to land on me, I thought. Annie should have done it in the first place.

"You know, it's a lot more fun to do that if you wear big old army clodhoppers," a throaty woman's voice said beside me.

"Boondockers," I corrected.

"Boon-whats?" came right back at me. I came out of myself long enough to see a tall blonde, her blue and silver shorts covering very little of what stood above her long, shapely legs. Her white top didn't come close to meeting her shorts halfway.

Quickly I went back to staring at my feet. "Boondockers is what they called army boots when I was putting in my four."

"Well, when I need to stomp my problems, I like to pretend I'm wearing those big black Doc Martens I had back in my college days."

"That couldn't have been too long ago. You still have them in your closet?" I said. Then wondered why I'd done something to encourage the woman.

"Your wife has taught you well," she laughed.

"She's a good teacher," I said, wondering even more why someone dressed like that was talking to me about my wife. "Makes it easy for me to learn."

"I have a good teacher at home too," she said, voice low, "when he's at home. He's halfway through a two-week business trip. How long has your wife been gone? Two, three weeks?"

"It only seems that long," I said, glancing her way only to find that she was working away at her own exercise program. Rivulets of sweat were running down her neck into her top. The white was now marked with near translucent streaks of perspiration. She looked like one of those magazine-cover swimsuit models, all wet at the beach.

With an effort, I pointed my eyes back at my feet.

"Does your wife call you? My Harry stops calling about halfway through a trip. That's how I can tell he's tied up with someone to keep his bed warm. Bet you your wife has quit calling."

There was a sly smile in that voice, but I didn't glance over to see what was on her face. I had a covenant with my eyes, and between the two of us, me and my Savior, we were going to keep it. I'd been surprised before; now nothing this woman did next would surprise me.

"You know, you turn the cutest red when you're embarrassed," she went on. Yes, my face was warm, and not just from the exercise. I glanced at the controls of the stepper to see my distance covered. Not much at all.

"I bet you think your little wifey is being a good girl. I bet you think she's keeping that big bed empty for you. What about all the guys she works with? Are none of them willing to keep her warm while you're miles away?" Now the voice was sly, like a fox. Or a snake.

But I had already started to wonder where Bob Roberts was these days. He'd visited Annie here in Baltimore when he could have just called. What were the chances he'd found an excuse to drop by Portland to see how she was making out in the new job?

*Making out.* Wrong words.

And my wife with an empty hotel room to go home to—not me or the kids. What would Annie be doing about now, now that she wasn't calling me?

*No, God. No, I don't want to think about all this. I don't want to go where this lonely and bitter woman is taking me.*

I bolted for the door; suddenly, the distance covered on the stair stepper tonight meant nothing. I had to get away from this woman and her purring surety about what Annie was doing without me.

Back in the locker room, I found I couldn't change, not in the condition I was in. I settled into the sauna. Someone had left the heat up high, watered the rock. It was hot in here. But not as hot as where that woman was leading me.

I settled on the lowest bench and tried to order my thoughts. Heavens knows, I'd found it hard enough to stay here, alone, among the familiar and safe—at least usually—places of my life.

What must it be like for Annie out there? Yes, I didn't trust Bob not to make a play for her. But I trusted Annie to walk away...no... run. Just like I'd run.

*Lord, I don't want to spend my life running away. Please, let me spend it running to Annie. Enough of this living separate lives. It's time to stop this craziness. I love that woman. Let's go to her.*

After all, Annie had once moved across the country to be with me when I was just an army lieutenant. Yes, it had been easier for her; she was just out of college and traveling was simple then. But she'd come.

It was now time for me to return the favor.

I felt calmed down enough to risk a quick shower. I made it very fast and very cold and was dressed in less time than I thought possible. *God, I don't know how I'm going to bring the kids around. Please help me find the words.*

I headed out of the locker room, my gym bag slung over my shoulder. In the foyer, where the staff checked membership, the woman sat, waiting.

She'd changed to a light blue mesh top that showed she wasn't wearing much of a bra. Her skirt was possibly appropriate for a tennis court, though even there I think it would be judged too short. "You took longer than I expected," she purred.

At their desks, two staff men were covering their mouths to hide smirks, chuckles, I don't know what. The one woman staffer in the area was looking daggers at my stalker.

The woman was out of her chair as I walked by her on my way

for the door. She tried to reach out for my elbow, but I managed to sidestep the familiarity without looking too much like a fool. Then again, maybe this was some of what the apostle was talking about when he mentioned being a fool for Christ.

Despite my best efforts, we went through the door together.

"You really are missing out on a good night's sleep," she assured me.

"I don't want to miss some quality time with my kids."

"Kids," she snickered. "Too young to know how to get what they want. Now me, I know exactly how to get what I want," she said, walking on when I turned to my car. No surprise, her car was a silver Porsche, top down to enjoy the night air.

It took me two tries to get my key in the door lock; my hands were trembling that badly.

In the army they taught me that the human eye is drawn to motion. You want to hide...stand still. You want to draw fire... move.

She bent over to put her key in her lock...and my traitorous eyes were drawn as her skirt hiked up and showed me what only her husband should see.

Growing mad at myself, at her, at my situation, I slumped into my car, started the engine, and found that she was ahead of me as I drove for the exit. Early, she flipped on her turn signal to go left. To make it more clear, she stuck out her left hand and waved languidly in that direction.

She revved her motor as she turned left. I paused at the exit, looked both ways. Only her tail lights were visible.

And turned right for home.

"Lord, why do I feel like I've been in a fight?" I asked.

Because I had. I'd fought for my honor, for my wife, for my life. And, at least for the moment, it looked like I was ahead on points.

The kids weren't home from school yet. I could have stayed at the club longer. Or dropped by her house.

"Lord, I don't want thoughts like this," I muttered to myself as I started the washer and fed my workout clothes into the hot water. I felt the need for extra soap, or maybe even running them through the machine twice. I shivered at where I'd been, what could have happened.

"Lead us not into temptation." Those words seemed kind of unnecessary tonight. We human beings were doing a good enough job of finding temptation with no help from anywhere else.

Sudden racket told me the kids were home. Joy was as joyful tonight as her name. She'd gotten a history paper back with a big red A on it. A red A for her was an honor. I didn't want to think about what it would mean for me.

"Let's hit Belgato's tonight," I grinned. "We can celebrate."

"I don't know if I can spare the time, Dad," Andy said. "I've got lots of work."

"I want to celebrate," Joy put in.

"And I want to talk to the both of you."

"Well, just don't talk too long." That was the kind of son Annie and I were raising. Some kids you had to tie to a chair to get to do schoolwork. Andy and Joy were hungry to learn. I like to think that having a mom and dad ready to talk about what they were learning made it easier for them to feel that hunger. This side of heaven, I wouldn't know whether that was true—as well as a whole lot of other theories.

Andy used his cell phone to call ahead and order a garbage-pail pizza. No, that wasn't what it said on the menu, but that's what we'd been calling "the works" since before Andy could reach the top of the counter to hand over his dollar for his dessert cookies. That was *if* he'd eaten enough to satisfy Annie's and my demand that he "eat something good for him" before he got a cookie.

Good memories.

"Hold the anchovies," Joy piped in, just like she had done since before she could get her little mouth around the word. Since she had grown into it, I'd tried and tried to get my mouth around the cute way she'd mispronounced it. Impossible. There is a time and a place for everything under heaven, and once it's time to pronounce *anchovy* right, there's no going back.

*Kind of my theme song for today, huh, Lord?*

I laughed as I turned into the parking lot. "There has got to be a pizza place as good as Belgato's in Portland."

"With a garbage-pail pizza?" Andy said, aping shock.

"I suspect so. And I'm sure Joy can continue to remind you to hold the anchovies."

"I'll always do that. You just can't trust boys." How often had Annie joked like that. Mother to daughter. Father to son.

We were all thoughtful as we made our way from the car to a table in the restaurant. As we had so many times, we waved at one of several familiar faces behind the counter, and they told us our pizza would be ready soon. I paid for it and sodas while the kids filled three glasses. The pizza, I saw, was a medium, what with only three mouths to feed. And only three drinks. I saved money.

But it wasn't enough of a savings to make up for the loneliness. Andy and Joy had a table for me when I was finished with the bill. Not our usual one, near the games. When we started coming here, the kids had loved to drop nickels and dimes in the machines. Now it was more often quarters.

Tonight, no one eyed the road races or ladybugs or building climbing monkeys. They sat, eying me, waiting for me to break the ice. I didn't waste their intensity on the usual questions about school. I took a sip from my soda, put it down, and looked across the table.

"Does anyone here miss Mom as much as I do?" I said.

"If chem lab had a reagent to test for missing or loneliness," Andy sighed, "I think we'd all turn blue if you dripped some on us."

"I know I would," Joy sighed.

"I'm thinking about moving sooner," I said, "rather than later."

"You hear about a job offer?" Joy asked.

I shook my head.

"You'd be willing to move without a job?" Andy said, but there wasn't much amazement in his words. Not anymore.

"Your mom's making more out there than we both were before she got promoted." I shrugged. "She didn't have a job lined up for her when she came out to Fort Lewis to join me. We managed to live on one paycheck very nicely," I said, trying to sound like there was no difference between the two. Like I'd be just as willing to be unemployed as Annie was, fresh out of college.

From the looks my kids gave me, I don't think I was very convincing.

"You do miss her a lot, don't you, Dad?" Andy said.

"Yes, but I also remember how much she was talking about her job the week I was out there. Now she has no one to talk to. Me, I've got you two knuckleheads to listen to. Mom has no one. I bet she's even lonelier than we are."

"Yeah." Andy nodded. "You know, I've never been the new kid at school. We do treat them kind of special. At least, none of them have keeled over dead, not any that I noticed in the last eleven years."

"But would a boy notice something minor like that?" Joy grinned. A straight line is never safe at our house.

Andy made a scrunched-up face at his sis. Joy stuck her tongue out...ladylike. But she got serious very quickly once the quiet fell.

As much quiet as you can get in a pizza place with games going off all around you.

"Dad, I've been wondering," continued Andy. "Would it be better to move now so we could make some new friends before summer comes? I mean, moving out there with two months of summer and no one around but the people on the block? It seems like it would be a whole lot easier to make some friends in school during the spring. What did you call it in your army days? 'A target-rich environment.' Yeah, better to get to know people at school than when you don't know where they hang out. Not the good ones."

That was something I hadn't thought about. But then it had been years since I needed to make friends outside the job and church. I was giving up the job. At least there would be church for a "friendly target-rich environment."

"I can call Mom and ask her to turn the moving company loose on us, then see what happens. Are you guys game for at least looking at it? Calling Mom and letting her know what we're thinking about?"

Two heads nodded back at me as the pizza arrived.

So it was decided.

And my cell phone rang.

I answered it, hoping it was Annie returning my calls, thinking it would be really neat to talk to her now. *Now that we were moving toward her, not away anymore.*

But it wasn't Annie.

In fact, it wasn't anybody whose voice I knew.

"Mr. Taylor, have you heard from your wife in the last two days?"

"No," I answered without thinking.

"Do you know where your wife is?"

"She's in Portland, with her new job," I said, still confused by the call and eying the kids. "Joy, has Mom called you in the last two days? Andy, has she e-mailed you or called?"

Both kids shook their head.

Suddenly something kicked in that should have the second this call started. Something was very wrong here.

"Who is this?" I asked. Nobody had a right to quiz me about my wife and how we were getting along. That was a matter between us and our God. Nobody else's business. At all.

"I'm sorry, Mr. Taylor. I should have identified myself." But the words had very little contrition behind them. Whoever this was, I was starting very much not to like him.

"This is Special Agent-in-Charge Brent Sanders of the Portland, Oregon, FBI office. I regret to inform you that your wife may be missing. She hasn't been seen by her co-workers for the past two days. Her boss tells us that this is quite unlike her. She isn't answering her cell phone. The hotel she was staying at says her bed hasn't been slept in since Thursday night. We found her car at the Pittock Mansion in Portland. Can you offer any explanation as to why she might have gone there and left her car? Do you have any information you can share about where she might be now?"

*Annie,* I thought. *Something's happened to Annie.*

The smell of cooking pizza twisted my stomach into knots, and the soda I'd just sipped turned to acid.

I held the phone at arm's length, unable to believe what I had just heard. Unable to believe that any phone could ever say such a thing to me.

And the nightmare began.

# 15

**"DAD, WHAT'S WRONG?" JOY ASKED ME.**

The pizza in front of me looked worse than revolting. I wanted to empty my empty stomach. I swallowed and tightened my leg muscles, knowing from experience that my blood pressure was plummeting. Knowing how my body was betraying me didn't make the betrayal any easier to handle.

Across from me, my kids' eyes were going wide, and they turned as pale as if they'd seen a ghost. Both were saying something, or at least their mouths were open. I heard nothing. Noise was also coming from my cell phone, but I couldn't make out the words.

I wanted…I wanted…I wanted everyone to go away and this call not to be happening. That was what I wanted.

*God, this can't be happening.*

The kids' voices were raised, asking me again what was wrong. The babbling still came from the phone.

It was happening. Happening to me. To Annie.

"Shut up," I muttered. When it had no impact on all the noise around me, I tried again. "Shut up!" This time I shouted.

Andy and Joy fell into a terrified silence. Their eyes didn't leave me. Neither of them piped up in their usual reminder that "shut up" was considered the worst of the phrases that their mother forbade them from using.

I think they knew we'd passed into some special zone where new rules applied.

Around us, other customers also fell silent. There even seemed to be a pause in the racket the game machines were making. A manager I knew was on his way toward us.

Into the silence, I spoke to the kids as calmly as I could.

"I need to take this call. It's very important." Then I put the phone back to my ear.

"What did you say your name was? It escaped me."

"Special Agent Sanders, Brent Sanders, Mr. Taylor."

"Hold on a moment," I said. I looked at my kids. "This is Special Agent Brent Sanders of the FBI's Portland office. He's calling about Mom. He wants to know if any of us have heard anything from Mom in the last two days. Or even three days."

"Nothing, Dad," Andy said softly. "Not a word."

Joy just shook her head, tears welling up in her eyes.

I put the phone back to my ear again.

"My son and daughter have not had any contact with my wife in the last seventy-two hours, nor have I," I said carefully, willing myself into that battle zone where a man did what he had to do.

I'd been there before. It was a familiar land.

The manager had stopped as I repeated the FBI question to my kids. Now he nodded and went over to the games area. Quickly they fell silent.

*For that, I was thankful.*

"When was the last time you heard from your wife?" the man from the FBI asked me.

My racing mind had expected that next. "I talked with her over the phone last Wednesday evening. I got an e-mail from her on Thursday at the office."

"You didn't hear from her over the weekend?"

The words didn't seem to have any sort of accusation behind them. They were just a question. So why did I feel defensive?

"The weekend got kind of busy, and we are three hours ahead of you. She's been calling me after her work, but it was past bedtime for us here. She was planning on doing a lot of shopping for furniture over the weekend, so I didn't worry when we didn't hear from her. I knew she'd be busy. In fact, we'd just decided, me and the kids, that this long-distance family was not working, and we were about to call Annie and tell her we were ready to move to Portland right now."

Across from me, the kids nodded enthusiastically.

Why did I bother telling the FBI that?

And why hadn't I tried to contact her over the weekend myself?

"You are sure she's missing?" I asked.

"We are sure that she isn't at the hotel, nor has she shown up for work. She isn't with her car. We've filed a missing person's report, but we fear that there may have been foul play in her disappearance.

So far, however, none of the bodies at the morgue or hospitals match her description."

"*What?*" I roared.

"We have reason to believe that this might be a kidnapping," he went on. "Mr. Taylor, we would appreciate if you would return to your home phone and wait for any call concerning ransom demands."

Before I opened my mouth, Andy was racing for the aluminum foil, but one of the workers was already tossing a box at him. Frisbee style. Andy caught it with one hand.

*Dear God, the teenagers you make are wonderful to watch. Just let me see Annie again.*

"We should be home in five minutes," I said. "Ten at the most. Where can I call you for details?"

Sanders gave me the number of his office in Portland and the nearest local office in Baltimore. "But you'll be filled in on what we know. Someone has been dispatched to your home. They will be waiting for you."

His tone left me suspecting that if I wasn't there fast to let them in, I'd find a broken door.

I was up and trotting for the exit even before Andy and Joy had slipped the pizza in its box. They followed at a pace that only teenagers can achieve.

"Good luck," the manager said as I went past him.

"Thank you, for everything," I said. "Thank all of you," I added, raising my voice to the entire, very quiet restaurant.

"Good luck," "We'll pray for you," followed us out the door. I'd noticed a few couples from church. If I somehow got too busy to call the minister, I was sure they would see that the church carried us on their petition list.

Still, all during the short drive home, the words, "Dear God, protect Annie," were running over and over in my mind. Just in case, I called Annie's cell phone. No answer.

Her cell phone was off. And her voice mail at the hotel was full. I was beginning, with horror in my heart, to suspect the FBI was right.

Somehow, discovering this for myself made Annie's disappearance even more real than the call from the FBI had. I prayed harder. Beside me, Joy's lips were moving too. Andy must have been praying as well, but he was present enough to ask me if I really intended to miss the street we lived on. I barely made the turn.

The night was dark, full of fright, and even my prayers struggled against what I could not let myself think.

We pulled into the driveway from the right as a nondescript green sedan pulled in from the left. I let two FBI agents, whose names escaped me, into my house, then waited for a third, who came up the rear with a large tool kit.

*Thank you, oh Lord, that I am here with my kids and that they are not facing this all by themselves. And that I am not wandering into this late at night with the scent of another woman on me. Now, Father, where is Annie?*

The FBI had no answer to that question. Which I asked them

more than once. They searched the house, dusted for prints, and did other things with some spray and a light. It took me a while before it dawned on me that they were searching for blood. Annie's blood.

We gave them free rein to wander through our house, our computers, our e-mail. To investigate the Web sites we'd visited. "I see you've ordered two tickets off the Internet for a trip to Portland?"

"Andy did," I said. I explained I went out with my wife to be with her the first week she was on her new job...and to job-hunt for myself.

"Find anything?"

"No. No job offers yet." Why did I have the feeling that they knew all the answers to these questions? That they were asking them to see if I knew the right answers? If I would get them right?

Inside, I felt as though I were being torn in two. What were these people doing, why were they wasting all this time with me, and why weren't they out looking for Annie?

They found a hairbrush in the bathroom with long blond hair twined through the bristles. "Your wife's?"

"Yeah. That's her home brush. She took a smaller travel brush with her."

"We'll need to bag this and take it," they told me. "DNA."

So they had what they needed to identify Annie. Were they already assuming that she couldn't tell them herself who she was? I would not let my mind wrap around the reasons why or the point when they would have to use fragments of hair for that purpose.

Tomorrow, I wanted desperately to believe, maybe the next day,

I would call Annie's name, and we would race for each other. We would.

*We would.*

I had to believe that.

It was late when they left. They took the disks and hard drives from all our computers. The kids' protests that their schoolwork was on them didn't go very far. I insisted the agents give me two sets of receipts: one for my records and one for the kids' teachers.

The FBI agent complied grudgingly, as though we were being unreasonable. The receipts we got only stated "HD involved in an ongoing FBI investigation."

*That should be reassuring to the school brass,* I thought. *Sure.*

"I hope my teacher accepts that," Andy said with a worried frown.

"Be quiet right now," I said. "We've got bigger worries right now than your teachers."

The agents finally left us.

With the house silent once more, we somehow ended up in the living room, them on the couch, me in the papa chair. The momma chair was so glaringly empty.

"What do we do now, Daddy?" Joy asked, clutching a pillow to her middle just as she used to clutch a security blanket. It had been years since I was Daddy.

I stared at the portable phone I'd had in my hand every second since we got home. It was just as silent as it had been while the FBI was here. What if it never rang?

"What if it never rings?" Andy said, echoing my thoughts. "I mean, what if the kidnappers don't know our home number?"

"Mom knows it," Joy snapped. "She'd tell them."

"Yeah, but will they call us?" Andy went on. "If they grabbed Mom because they thought she was rich, they're so in for a surprise. I mean," he said, looking around, "we aren't exactly rolling in dough here."

"Could be they grabbed Mom because of her job," Joy added. "Didn't some guy from the company go missing overseas a couple of years ago? The company paid to get him back, right? So that must mean that Mom's office has a pot of money for handling this kind of thing, right? People are being kidnapped all the time from companies like hers. It's on the news, right?" Joy's voice slowed as she found it harder and harder to imagine the place she now found herself in.

I stared at my kids. Normally, Andy's diction was as perfect as any college English major's. His repeated "I means" showed me more than anything else just how much this was tearing him apart. And Joy was always so sure of herself. Now every other sentence ended in "right?" My poor kids.

I moved from the papa chair to the middle of the couch. Suddenly I was one terrified husband with two very scared youngsters huddled together in a strong embrace.

"Dear God, help us," I prayed aloud.

"But how, oh Lord?" Andy prayed right behind me.

"God helps those who help themselves," Joy said, hugging me with one hand and clutching the pillow with the other.

"That's not Christian," Andy shot back. "It was pagans who said, 'The gods help those.'"

"But Jesus never says anywhere that we shouldn't help ourselves, does He?"

"She has a point," I told Andy. "How often does the minister ask us to act on what we've just prayed for?"

"Okay," Andy snapped. "I'm praying. You're praying. We all are praying. So, let's say for the moment, I concede that Joy does have a point. All I see is another question: what *can* we do?"

I pulled the portable phone out from between us and set it on the coffee table, next to the family Bible. "The FBI said we should stay ready to answer any phone call." Had my marriage vow come down to this—sitting, staring at a phone, waiting for it to ring, and praying that the people on the other end would ask me for money to save Annie's life? I'd pay whatever they wanted.

But all I could do for now was wait?

Joy scrunched up her face as she stared at the phone. "But I didn't see the FBI leave any gizmo behind to trace and record any call. They always do that in the movies. So...are they really expecting us to get one, or what?"

We stared at the phone, as if it might speak and give us the answer we couldn't seem to find for ourselves.

After what seemed like a year or nine, I shook my head. "You've got a point. I think you're onto something. I don't want to sit here waiting. I know Annie better than any man alive. The FBI can't begin to understand her like I do. They don't know why her car was left where it was. They don't know what she'd do if she was worried about her safety. They don't know anything about your mom except that she's gone. I know her. I should be there," I said to no one in particular.

"You should, Dad," both kids said at once.

"But we'll go with you," Andy said.

"You have to go to school tomorrow."

"Like it's going to do us any good, Dad," Joy shot back. "Do you think we'll be in any mood to learn?"

"Dad, I don't want to be in school, wondering any second if my phone's going to ring and you're going to tell me…" Andy's voice trailed off, unable to put in words the worst of the things I might have to tell him from Portland.

"I wouldn't tell you over the phone," I said.

"Yeah, and what are we supposed to think when you call to say you're coming home, Dad?" Joy could really slap you around with the obvious.

"Besides, Dad, who's gonna stay with us? Mom's folks are somewhere in the Caribbean already, recuperating from a week with us. And your mom. Well…"

Yes, better not to talk about her grief at the loss of my dad. Dropped into the middle of this, having her come watch the kids in her current state would be far worse for her and my kids than leaving them alone and unsupervised.

"I could call someone from church," I suggested.

"That'll take time. You want to be on the next plane out of here, Dad," my son said, getting off the couch.

"We want to be on the next plane out," his sister said, joining him to stand in front of me.

"Can we do it?" I said, still sitting, but catching their determination. "You can't call—we need to keep the house line free. And you can't book us over the Internet, because they gutted your computer."

"They didn't take my old one," Andy said.

"My old one," Joy said, elbowing him.

"Your mother's old laptop," I corrected. It had been a hand-me-down from Annie's first effort at portable computing. It was ancient...and a charge up the stairs showed that it was still buried in the bottom of Joy's closet, mixed with her shoes and the stuffed toys that had been crowded off of her very crowded bed.

"Can you hitch it back up to the router?" My son gave me one of those teenager looks, like I'd asked him if he remembered how much two plus two was. He even rolled his eyes when he thought I wasn't looking.

"But we can't leave the phone unanswered," I said, realizing the flaw in our plan. I turned to Joy. "Could you do that thing you did last summer?"

She'd gotten in deep trouble for forwarding the house phone to her cell...without telling the rest of us. There'd been this guy, she told us. She was *so* waiting for him to call her.

Joy was grinning like she was finally being told she could eat the canary. "If computer boy here can get us on the Internet, I'll have us back in business with call forwarding in two shakes." Then she paused. "To whose cell phone?"

"Mine," I said, blinded by the obvious.

Both kids were shaking their heads. "Nah. You have to have your phone ready for anyone else who calls," Andy said.

"Use mine," Joy said.

"You really mean that?" both Andy and I asked at the same time. Whoever's phone we used for the forward would have to be kept free at all times. No outgoing calls. Was Joy, the queen of continuous cell phone talk, really offering to give up her phone for the duration of this situation?

"Yeah, mine," Joy said. "And, besides, if I just have to make a call, bright boy here will let me use his cell, and he'll get socked with the usage," she said, sticking her tongue out at him.

It felt good to see the kids being kids, even if there was tension around the edges on all of us.

It took Andy only a few moments to reconnect the old computer to the net and get our plane tickets. "We've got an hour and a half," he shouted to where I was throwing clothes into a suitcase.

"We can make it," I shouted back.

Five minutes later Joy shouted, "I've got the phone forwarded."

I dialed the familiar number. No ring on the bedside phone.

Down the hall from Joy's room came a quick rendition of "I've Got You, Babe." That was Joy's contribution to the family's humor. I punched off.

We made it to the airport with no time to spare, but the line at security was short this late at night, so we moved through quickly. In the boarding area, I made a quick call to the office phone and left a message on the general mailbox. "I have a family emergency. I need a week off, maybe more. I'll call in the morning and give you the details," I said before punching off.

I put off dialing the Portland FBI office until after we boarded. When they connected me to Agent Sanders, I quickly told him we were on a plane headed for Portland.

"You can't."

"We can. We are. We've forwarded our home phone calls to our cell."

"Cells phones don't work on planes."

"Not true. Airlines just don't like to have them on," I said.

That was true. Airlines request that fliers turn their cell phones off because they can mess with a plane's navigation frequencies. But we were going to ignore that little piece of advice tonight.

"We're on our way," I said. "Deal with it. If somebody calls, we'll probably hear. If we don't, you can't tell me you don't have our phones tapped. It'll be early morning when we get in. We'll check into a hotel and see you in the morning. Got to go. Bye."

He might have been still talking to me when I punched off. Or maybe he wasn't. It didn't matter. We were on our way.

## 16

IT WAS DARK—THE MIDDLE OF THE NIGHT. SHE COULD TELL by the lack of ambient light in the small room where they kept her. Her blindfold was gone, but in no other way had her situation improved. Annie Taylor bit her lip and tried to keep from crying. She was tied to the bed she was lying on, and she'd pulled at the bonds until her limbs were bloody and her muscles screamed from the pain. All she'd done was wear herself out. She'd been warned to keep quiet or she'd regret it. After a couple of cuffs to her head that had nearly knocked her out, she was afraid to make a sound.

She'd been praying to God—praying for a miracle, praying for inspiration, praying for rescue, praying to see her husband and family again. God's peace and the love of her family had never seemed farther away in her life than at this lonely and terrifying moment. She longed for her husband's warm arms around her, to hear his voice in her ears.

But all she could hear was the sound of her captors arguing in the distant living room. It was, she thought, the most terrifying noise she'd ever heard...until she heard the sounds of their steps echoing through the hallway, growing closer.

Her heart almost stopped in her chest, her fear was so great.

She prayed for the strength to endure.

"The Lord is my shepherd," she began, and listened in horror as the knob to her small cell began to turn...

Special Agent Jennifer Hunter hated it when Special Agent-in-Charge Sanders started treating her like one of the boys. It usually meant he intended to use her as a girl. Growing up with four brothers and no sisters had taught her a lot about boys. Being one of the few female MPs in the Marine Corps had only added small finishing touches. The FBI held no surprises for her in that arena.

Just frustrations.

Take this latest assignment, standing at the airport at two in the morning, holding a sign saying "Mr. Taylor." Officially, Brent was steaming mad that his chief suspect was hightailing it out here. With his kids! Actually, it seemed to her that Brent was delighted to have this guy close where he could keep him under surveillance. The DC office had tossed his house and found nothing. No one had really expected to find a body under his bed. Still, the total lack of any sign of any wrongdoing whatsoever was bothersome to Brent.

The first take from the East Coast office described the Taylors as a nice, churchgoing couple. Two kids who were almost too good to be true these days. Respected at their places of employment. A husband who'd gone out of his way to support his wife's career. And whose own career didn't seem to be going anywhere.

What did it add up to? Do nice, churchgoing husbands snap and kill? Sure they did. A case made the papers at least once a month.

Which was where "Dear Jenny" came in.

"Get him in here where I can talk to him," Brent said. "While he and the kids are still jet-lagged from the flight out" didn't get mentioned but was clearly intended.

"And see what makes this guy tick. Apply some of your sharp instincts to Mr. Taylor. This disappearance could be nothing but a domestic row, have nothing to do with her job. Show him some of your feminine wiles. See if this husband's screws are in right. Do they turn the right way? Could he have just killed his wife?"

So Jennifer was standing here, with only a few hours sleep under her belt, waving a sign...and with the top two buttons of her blouse undone. She'd been told often enough she was a looker. Let's see how this guy looked.

She'd seen the manifest; this plane was over half-empty. She wasn't really surprised when a middle-aged guy, with a teenage boy and girl in tow, was the first person up the passenger ramp.

Her mind categorized him. White, male, about six foot. Hundred and sixty pounds. Brown hair showing gray at the temples. The boy was a tad taller and a gangly one-twenty. The girl was maybe five foot eight, short blond hair, and had the makings of looks that would never fail to attract men.

All three looked drained. From the trip? From the news? The man spotted her about the same time as the kids. He sighed and pointed but still said nothing.

Jennifer stepped forward. "Mr. Taylor. I'm Agent Hunter."

"Ben," he said, sounding friendly enough for a guy with his troubles, then added, "The tall guy is Andy. Short stuff is Joy."

"Mom's shorter," the girl blurted out, then seemed horribly embarrassed that she'd mentioned the missing woman.

"I have a government car waiting," Jennifer said and reached for Mr. Taylor's carry-on bag. He declined and turned it into a roll-along, heading off down the corridor. Was there something in the bag he didn't want her close to, or was he just too much of a gentleman to let a young woman carry his bags? The two kids took time to do the same; they looked like a family of self-reliant folks.

But Jennifer had learned not to trust appearances.

She made small talk as she led them through the airport. Her carefully phrased "Did you get a phone call on the plane?" got a negative response. As did her inquiry about sleep. Her charges all looked a little shell-shocked. So far, no surprises.

As they passed by the security checkpoint and into the main body of the airport, bright lights came on and cameras whirled. A woman reporter stuck a microphone at Mr. Taylor and demanded to know how he felt.

The man blinked in the glare, surprised and irritated, and muttered something about just wanting to find his wife. The kids looked like they might try to run back into the safety of the airport concourse.

Jennifer had seen nothing of this reception when she passed through security. If she had, she'd have asked the media to lay off. She increased the speed of her steps, and the Taylors took the hint and passed quickly on by the crowd of reporters. Blessedly, the reporters actually got the hint and didn't dog them further.

"Where did that come from?" Taylor whispered, eyes straight ahead.

"The local paper broke the story of your wife's disappearance in the afternoon edition. We don't know who leaked it. Could have been somebody at the company or at our office or the perps. We don't know. If it's our office, though, somebody's rump is going up in flames. Welcome to your fifteen minutes of fame."

"Well, I could have lived my whole life without that," the teenage boy said.

"Me too," the girl added.

With no further surprises, Jennifer got her charges in her car and headed downtown. She checked out her passengers when they weren't looking. For most of the drive, they ignored her. Ben sat in the front passenger seat, staring out at the dark city passing by. The boy played a handheld computer game nervously. The girl, like her father, stared at the world as if she hoped to catch sight of her mother at any time.

Jennifer found herself feeling sympathy for the girl. Joy, that was her name. No joy in her tonight.

"Do you want me to take you to a hotel or to our office?" Jennifer asked, knowing full well that she would not accept the hotel option if he took it.

"Office," came from all three of them.

"We'd really like to know what you've done so far," Ben added. "I was only out here for a week, but I might have stumbled upon something that will help you find Annie."

Spoken well...or was the guy just well rehearsed?

Jennifer parked in the underground garage at the bureau. Her conclusions were few as she took them upstairs. The possibility that Ben Taylor had just killed his wife was still a viable option as far as she could tell. He'd spent most of the airport walk and the drive not looking at her. Was he guilty or just a good churchgoing man uncomfortable with the amount of cleavage she was showing? The young boy had just about popped his eyeballs out at first, then concentrated on his video game.

While they got their luggage out of the trunk, she'd buttoned up both buttons. Father and son seemed much more comfortable in the elevator. It had been years since she'd been around church folk. Maybe what she was reading was just that.

Jennifer Hunter left the three exhausted Taylors in the waiting room and went to find Sanders. Her gut told her that Ben Taylor had probably not just killed his wife. But it was only her gut, and that "probably" was nowhere near strong enough for her to use as an operational thesis.

# 17

I WAS NOT HAPPY. I WAS TIRED, WORRIED, AND RAPIDLY START-
ing to boil at the strange ways of the FBI. I did not need to be
baby-sat. Neither did my kids. And if they were going to send an
agent to meet us at the airport, the least they could have done was
send somebody fully prepared to brief us.

And what was it with those undone buttons? That girl looked
more like a woman in the world's oldest profession than a federal
agent. Did federal agents on the West Coast regularly go around
showing off their latest Victoria's Secret buys? Even Hollywood
films showed the lady Feebs wearing conservative clothes. If she
wanted to strut her stuff in front of me, I could just look elsewhere.
But in front of Andy! And Joy!

It was more than I was prepared to handle.

I was worried about my kids. Andy had buried himself in his
video game, just like he had during the flight out. Joy, however, was
taking this all in and probably filing it in her fertile brain under
"how a powerful young woman acts in this world." Her mom and
I were going to have to talk to her about some things after this.

Assuming Annie and I ever got to do anything together again.

*Don't think that. Don't ever think that! Dear God, help us find Annie. Find her safe and okay!*

So I charged into the FBI's office tired and mad and looking for someone to take it out on.

And got left with the kids to cool my heels some more.

Blast it, how's a man supposed to keep a Christian tongue in his head when everyone around him is doing everything they can to drive him to cuss like a trooper?

*Right, Lord, it's not what we do when everything is fine but what we do when this whole world of Yours is driving us to, well, join it in doing everything wrong.*

So I sat in their uncomfortable chairs and tried to pray again for Annie's safety.

"Dad, what's going on?" Andy asked.

"Yeah," Joy added. "Why aren't they talking to us?"

"You watch the cop shows on TV," I said. Joy was addicted to *Law and Order.* "You tell me."

"I can't." Joy shrugged. "This isn't the way it goes on TV."

"Kind of like watching TV to learn how to shoot a pistol," Andy said, managing to chip off something close to a smile at the memory of a better day.

"Good point. I don't think you can trust television, even reality TV, to show you what will happen for real," I said and frowned. So, what was going on...for real? *Somebody better tell us soon.*

A man in a blue suit that screamed Men's Wearhouse with a smile that was way too wide but far too shallow came out of an office and offered me his hand.

"Hello, Mr. Taylor. I'm Special Agent-in-Charge Brent Sanders. I must say, I'm surprised to see you here."

I took a moment to listen to what he said. Really listen. He was surprised I was here? That made no sense. I'd told him I was coming. My *wife* was missing. I blinked twice and tried to understand him.

And came up blank.

"I'm sorry," I said, in my most calm, most soothing intervention voice. "Your surprise surprises *me*. My wife is missing. The woman I love. I've lived with Annie for twenty years. I am the person who knows her best," I went on, trying to sound logical and rational. "I'm hoping that I can help *you*. See something your investigation has turned up that means nothing to *you* but something to *me*."

Brent nodded along with my words, but his eyes kept wandering from me. He wasn't listening. Why?

When I finished, he turned to Agent Hunter. "Jennifer, why don't you take the kids and talk to them. I'll brief Mr. Taylor myself."

The woman agent motioned Andy and Joy to a room to the left of Agent Sanders's office. They went, but under protest.

"I know Mom well too." Andy insisted. "I could help."

"Both of us could," Joy insisted.

"I'll give you the same briefing they give me," I assured them.

"You'd better, Dad," was the last I heard from them as Ms. Hunter shooed them into what I took to be her office. Brent led me into his.

"Would you like some coffee? Something to eat?" But somehow the agent's words managed to have nothing solicitous behind them. I'd dealt before with people whose words said one thing but whose actions had nothing to do with their words.

I'd dealt with them, but I never liked doing it.

I took a deep breath and prepared to do it again. For Annie's sake I'd do anything. *Dear God, help us.*

Sanders showed me to a seat in an office that looked like standard government issue, decorated by the lowest color-blind bidder available. What wasn't a boring gray was a sick tan. I settled into the offered chair and tried to get comfortable. I don't think the furniture was designed with that in mind. But I'd sit on hot coals to find Annie.

Sanders took two steps back from me, folded his arms across his chest—not a good sign—and said, "So, what have you been doing while your wife was out here?"

I folded my arms across my chest, since the chair lacked any armrests, and decided I did not like this man. It was time to let him know he was stepping very hard on my toes. "Do you want me to account for the entire last two weeks, or are you mainly interested in the last forty-eight to seventy-two hours?"

"Either one," he said diffidently, but his eyes bored into me like hot iron drills.

"Since I've heard that the first twenty-four hours are the most important in finding a missing person alive"—I may not watch much TV, but that didn't mean I didn't know what was going on— "and since we are well past twenty-four hours since Annie was last seen, and maybe into seventy-two hours, I'll pick the shorter option. At some point, though, I'd like an explanation for why you allowed so much time to go by without notifying me of her absence." I quickly filled him in on my Monday at work, our Sunday at church, and the family's Saturday trip to the rifle range.

"You shoot a lot?"

"Before Saturday, I hadn't shot a weapon since my army days."

"Why'd you go shooting Saturday?"

How much of that one to answer? "Jeb Shepherd, a foreman at the plant, collects weapons. He invited us. My kids thought that shooting a black-powder rifle, a black-powder pistol, and some World War I and II army rifles might be fun and educational. So I took them shooting."

"What does your wife think of shooting?"

No way to avoid answering that one now. "She doesn't like weapons. We don't have anything more lethal than a baseball bat or a kitchen knife around the house."

"Weapons. You say weapons, not guns."

"I put my four in the army. My DI taught me early that it's a weapon, not a gun," I said.

"You ever kill anyone?"

"That is not a question you ask a soldier," I shot back, feeling anger rising in my face. "Have you ever killed anyone in the line of duty?"

"This will go a lot faster if you let me ask the questions and you concentrate on answering them." The words rattled out as if Sanders were reading from a script he'd memorized so long ago he could say it in his sleep.

I took a deep breath and leaned back in my chair. "By the grace of God, there was no war during my four. I deployed for six months to Bosnia, but things were quiet while I was there. I saw no more action than a suburban beat cop might." I thought for a moment, then added what was going through my mind. "And I have praised God every day for that blessing. I've looked into the eyes of soldiers who've killed. I don't want those dark shadows haunting my days and nights."

Sanders scowled and turned away. His body language shouted that he wasn't buying a word I said. Assuming his body language was no different than the union and management types I usually dealt with. *Watch your assumptions, Benjamin,* I warned myself.

"Did you spend all Sunday at church?" he said, without turning back to me.

"No. We attended morning services, had a nice lunch, and then the kids spent the afternoon catching up on schoolwork. Joy had a team project, and she needed to meet with three of her friends about it. They met at our house, used our computer. You should have their Internet searches date-stamped on that hard drive you walked off with. Andy wanted to get in some extra jogging. I spent some of the time at the health club, then tried to catch up on my reading. Maryland has issued some new rules for employee safety. I have better things to do with my time at the office than read safety memos. So I read them at home on Sunday."

"Were they online?"

"No, paper."

"So your Sunday afternoon is not accounted for."

That was not what I said. And he knew it. "My kids know where I was. I was at home."

"So you say."

"Yes. And so do my kids. And their friends."

What kind of proof did this guy need? My slow burn was rapidly reaching the boiling point.

Agent Hunter knocked on his door, and the two of them went out to talk for a moment, leaving me to get even madder. He returned after only a moment. "You might like to know that your kids agree on how the three of you spent the last three days."

"Good. *Now* can we get down to finding Annie?"

"No, Mr. Taylor. I am not yet willing to tell my prime person of interest all the internal details of my investigation."

"I'm *still* your prime suspect?" I exploded. With an effort, I stayed in my chair, kept my hands away from his throat. *I'm not a violent man,* I kept telling myself. I may not be a violent man, but I might make an exception for Agent Sanders.

"You are not my prime suspect, only a person of interest," Sanders said with maddening ease. "If you were, I'd be reading you your Miranda rights. You aren't yet proved to be involved, so we're still talking."

"This is absurd," I said, letting my anger run for a moment. Normally, I don't let emotions show in a negotiating session. But there are times when people need to know what they've done to you. Holding a steady, gentlemanly demeanor can be the worst thing you can do to your chances of reaching agreement. It was time Sanders learned just how disgusting I found his whole line of reasoning. And how devoid of any facts it was.

I held up my hand and raised one finger. "One, you know that I booked a flight out here with my wife...and that I returned." Up came another finger. "Two, by now, you've checked my credit-card records, and you know that I haven't booked a second flight out here until tonight." Sanders's face was an unreadable mask.

I thought for a second longer, then held up a third finger. "You've also checked my bank balance and know I have not withdrawn enough money to buy a ticket under a different name."

I dropped my hand into my lap. "Face it, Sanders. There is no way I could have come out here and done my wife any harm." That should settle that.

But Sanders just eyed me for a long minute. Then he shook his head. "You really think we're that easy to fool?"

Now it was my turn to frown. What else could a criminal mind come up with? I thought a while and came up blank. Empty-handed, I shrugged at Sanders.

"You are a personnel officer, aren't you, Mr. Taylor?"

I nodded. Actually, I was the chief of Human Resources, but most of the Feds that attended our monthly meetings still used that obsolete term.

"You have access to the personnel records of everyone at the Carter Cutlery plant, don't you."

"I have to, to do my job," I agreed.

"Indeed, a look at your hard drive shows that you recently loaded the entire personnel database onto your computer. Names, addresses, Social Security numbers. All the data on everyone. What were you doing, Mr. Taylor, with everyone's personal data on your computer?"

I didn't like where this was going. "I had it only temporarily, and I immediately erased most of it," I shot back. Then I put on my most reasonable voice. "I was doing my job. Our workforce is aging, Agent Sanders. I needed to estimate the retirements that would face us over the next ten years. So that we could hire trainees and bring them up to our level of quality before all our old hands are gone."

"Interesting project," Sanders said, sounding almost persuaded. "For that, you'd need name, date of birth, maybe the date they started with you." He paused for a moment, and his faced changed, now looking like a guillotine blade slamming down. "But you downloaded everything. Why?" His question had as much force behind it as a minie ball from that black-powder rifle.

I took a deep breath and let it out slowly. "I had to take it all. The plant has everything on one ancient computer. Billings, pay, personnel, markets. Everything is on one old computer that should have been replaced ten years ago but wasn't. All of us who use computers in our work take regular downloads off the decrepit thing, then do the actual manipulation of data on our own personal machines, or the ones at our desks. Ask Rod Montgomery in procurement or Mary Oppie in accounting or anyone at the plant. Mr. Montgomery has hired a computer geek to bring our main data into the twenty-first century, but we aren't there yet."

"And you couldn't have made a quick pull of just the few data points you needed."

I shook my head. "Tasking the old mini-mainframe to do that would have brought it to its knees for half a day. I'd have had every manager in the plant on my case. Excuse me, Agent Sanders, but I'm the geek who showed everyone how to do the export and work the data on their own machines."

Clearly, judging by the triumph in his face, that did not help my case with Sanders. "I showed them about six, eight years ago," I added. "And as for the recent download, I deleted the extra data immediately. My hard drive should show you that."

"Oh, it does, Mr. Taylor." That should have sounded good, but somehow Sanders made it all come out bad.

"And?" I said.

Sanders reached into his pocket and pulled out a small USB drive. About as big as my thumb and half as thick, I recognized it as a nifty innovation my kids and I had been using for much of the last year or so. You could load a huge amount of data and walk it over to your friend's or to the office.

"Ever use one of these?"

"We have several in the family."

"None were found by the FBI team that went through your house."

"They're kind of small," I pointed out. "Joy or Andy are misplacing them all the time, taking them to school and leaving them in their locker or in the school computers."

"But you could have downloaded all that personal information to one of these," he said, tossing it in the air and catching it. "Then you could have erased it from your hard drive and still had it available anytime you plugged this into your computer."

I nodded agreement and sighed. Proving you're innocent is not easy. So whatever happened to innocent until proven guilty?

Sanders seemed to be in the business of proving someone innocent—me—guilty.

"Your credit-card records show that you've bought seven of these nice gizmos in the last two years. Where are they, Mr. Taylor?"

"I wish I knew," I said, slumping into my chair. "They aren't where they're supposed to be."

*Dear God, we could use some help here. Annie needs help. And now it seems I need help. Oh Lord, help us,* I repeated, eyes closed, slowing my breathing. I knew the agent was here to raise my stress level. Maybe raise it high enough for me to confess.

Unfortunately... No, fortunately, I had nothing to confess. *Jesus, help us. Lord God, help us,* I repeated over and over. *Holy Spirit, enlighten us.*

My eyes popped open. Yes, that should answer a heap of questions.

I looked at Sanders. He seemed a bit surprised by whatever I'd been doing.

"Let's suppose a few things, just for discussion, Special Agent-in-Charge Sanders." *Keep the sarcasm down. It won't help anything here.* "Suppose that I did abuse the privileges of my position. That I took advantage of my job to gain access to everyone at the plant's personal data." I shivered as I said those forbidden words. "I can't tell you how much those in my profession find that repugnant and unthinkable, but you're after a criminal, and let's say that I'm willing to destroy all the trust and goodwill I've built over fifteen years. I use the data to order credit cards that I then use to fly out to Portland and do something horrible to the woman I love."

The man nodded happily along as I uttered words that it hurt me to even let out of my mouth. *Dear God, I am so glad You guided me into my job and not his.*

"So, there are two hundred and fifty-seven people at the plant. And a month or so ago, new credit cards started coming to them. No, they couldn't have arrived at their home addresses. They'd have them and not me. Did they show up at their work address? In that case, I would have had to fish them out of the mail room before they were delivered to the correct people." I frowned at Sanders. He was frowning back at me.

"Or maybe I had them mailed to post office boxes? But I thought credit-card companies didn't like to mail new cards to those things?" I gave Sanders the fish eye.

He blinked and conceded nothing.

"But if four, five folks at the plant had gotten new credit cards in the last five, six months, it would show up on their credit rating. Wouldn't it?"

That time, he did nod.

"So the Washington FBI office can just pull the credit report of everyone at the plant, check with anyone with a new one to see if they have it or if it's a surprise." *Dear God, please don't let anyone at the plant be a recent victim of identity theft. Oh please, God.*

"The Baltimore office will do it, and it will take some time."

"Hopefully not too much time," I said, struggling out of my chair. "Now, I'd like to know what you can tell me about my wife's disappearance."

"I'm afraid I can't tell you anything right now."

"Then I think it's time my family gets some sleep. And, hopefully, in the morning, you and I can start off on a better foot. I want you to start pouring everything you have into hunting down whoever did kidnap my wife. Because I had absolutely nothing to do with it."

For a moment, Sanders chewed on his lower lip. Not much,

but I'd seen some pretty cool negotiators give away their indecision by just a small tug at a lower lip or ear.

Then he offered me a hand up. That was when I realized just how exhausted I was. I needed that hand.

Out in the open office, Andy and Joy were hunched in chairs. They were half-asleep, but they shot to their feet when they saw me. Agent Hunter was with them. Looking out for them? Making sure they didn't make a break for it? I hated this middle ground between being not yet guilty but not yet innocent, either.

"Jenny," Sanders said, and the woman agent came to a kind of attention. "Why don't you run them up to the Hilton? Get them settled in, then call it a night. Get some rest. I'll see you all in the morning." Which was what? Three, four hours away? I'd hate to have Sanders for a boss.

Agent Hunter took us back to the elevator and down to the garage. But the kids didn't want to wait to learn what I'd been told. I eyed the agent for a moment, but the way she didn't meet my eyes told me that she knew how my interrogation had gone. Did it also tell me that she was on our side?

She said nothing.

"I didn't learn anything. Agent Sanders is keeping his evidence to himself right now. He thinks I may have killed your mom," I said.

"No!" Andy snapped.

Joy was slower to react. When she did, it was with a shake of her head. "That's what they say on Court TV. Close family members are usually the prime suspects when harm comes to other family members. Of course, they don't know you. I do. You didn't do it." It was a powerful statement, but it was weakened by a yawn.

Which got us all yawning.

"But you couldn't do it," Andy got out through his own yawn. "Mom was out here. We were back home the whole time."

I nodded. I didn't want to dump on my kids what had been poured over my head during the last hour.

"They must think that we're covering for Dad," Joy said. "Saying he was at home while he flew out here and...you know."

"They think we're liars?"

"Criminals usually are," Agent Hunter said as the door opened on the garage.

"So you think we were lying?" Joy snapped. I think Joy had taken an immediate liking to the woman agent. To be called a liar by Agent Hunter would hurt Joy. Hurt her a lot.

The agent looked uncomfortable, but she stopped to face us, didn't flee for her car. "I don't know. In this job, I meet a lot of people who are good at saying things that aren't the truth. It makes it hard to believe anyone is a straight shooter." The woman turned, took a few steps toward her car, then stopped when she realized the kids were frozen in place.

She turned back to eye Joy, then Andy. Her lips grew taut, a thin, narrow line of pink in her tan face. "For what it's worth, I do believe you."

"So you'll tell your boss we're telling the truth, that he's wasting time and needs to be looking for Mom out there, not sniffing around my dad," Joy shot back.

The agent shook her head.

"What she thinks doesn't matter," I said, sadness and exhaustion competing for top billing. "Sanders is in charge. He has to find his own faith in me."

We got in the car, and Hunter put it in gear.

"Where's the nearest motel?" I asked. "Is there one within walking distance?"

"There's one across the bridge on the other side of the river, but it's not a nice place."

"How close?"

"Four, five blocks. One of them is a long walk across the bridge."

"I'd rather be close enough to walk over to your office tomorrow. The place too bad of a fleabag? Shootings, drugs?"

"No, just a three-star joint. The rats and cockroaches aren't so big you can ride them. At least, not Andy. Joy, maybe?"

*An FBI agent with a sense of humor. Dear God, I didn't know You made any of them. But maybe, after an hour or so around my kids, it was just contagious.*

The place didn't look that bad, and we checked in. Maybe having an FBI agent flash her badge and ask for a room for family members got us the best rooms they had available.

I got Joy bedded down in the room next to Andy and me. She

asked to keep the adjoining door open, and I agreed. Andy was sound asleep before he hit the bed. I left him there, fully clothed.

I doubted I would sleep. I hadn't on the plane. How could I sleep while Annie... I would not go there. I could not. Annie was a tough gal. She'd find a way to take care of herself.

*Dear God, help her. Help me find her. Help me never leave her side again so long as we both shall live.*

I'd pray all night if I had to.

So I lay down on the bed, folded my hands, and started to pray.

## 18

BILL PARTON SAID, "I'M SORRY, BUT THE SHIPMENT SEEMS
to have vanished." Bill put all the sincerity into that lie that a life-
time of experience with half truths and untruths had taught him.
His life depended on it.

The Boss shook his head. "Billy Boy, my friend, I appreciate
your regrets, but I really need that shipment." Unlike Bill, the Boss
didn't put any sincerity into his words. He left no doubt that he
sincerely wanted this shipment.

Gold glittered in the morning light from the rings on every finger of both of the Boss's hands as he waved them diffidently. The
well-muscled man driving the limo glanced in the rearview mirror
at Bill and gave him a look. Bill had seen that look before on the
Discovery Channel—on feeding sharks.

"Listen, I have this new boss—uh, woman—at the office."
That was a mistake. Around the Boss, there was only one Boss. Bill
rushed on. "She's new, and a real snoop, wanted to see everything,
visit the docks, get to know the shippers, into everyone and everything. Big pain, you know the type?"

"No," the Boss said, shaking his head. "Pains don't last long around me. They either learn not to be a pain"—his grin showed gold teeth inset with diamonds—"or they suddenly aren't a pain anymore. Right, Reinaldo?"

"Right, Boss," the driver said. "You run a tight business. Might even say you're a cutthroat competitor."

Bill shivered to let them know he got the point—and because he really needed to. He hurried on, "Well, this woman is all over everything, just like I told you, and then she disappears, and surprise, surprise, the horse isn't where my contact said it would be. Gone. Totally. I'm thinking she spotted it. Maybe was looking for it and grabbed it before I could get it off to you."

"You think so?" the Boss said slowly but with emphasis. "Reinaldo, what do we know about this woman?"

"Just what Billy Boy here told you, Boss."

"And what was it you said about her, Billy Boy?" the Boss said, turning his full attention to the main shipper of his top-quality Golden Triangle heroin. The Boss earned millions on that heroin, and he was very, very serious in his attention to detail when his investments were on the line. He might look like a movie stereotype, but the gleam of hard intelligence and menace in his eyes was all too real.

Bill gulped, desperate to remember exactly what he'd said about his new manager before he'd gotten his greatest idea ever. Or so he thought. That was assuming he pulled this off and lived to spend all the money he stood to make if he did. His second thoughts had long ago become third ones, then fourth, and so on. He swallowed again.

"She's from Baltimore," he started. "She handled shipping stuff from the Balkans, former Soviet Union places." Inspiration added itself to the perspiration freely flowing down Bill's back. "I heard she had contracts with the Russian Mafia, the Serb cartel. Wouldn't they love to get a load of your stuff? It's better than theirs by far."

The Boss didn't look pleased at the backhanded compliment. The new world order was making for disorder among the folks who dealt in smuggled goods. Especially the illicit variety of goods. Disorder among the criminal elite tended to result in bodies lying around bleeding freely. The Boss hated a messy workplace. Almost as much as he hated losing a shipment. But not quite. He sat silent, waiting for Bill to go on.

"And this Annie Taylor has disappeared. Somebody found her car over at the Pittock, and now the FBI is looking for her. I saw in the news that her husband is out here to look for her. Or so he says."

"He didn't say much on TV," the driver said quietly to the Boss. "My girlfriend recorded it. She's always doing that to stuff she thinks I might be interested in."

The Boss just stared at Bill.

"Well," Bill said, rushing this little talk along, "we've got the FBI crawling over our offices. They're finding nothing," Bill quickly added when the Boss raised an eyebrow. "The shipment is as gone as the woman."

Bill fell silent, not wanting to babble in the Boss's presence. He'd learned long ago that babbling was a liar's worst friend. The Boss eyed him across the Moroccan leather upholstery of the limo. Outside was a vacant lot; they parked so that nothing could get close to them without the Boss seeing it. Once a year when the Cirque du Soleil came to town, this lot was their camp, their parking lot. But for now, it was just a big bunch of empty.

"Reinaldo, there any word on the street about this?"

"Nada, Boss," the driver answered. "Nobody's talking. Nobody's seen anything unusual."

"I've got a shipment missing. I don't like that, Billy Boy. I don't like that at all. I want it found. I'm holding you responsible for looking for my shipment. If the woman has it, I think you would like to find her, too, Billy Boy. Now wouldn't you?"

"Yes. I definitely want her found." Bill felt the sweat on his brow begin to bead up and pool on his forehead. He resisted the urge to wipe it off.

"And when you find her, you'd better find my shipment."

The boss didn't do anything as crass as making threats. He didn't have to. Bill knew exactly what he meant.

The door behind Bill clicked open. He took it as dismissal. "I'll see that every rock I can find is turned over. If she's hiding under one, I'll find her, Boss," he lied with fervor as he got out of the vehicle with as much speed as he could.

The limo pulled away, leaving Bill to walk the few steps to his own car. He walked on shaking legs, trying to show just enough shaking to let the Boss know, if he looked back, that he took him seriously, very seriously. But not so shaky as to show that he had more than the usual to fear from the largest dealer of heroin on the West Coast.

*I've got to look like I'm sweating, but not the terror I'd have if I had been dumb enough to walk off with twenty kilos of pure heroin,* Bill lectured himself.

But once he was in his car and the limo was gone, Bill let the shakes take him. He was playing for big stakes. Huge stakes. If he helped Ringo take over the Boss's territory, Ringo would owe him. Assuming Ringo won. Ringo was young and hard-charging, like Bill. The boss was too old. Too meticulous. Too careful. Everyone knew the Boss. Bill was willing to bet even the FBI knew him. But they had never gotten enough evidence do anything about him. Every lead they'd ever turned up had gone cold. Dead cold.

Bill shivered.

Ringo was another matter. Ringo would pay Bill through the nose for forty-five pounds of H. It would let Ringo corner the market here in the Northwest this season. Ringo would owe him big. Ringo would let him in on the gravy train, not just keep him as some little cog in the transportation sector.

Of course, that would only happen when Bill delivered, something he was holding off doing until things settled down. If that shipment of pure heroin turned up too soon in the neighborhood, the Boss would know just where it came from.

With luck, the Boss would soon be chasing Ms. Taylor just like the FBI was chasing her. The Boss had his hooks into the FBI—he'd get their data almost as soon as the agents gathered it. Bill had arranged a few careful threads of evidence that would lead everybody right to the new and nosy Ms. Taylor.

No one would find her where he had her stashed. And since the three guys he had holding her were his own guys, not part of the usual underworld that the Boss and the FBI knew so well, there'd be no leads back to him. It was no surprise that the street had nothing to say about Taylor. Nice of Reinaldo to drop those good words.

So long as they didn't find Ms. Taylor alive and talking, so long as everything held together, so long as Bill lived on as a valued employee of the Boss, his story would hold up very well. Until the time came to show his hand and get his share of the pot of gold at the end of the rainbow. When the Boss toppled, he'd make his play.

In the meantime, he needed to keep the lady under wraps in case he needed her.

How long could he keep her disappeared? And what would happen when he let her resurface? That was the rub, a rub he'd been dodging ever since he took the twenty kilos of horse. And Ringo might be good, really good, with a fine head for organization, but he wasn't planning to pop the Boss immediately.

Bill sighed. Ms. Taylor would have to stay disappeared until the heads of a few important criminal organizations reorganized themselves. Maybe she'd have to stay under wraps longer than that. Permanently? No—probably more valuable alive than dead.

That was one question he hadn't wanted to answer. The idea of walking off with a fortune in heroin and using it to buy in with the new up-and-coming crime lord of the Northwest had sounded like a great idea a week ago. Blaming it on the woman who'd stolen his promotion had sounded even better.

And he'd known exactly how to pull it off. He called in some old friends who weren't exactly model citizens. More like losers on the edge of society, ready for any kind of trouble. He'd grown up with Dwayne, Harry, and Oz back in Twin Forks, Nebraska. They were on the edge even when they were all kids. But he kept them out of trouble more than once, and they still hadn't landed in jail when he last went home for Christmas. During that visit he hinted that he might have a job for them, and they swore they wouldn't tell anyone. He'd busted Oz's jaw back in high school for talking big around girls, and apparently the lesson still held. When he called them up two weeks ago, they were willing to listen and eager for any way to make a quick buck.

He gave them an opportunity, and they jumped at the chance.

Now they had Taylor hidden away in a coastal-range cabin. Keeping her on ice. He wasn't sure yet how to use her. He had the luxury of not having to decide just now. All he had to do was make a phone call, and her body would end up in a shallow grave somewhere back in the woods where no one would ever find her.

Bill glanced at his cell phone—he'd left it in his car for that little talk. But what if he needed Taylor to die more visibly, say in a shootout, maybe in an incriminating way witnessed by Ringo or the Boss? Killed in the cross fire? Or in an accident with a sample of the missing goods somewhere on her person?

Bill shook his head; Taylor dead was Taylor dead. There were all kinds of ways for the feds to tie her death to a place and a time. And there was no going back. Alive, he could manipulate her and everybody looking for her. His options were wide open. He was sure she would serve a purpose in his plan to get away clean with the theft of the goods and a move up the criminal hierarchy. He was good at playing all the angles. He figured if he let her live a bit more, he could keep his eyes open and his ears to the ground. The right opportunity would present itself. He just had to wait and watch.

One thing he really wanted to watch was that nosy woman's exit from the world in a blaze of glory.

While he took her life, her reputation, her job, and rewards of his labor, all at her expense.

## 19

I AWOKE WITH LIGHT STREAMING IN THE HALF-CLOSED BLINDS.
Somehow I'd slept. And I felt guilty that I had.

Then again, maybe I'd be of better use to Annie with a bit of
rest in the bank. All things work for good to those who love the
Lord. *God, help us,* I repeated the prayer that seemed to be on my
lips every waking moment.

In the bed next to me, Andy was stirring. Quietly, I called work
and told them what was going on. Bea was horrified and promised
to hold down the fort and pass the news to the appropriate people.
And she made one more promise, one that meant a great deal to
me. She promised to start a prayer chain for Annie's safe return.
The plant, she said, would ring with prayers for us all.

I gave her my thanks in a broken voice and said good-bye.

With that taken care of, I headed for the shower. By the time I
was done, Andy needed the bathroom, so I shaved in front of the
mirror over the sink. Noise was coming from the shower in Joy's
room. There were no sleepyheads this morning. Thirty minutes

from the time I rolled out of bed, we were sitting down to a quick breakfast at a small restaurant across from the motel.

Today I didn't complain about the way my teenagers inhaled their food. After thirty minutes we were back on the street and walking across the bridge. The kids set a rapid pace, but I didn't have to struggle to keep up with them. My time at the health club did do some good for this middle-aged man. The night's rain had brought sea gulls in with it and cleaned the air. Even with the morning rush-hour traffic rumbling along beside us, I could still get a faint taste of the Pacific; it reminded me of Annie at the beach on our honeymoon.

*Oh God, how I miss her. Please keep her safe. Help us find her.*

This morning we didn't get to ride up the elevator from the parking garage, so we had to walk into the FBI's front door. This meant stopping at the security checkpoint in the first-floor lobby and waiting while the guard called upstairs to see if anyone would come down and vouch for us.

Agent Hunter showed up after only enough time for a small argument with her boss. She had a smile on her face and was wearing a loose-fitting powder blue sweater and skirt arrangement that was similar to what I so often tried to get Joy to wear.

I wasn't the only one who noticed the change in her attire.

"Yes, Dad, I see it," my daughter whispered beside me.

The agent vouched for us and said that we might be needed upstairs. We were issued visitor's passes good for today and only on the floor Agent Hunter cleared us for. On the ride up the elevator, I kept quiet, but Hunter seemed willing to talk.

"That was some idea you came up with last night, Mr. Taylor. I don't often see Sanders outmaneuvered, but you got him good."

"What did Dad do?" both kids asked.

"My boss thinks your father may have created a number of credit cards from the personnel files at the plant," the agent said.

"Dad would never do that," Andy snapped.

"Those files are a sacred trust," Joy finished.

"Your father has integrity—something a lot of the people we deal with lack," the agent said. "We don't have a report from the Baltimore office yet. But I persuaded my boss that we could keep an eye on you better if you were sitting in our office. Besides, you couldn't be doing mischief if you were right under our eyes, now, could you?"

I grunted agreement. Andy and Joy frowned at each other and at me, but neither said a word in front of the agent. I think they were arriving at the same conclusion I was. For better or worse, we were on our own among these people who were supposed to defend us from evil. They weren't trying to help us. They might even be trying to hurt us.

In the FBI office, Hunter introduced us to the secretary, who offered to get us something to drink. We passed, explaining that we'd just had breakfast. Sanders came out just long enough to express surprise at seeing us this early and to repeat that they had no report from back East.

Andy opened his mouth, I feared to tell Sanders that we already knew that. I nudged his foot before he said a word and interposed. "Thank you. We'll wait here for the news, if you don't mind." I think he did mind, but he said fine and went back to his own office.

Hunter rustled up a chair for Joy from one of the desks scattered around the bull pen. No longer blind from exhaustion, I settled into another chair, half closed my eyes in prayer, and took a good look at my surroundings.

"Dad, what's going on?" Andy immediately whispered.

"Nothing. Sanders still doesn't trust me. Until he does, we just sit here and pray," I told him. "We volunteer nothing."

"I want to do something," Joy pleaded.

"So do I. But we can't do anything right now but pray. So pray," I said.

Joy took Andy's right hand. I took his left, and we all prayed silently.

Though my first prayer was a short one.

*Forgive me, Lord, I do intend to pray, but give me a few moments to get a feel for this place,* I thought as I kept my eyes half-open and now did the survey of the environment that had been interrupted by Sanders's entrance.

The room was an open space with several desks, computers, and ranks of file cabinets. The decor was utilitarian; the colors tended toward gray and tan, with occasional bright spots of family photographs and sparsely placed plants. It looked well worked in, but most of the desks were empty now.

*Everyone on the road, Lord?* I wondered.

There was a soft buzz from a conference room off to my right. Its walls were mainly glass, so I could see that about a half-dozen agents were working there, poring over materials spread out on a table and examining the screens of their portables. *Is that where everyone is?*

No answer.

I moved my head just enough to get a better view of the left side of the room. Sanders's window office had solid walls blocking my view; his faux oak door was closed. Next to it was a solid walled conference room, its door open. That was probably where Agent Hunter had interviewed my kids last night.

The left, what I was starting to think of as "our" side of the room, was quiet as a sepulcher. The other side was alive with talk. Talk I could not understand.

Was it any of my business?

"Dad, what's going on over there?" Andy asked, nodding toward the right. It seemed that I wasn't the only one not doing a good job of praying this morning.

"We are not among people who like for others to take an interest in what they do. If we don't want to be sent downstairs, it's best we keep our nose out of their business," I whispered. "Pray."

I bowed my head again, and the kids did likewise.

For a moment, I actually prayed. *God, help me. Please don't let me do anything to make things worse for Annie.*

Again our Father was quiet.

So I cleared my throat and stood up. "Is there a water fountain?" I asked the secretary. She smiled and nodded toward one, across the room...on the right.

I gave the kids a firm look, and they ducked their heads and went back to praying. They looked even more worried, if that was possible, and bowed their heads as I sauntered toward the water cooler, my stomach doing flip-flops.

There I pulled a drinking cup from a dispenser, filled it, and drank slowly, edging a bit out of sight of those in the glass-enclosed room. With no water running, I could hear better, but still not clearly enough to decipher the talk among them. But I thought I heard "drugs" and "heroin" mentioned several times.

Oops, drugs. Not our issue. And not something I wanted to get mixed up in. About to crush the paper cup and toss it in a nearby trash can, I heard something that sounded like "tailor" or maybe "trailer"...or maybe "Taylor."

I refilled my water cup, searched in my pocket for some breath mints I'd bought for the flight, and took one. If someone thought it was medicine, or vitamins, I wasn't actually lying. *Was I, Lord?*

As I slowly drank the water, I heard more talk of drugs. I thought I caught that *t* word once or twice more. Then someone looked up. Our eyes locked for a second, then he looked away.

But the talk from the room quieted. Now I could make out

nothing. I took a final drink, crushed the cup, tossed it, then slowly made my way back to where the kids were praying. They both looked up, questions in their eyes, but I gave them a fast shake of the head, and they went back to praying, or what we hoped that the good Lord would accept as prayers from our distracted selves this morning.

I sat, took Andy's hand back in mine, and prayed. And thought. *Father God, what is going on here? Seated across from the people making haste very slowly to find Annie is a much bigger bunch of people worried about drugs.* That was definite. *Were they also talking about Annie Taylor? My wife. The center of my life here on earth, Lord, my beloved right. The love of my life, next to You.*

Was finding my wife somehow being put in second place next to some drug bust or sting or whatever they called it these days? I took a few more moments to pray and to go over in my mind my evaluation of that side of the room. Further examination didn't lend itself to a different conclusion.

Enough of this. I stood, pulling Andy to his feet. Joy followed immediately. Their eyes were on me, but there seemed to be less worry in their faces, at least for the moment. Doing nothing was doing, well, nothing. Doing something seemed so much better.

I headed for Sanders's office. I could demand that Agent Hunter tell me what was going on, but she could only pass me along to Sanders. And if she broke and told me anything, it would just get her in trouble. She didn't deserve that. Certainly not so long as she was the closest person we had to an ally here.

I rapped on Sanders's closed office door. Hunter was around her desk and sticking her neck out her door before I got a "Who is it?" from inside.

"Taylor. The husband and kids. We need to talk."

A second later the door opened, but Sanders stood as a solid block in it. No invitation in. I made an effort not to look at what was on his desk.

Not that it would have helped. It looked pretty clean. Not at all like a working man worked there.

"You have a problem?" Sanders said.

I started to snap out a detailed answer to his quick question, then swallowed it—*Praise You, God*—and started softer. "My wife is an importer. Whenever anyone brings things into the country, there is always a risk of tagalongs, things they didn't order coming in. Bugs, maybe. Drugs...maybe."

I let that hang there for a moment, waiting to see if Sanders would take the hint. Out of the corner of my eye, I think I saw Hunter swallow hard. Both my kids were looking at me, the word *drugs* on their lips in an expression of horror but left unsaid.

Sanders eyed me but said nothing into the stretching silence. This man was good. Not someone I'd want to negotiate with regularly.

"Is there a drug operation going on here," I said, "that in any way involves or is related to my wife's disappearance?"

Sanders's only reaction was to raise an eyebrow at me and then glance at Hunter. She shook her head and shrugged as if to say, "Not me."

Sanders opened his mouth, but he was interrupted by the door opening in that glassed-off room and three agents hustling toward him.

"Sanders, we got a ransom demand from whoever snatched the Taylor woman," the one in the middle with a portable computer in front of him announced.

"We intercepted it coming into her home computer," his supervisor said.

*Dear God, thank You,* I prayed.

# 20

ANNIE TAYLOR TOOK A DEEP BREATH AS THEY TIED HER BACK onto the bed in the cabin. It was a metal bed, just an army cot, and for the last four days, except for trips to the bathroom, it had been her world.

*Dear God, let the message get through,* she prayed.

She kept her face to the wall, not risking a look at her captors, not wanting accidentally to do anything to set them off. It didn't really matter, though; she'd seen their faces. She knew enough about kidnapping to know that their allowing her to see them meant they either intended to kill her...or they were horribly inept.

After four days of listening to them bicker among themselves, she was beginning to think they might just be inept and not too bright on top of that.

It was her only hope right now.

The two big guys headed downstairs, gleefully talking about how they'd spend their third of the million-dollar ransom they'd just demanded. The third fellow, Oz, hunkered down with his video game and continued his endless search for the next level.

That thing just might have saved her life.

Ever since she had given Andy his brand-spanking-new, top-of-the-line Barracuda IV gaming platform, she'd regretted it. The boy was addicted to playing it.

Worse, he was addicted to talking about it. Almost more than he was about the other boys and girls on the track team. Definitely more than talking about school. She heard so much about Cross Country Rally that she just knew she could go through the first five levels blindfolded.

And she had. The last few days, lying on the back floor next to Oz's muddy boots, she'd listened to noises that sounded more and more familiar as the young man cursed his luck and sometimes just cursed. He'd drive off the road, end up in the mud, and hit deer, though he seemed to like that part. He had his game set for bloody, she'd learned, and it seemed that a deer antler in a driver's eye was not a pretty sight, though Oz liked it.

That was not the way Andy played that game.

For a day they kept the blindfold on her. But when it slipped off during a bathroom trip the second day, they didn't bother to put it back on. Annie knew that was her death warrant, but they seemed to either not know—or not care.

That was when it came to her. *Lord, I think it's just You and me on this. If I'm going to get out of here, it's going to be You and me work-*

*ing on this one together. I'm in Your hands. Any help would be grate-fully appreciated.*

For a long afternoon, no help came in sight.

Then, as the two fellows downstairs got liquored up, Annie spotted what might just be an opening sent straight from God. It took a while to recognize it. A video game, especially one with such bloody pictures on it, is not usually where a woman of faith expects to see the hand of the Lord. Still, it started to look like the situation was working out that way to Annie.

She'd found enough play in the ropes tying her to the bed to almost sit up. That gave her a better view of what Oz was up to.

"You know, it's easy to make it to the next level," she said as he crashed and burned once again.

"You play this game?"

"My son does. He talks about it a lot."

"And you pay attention to what he has to say?" That seemed to shock the pudgy young man.

She suggested a maneuver Andy had bragged about. *Please God, let this be the right level and the right time.*

*Praise God,* it was.

And her next suggestion got him to the level he'd been cursing his failure to achieve. Then he turned into her protector when the two other guys staggered upstairs late that night, or maybe the next morning, with things she didn't even want to think about clearly on their minds.

"The boss said not to bother her," Oz said, standing in the doorway between them and her. Somehow he stared them down. They left. Oz had his weaknesses. The game for one. Junk food for the other. His nest at the door was surrounded by empty chip bags. Even his finger marks on the game controller were greasy.

But that night she believed that he saved her life.

After they left, Oz played happily on his game, and Annie risked some sleep.

The next morning she awoke early. The smell of cedar wood and ocean reminded her of the honeymoon cabin she and Benjamin had shared somewhere along this coast. The drive from Portland hadn't been any longer with her captors than it had been with her new husband. Nowhere near as pleasant, but...

Where was she now?

When the wind died down, it seemed she could almost hear the surf. They couldn't be too far inland. Any sounds of traffic were distant, so they weren't close to the coastal road. As Benjamin the infantry officer would say, not a lot of data to correlate for targeting.

But then, she had no idea why she'd been kidnapped. Nobody in his right mind would kidnap her. She thought about what a wonderfully empowered woman she'd been. Not anymore. Now she was lying here like some old-fashioned fairy-tale heroine waiting for a prince to come along and rescue her. Her hair wasn't even long enough to wave out the window, Rapunzel-style.

Oz interrupted his snoring just then, almost waking up, but

then he rolled over on his air mattress and went back to sawing wood.

Annie eyed him for a moment. Then her glance fell to where his game system had fallen. Very slowly a thought dawned on her. Embarrassingly slowly for a professional importer.

That wasn't the video-game system her son had just about worn out. No. Oz was playing the new upgraded version that was only available in Japan at the moment. The Barracuda Vn that Andy had begged her with tears in his eyes to get for him. The one that, according to Andy, did everything except cook dinner and take out the trash—which he'd offered to do every day for six months if she'd just get him that game system.

In fact, Andy had been so desperate for her to import one of those for him that he'd practically been willing to barter away his future and his freedom for it. She'd explained that the units were still going through their FCC testing. She could probably have gotten one for her son, but she hadn't wanted to have him sink into a new game system just before final exams. This summer would be soon enough for him to disappear into the glittering world of new twists and turns available in virtual game space. So the system hadn't yet become a part of the Taylor family.

But Oz had the new version. And it wasn't just a gaming box. No. Annie's Palm Pilot had games to play on it. And so did her cell phone. And some PDAs now included phones and Internet capabilities.

So the folks who made the Barracuda Vn system had decided

to jump for the whole enchilada. Games, phone, daily scheduler, wireless communication platform for text messaging and the Internet. Heaven help the poor teachers. Kids would be playing games in the back of the classroom, or gossiping with their friends, and then switching them over to schedulers as the teacher walked up.

*This generation will never learn another thing!* the mother in her sighed.

But if Oz had access to the Internet on that gizmo? No one had said a word about a demand for money. Were they that dumb, or was that being left to the "Boss"?

When Oz awoke, much later, did his own morning stuff, and then oversaw her trip to the bathroom, Annie let slip to him that his gizmo could access the Internet. That blew right by him.

Annie gulped and decided to go the rest of the way. "Have you fellows asked for the million-dollar ransom?"

"What million-buck ransom?"

"When I was promoted with Triton Imports, they took out a million-dollar insurance policy on me so they could pay out if I was kidnapped."

Oz dropped his game and bolted downstairs. Fifteen minutes later all three of them made the trip up to see Annie. They seemed a lot more respectful of her comfort. At least they brought her a glass of water without her asking for it.

"You're worth a million bucks?" the tall one she'd decided was in charge said.

"That's what the policy I signed for two weeks ago said."

"And he didn't tell us nothing about that," the shorter one said.

"Probably planned to give us the five thousand he talked about and keep the rest," Oz put in.

"Bill wouldn't do that to us, his old buddies."

Bill? Not the Bill that worked in her office? The one who'd been turned down for her job and had been making a major pain of himself ever since? Annie kept her face deadpan. There would be time later to check out who Bill was. But only if she kept herself alive.

*Dear God, help me.*

The tall one nudged the game with the toe of his boot. "And you say this toy can get on the Internet."

"It should. It's designed to do it. I don't know what that one has been rigged to do."

Oz carefully picked up his favorite toy and handed it to Annie. She'd never read the manuals for this rig, but she'd seen the advertising. And they were supposed to be as easy to use as you'd expect them to be for six-year-olds.

They eyed her. She figured it was better if she did things slowly and showed them what she was doing. She explained the machine to them as she converted it from game system to scheduler to phone.

No dial tone. "I guess that's not activated," she said. They answered with blank stares. She switched it to the Internet setting and prayed it would come up.

The home page of the system was on some porn site. Which said something about the original owner. But it worked. "And, see, it also has e-mail. That allows you to send mail to whomever you'd like to write."

"Who would I write a letter to?" the shorter one said.

"Who'd waste the time answering you?" the taller one said. Friendly bunch. "Could we send a message to your office for the ransom?" Aha. They'd made the mental leap she needed them to make.

"Might work better if you sent it to my home," Annie said. If their Bill was her Bill, any message to the new office could bring a very upset boss down on them. And on her! She probably wouldn't survive the visit. "I'm new out here. They may not be too worried about me at the office. But I know my husband will do anything he has to do to get me back. And Benjamin knows Mr. Roberts, our company's CEO, very well." *And dislikes him immensely, but that is a personal matter.*

Annie typed in her home computer addresses, both of them, and waited.

"Can't they tell where we are from this? Trace it back?" the tall one said, showing just how smart he was.

"Don't I wish," Annie said with an honest sigh. She'd been studying the return e-mail address. It wasn't the usual dot-com, she explained, but dot-sb. "I think it's going to Serbia. That's where the mafias—Italian, Russian, American, whatever—are operating their underworld Internet servers. There and in Russia. My son read something about them. Told me."

"And this can't be traced back to us?"

"No," Annie said. "At least, dot-sb addresses are not supposed to be traceable. How much are you willing to risk for a million dollars?"

"A lot."

"Maybe we ought to talk this over with the boss?" the short one said.

"He was going to stiff us. You think if we tell him we know what he was doing to us, that he'll be happy about it?" Oz contributed to the discussion.

"A million bucks of insurance money. It ain't like it's anyone's," the taller one said. "What do you think we should say to get the cash?"

Hands trembling, Annie quickly wrote out her message. She didn't even go back to correct typos. The three of them looked at the message.

"Send it," the taller one said.

*Dearest Father, into Your hands I commit myself,* Annie prayed as she pushed the Send button.

## 21

"THEY WANT MONEY FOR MOM," JOY WHISPERED BESIDE ME, pain in every syllable.

"Yes." I turned to hug both my trembling children. "It's a good thing. It means that she's still alive. And the kidnappers are talking to us," I whispered to them. "Now we can talk back. We can save her."

"He's right," Hunter said, coming to place a hand on Joy's shoulder. "If they want money for her, that means they know she's worth something to them alive. Maybe they even sent along proof that she is alive. Kidnappers often do."

I looked up, my gaze going from Agent Hunter to the one with the computer in front of him. Quickly he shook his head.

"What did they send? Please tell me," I pleaded.

Now there was a lot of wordless discussion between the agent beside the computer fellow and Sanders, with a few quick glances at Hunter as well. Nothing aimed my way.

"Please, for God's sake, don't leave us out here dangling. We know Annie. Give us a chance to help," I pleaded.

The guy with the computer did a few things to it. My guess was that his keystrokes were closing down several windows that told them things they didn't want me to see. He showed the screen to his boss, who nodded, and then turned the computer screen toward us.

I didn't have to say, "Don't touch." Both my kids put their hands in their pockets and, if anything, edged away from the computer. Still, we were all leaning forward to get a better look.

We saw an e-mail.

WE GOT TAXLOR. WE WANT 1 MIL R SHE DI. REPLY WHN U HV MIL 4 ORDERS.

I glanced at the header. The return address was long and involved. "Russian," Andy said. "Did it come through Serbia or North Korea as well?"

"You suddenly know an awful lot about the Mafia's Internet," Sanders muttered.

"Of course he does. He's seventeen," I snapped. "He lives on the Internet. But I monitor his messages. You've seen his hard drive. He doesn't abuse it."

"I just read a lot," Andy said with a quick shrug.

"But he's right," the agent with the computer said. "Whoever these jokers are, they got the message to us through so many cutouts that this thing will tell us nothing. The address is a dead end." Sanders looked like he wished the agent hadn't told us that, but the agent's boss only nodded.

"So, what do we do?"

The others looked at Sanders. "You have a million dollars?" he asked me.

"Of course not. Where would I get that kind of money?" I thought furiously for a moment. "You know, Annie signed papers for some kind of kidnapping insurance when she got this promotion. I remember her laughing about it over dinner Monday, no, it was Tuesday evening." I didn't like the look Sanders was giving me. "I don't know anything about it, but I do know who we can ask."

"Who?" Sanders asked, with Joy and Andy chiming in a close second.

I whipped out my cell and speed-dialed Annie's old office, explaining what I was doing to agents who looked none too happy to have cell-phone calls originating in their office from visitors. But then, none of them had been all that overjoyed about having visitors in the first place.

The secretary answered and put me right through to Wilson as I put the cell phone on speaker. "Willy, how're the kids?" I asked.

"Fine. I'm more worried about you and yours. I'm sorry to hear about Annie."

"Not as sorry as I am," I said. "How'd you learn about her?"

"Got a call from the Portland office. Normal business."

"Well, I was wondering if she has some kind of insurance against kidnapping. Under the circumstances, well, it might be time to get some details. "

"Yes, she does. So do I. All our major managers are covered by that policy," he said. "Obviously it's not something I can talk about. You'd have to talk to the big boss."

"So how do I get in touch with Bob Roberts?" I asked, and he patched me through to the CEO's phone. It rang several times and I started to wonder if it was ever going to be answered. Then, at last, he picked up.

"Roberts here. Who is this?"

"This is Ben Taylor. I'm Annie Taylor's husband. You just promoted Annie to your Portland office."

"Of course, Ben. What can I do for you?" Roberts said, so smooth, so controlled...so usual.

"My wife has been kidnapped."

"I'd heard. You have my sympathy," he said, without meaning a word of it.

"I'm in the FBI's office in Portland, and they've just intercepted a request for a million-dollar ransom for my wife. I understand Triton Imports has an insurance policy for just such situations as this." The kids eyed me, hopeful. In fact, hope bubbled all around us, leaving me feeling almost giddy. We could pay the ransom. Annie would be safe.

"I'm sorry, Mr. Taylor, but you seem to be misinformed about our policy," Roberts said with the same glib coolness he always showed.

I shook my head as if to shake off a blow.

"What?" I said, trying to keep my voice smooth, calm, even as I felt as if I was hurtling head first into some deep, ugly pit.

"We do have a kidnapping policy," Roberts said with the infuriating smoothness of a kindergarten teacher trying to help a particularly slow five-year-old. "But it is only to ransom senior associates if something happens to them while they are on foreign business trips. We consider that risk part of our corporate mission in some, uh, locations. However, when our people are here, in the States, it doesn't cover them. Domestic kidnappings, well, they're rarely business matters," he finished, as if having explained it would solve everything.

"There must be some way you can extend the policy to this, uh, situation of Annie's. She doesn't know anyone on the West Coast. She's only been there a couple of weeks. She had to have been taken for some business reason," I said, my voice as flat as I felt. Joy collapsed cross-legged on the floor. Andy at least made it to a chair. I stood, because I was the father. I had to keep going. My stomach was twisting, revolting; I struggled to keep my breakfast down.

"No, I truly am sorry," Roberts said, sounding not the slightest bit concerned, "but you must understand, we can't change insurance policies in midproblem. You, a personnel manager, must know that."

I would have slugged the man if he hadn't been on the other end of a phone line. *Dear God, help me.*

"However," Roberts went on, "if you do need to arrange a loan, I can put you in touch with one of our lenders who can probably arrange something at a reasonable interest rate. Of course, they will require substantial collateral if the amount is too high."

"Like a million dollars?" I said, calling on every second of my years of walking with the Lord to keep a civil tongue in my head. *Maintain control, Ben. You may need this man.*

*Dear Jesus, help me find the meekness You found before Pilate.*

"That's the exact amount of insurance we pulled on Annie. She must have misunderstood the policy and told her kidnappers about it," Roberts said, a light dawning in his voice.

"I'm afraid so," I said and glanced around me. At least Agent Hunter looked sympathetic. My kids looked crushed.

"Is there anything else I can do for you? I'm a busy man."

"I'm sure," I told him dryly. "I'll call you back if I need help."

"Please do" was followed by a click as he hung up on me.

I collapsed into a chair. Several deep breaths later I was still trying to calm my sick stomach, my sick heart, my anger. Finally, I mastered myself enough control to explain to everyone the problem with the insurance policy.

"That may complicate matters," Agent Sanders said when I finished.

I eyed him as I weighed his understatement and suppressed the temptation to take out my rage on him—barely. Annie was in trouble, and I needed everyone's help. This was no time to let my rage burn any bridge she'd need on her journey back to us.

"Is there any way you could raise a million dollars?" Hunter asked.

I took another two deep breaths before I risked a word. "Our house is almost mortgage-free," I said. "That was how we were planning to pay for college for the kids in the next few years. Re-mortgage the house. And we've got 401(k) accounts through our jobs."

"Dad, I've got some money saved," Andy cut in.

I shook my head at my son. I didn't want to be using our kids' money if I could help it. "Between those assets I might cover just over half the ransom demand."

"And the other half?" Hunter asked.

"Will be hard to find on my own," I said, then started dialing my cell phone again. Sanders looked like he was about ready to yank the phone from my hand, but Hunter stepped between us.

I listened as the phone rang twice at our home church before Pastor Evans picked it up.

"Pastor, this is Ben Taylor."

"Ben, I was so sorry to hear about Annie. We've been praying for her all week." There was no doubting the sincerity behind that voice.

"I can't tell you how much I appreciate that, Pastor. Me and the kids are doing a lot of praying, too, out here in Portland, at least we are if the good Lord counts our desperate renditions of 'Please help us' as prayers."

"Sometimes those are the only prayers we can utter and the best that He hears."

I appreciated that more than I could say, but what I said was, "I'm afraid I'm calling about a problem that needs more than prayers." Quickly I filled him in on the ransom demand and the discovery that we couldn't raise the money on our own.

"Annie's job hasn't offered any help?"

"No. The CEO has offered to introduce me to some bankers who'll demand collateral that I don't have and make me fill out paperwork that will take time that I don't have. I can mortgage the house for about half of the amount I need. Our retirement accounts might cover a major chunk of the rest, but not all of it. And I'm not back home to arrange all of this. To do all the paperwork. You were the first person I thought of when I realized that I needed help."

"I'm pretty sure I can help. Are you asking for gifts or for loans that will be paid back?" Pastor Evans had built a church, two schools, and a summer camp since he'd been our minister. A man of the cloth, but he knew business.

"I will pay back every cent. And if I can't do it immediately, I will pay interest."

"Can you give me two, three days?"

"Pastor, if it were up to me, I would give you forever. It's Annie I fear for."

"And rightly so. You're calling on your cell, and I can reach you there, right?"

I said yes.

"There are several members of the congregation I will need to talk to. I'll get back to you in a couple of days. Maybe sooner," he said.

"I can't tell you how much I appreciate this."

"We are all in God's hands. My advice is to pray as if everything depended on God. Work as if everything depended on you. In the end, our Savior will bring good from all this."

"I live in that hope," I said as the phone went dead.

"We prefer that you don't pay the ransom," Sanders said.

"We can't lure them out of whatever hole they're hiding in without money for bait," I said, but that was not my main concern. Annie had told them to expect a million dollars. I was sure of it. Insurance companies should have that money at their fingertips; they did in all the movies.

But this wasn't a movie, and the money wasn't coming from some big vault. Annie needed to know that. Her kidnappers would know it soon enough.

I locked eyes with Sanders. "I need to send an e-mail back to my wife." He was shaking his head before I even finished. "I need to let her know that the money is coming, but not as fast as she thought. If we leave her hanging with no word to the kidnappers, things could get ugly."

"It might be nice to have another message going back down that track, whatever it is, to them," the agent with the computer said.

Sanders scowled at him, then turned to me. "It's on your head if you do it and something goes wrong."

*Oh Lord, which was the right move? Doing something? Doing nothing?* Once more, my Savior was silent.

Everything in me, everything I'd lived by, said that Annie deserved to know what was happening. Because out of ignorance came error. "The truth will set you free," was both scripture and the touchstone upon which Annie and I built our marriage.

I reached for the computer. The agent tapped it to open up a reply window, then handed it over. As I let my mind wander in thought, my eyes drifted over the machine and came to rest on a property tag that said DEA. So the FBI *was* working with the Drug Enforcement Agency. Yes, this mess might be domestic, but I was coming to believe that it surely was business related. Though perhaps not in the way that I originally suspected. The business involved was probably not listed in the yellow pages.

Joy and Andy came to stand beside me. I took a deep breath and began to type.

Annie, love, I am mortgaging the house and raising the full million. The insurance policy was only for foreign kidnapping, not domestic. We will need a bit of time to raise the money, but it is coming. Love from the kids. Church is praying and helping. Love from us all, Benjamin

"It needs to be shorter, Dad," my son suggested.

" 'Annie, love,' stays," I said. But I cut "full." Then I backspaced over "not domestic."

" 'Need a bit of time,' is vague. Not good," Hunter said.

I replaced it with "We need two or three days" and dropped "but it is coming."

I glanced at the agents surrounding my tiny family circle. I found little hope in their professional gazes.

This was my risk to take, so I focused on my kids. They gave me short nods. Behind Joy, Hunter seemed to be truly hurting with us. She nodded along with my son and daughter.

I handed the computer back to the agent who rode herd on it. "Do what you think you have to do to track this, but please send it."

The agent looked around. Sanders gave the kind of shrug Pilate might have given as he washed his hands of a troublesome Jew. The agent did several things, then, pausing for a moment in what might have been a silent prayer, hit the Send button.

"Into Your hands, oh Lord, we commit ourselves," I prayed out loud. Joy and Andy answered with a quick "Amen," followed a bit more raggedly by several of the agents.

"Now what do we do?" Andy asked.

"We wait," Sanders said. "There's a cafeteria downstairs. Why don't you settle in there? Jennifer, do you have their cell-phone number?"

Agent Hunter nodded.

Joy pleaded for a chance to participate. "Isn't there anything we can do?"

Sanders looked at Hunter.

She shook her head and put an arm around Joy. "We're still waiting for a report from Baltimore, and besides"—here she glanced at Sanders, and I got a mental image of her sticking her tongue out most unprofessionally—"the file on this case is terribly thin. I'm not sure there's all that much that you could help us with."

We went downstairs and settled at a table in the small cafeteria. For a while we prayed, but distractions were rampant. Andy took to pacing, and I was tempted to send him out to run around the block. Joy curled up in a booth and seemed to go to sleep.

The table next to us had an abandoned copy of the morning edition of the local newspaper, the *Oregonian,* and I leafed through it. I found myself looking through the ads, wondering if anyone might be advertising for a personnel specialist...or a kidnapper. I noticed that there was going to be a gun show Wednesday through Saturday at the state fairgrounds.

I thought gun shows were weekend things, but this was the West and all that.

About 11:30, Agent Hunter came by in running clothes: an oversize T-shirt that said Run for the Cure and running shorts. "Would any of you like to do a lunch run with me?" she asked.

Andy about jumped out of his skin, he said yes so fast. Joy was a bit slower. Now I saw the tears running down her face; she hadn't been sleeping but crying.

"I'll go too," my daughter said.

I glanced down at my leather shoes and shook my head. "I didn't come prepared for running."

"Why don't you come amble along with us?" Hunter said. "Lots of people just walk along Waterfront Park. It's not raining."

I followed the agent and my kids as they walked the three

blocks to the waterfront area. A long green swath separated the closest road from a sea wall that had a good fifteen- or twenty-foot-wide sidewalk full of walkers, runners, skaters, and folks on bikes, all respectfully avoiding running into one another.

There was a large gray tower, so while my kids took off south jogging along with the FBI agent, I walked over to discover that the gray thing was the fighting top of the battleship USS *Oregon*—all that was left of it—and read more about that bygone warship than I really wanted to know. I took off again. Maybe I could walk the jitters out.

An hour later Hunter and the kids came jogging back my way. Hunter trotted back to her office, and the kids and I decided to walk back to the motel. We had a light lunch, and I arranged to rent a car.

"What do we need with one?" my son, always intent on saving a dime, demanded. "It's not like we're going to want to go sightseeing."

"I don't know. I just want to have a car handy in case I need one," I said, maybe a touch defensively.

"It's a grown-up guy thing," Joy said, and elbowed Andy, who elbowed her back. It was good to see they could still find a bit of humor, even in the middle of this nightmare.

The day dragged on with us watching more television than we wanted to. There was nothing on the local news about Annie. We talked about that and decided it was good. I offered to rent the kids a first-run movie, but we didn't see one that we wanted. The usual violent fare just looked repulsive to us. We channel surfed and got on each other's nerves. Joy ended up in her own room, watching someone sell jewelry or maybe just spacing out. Andy settled on a cartoon station that was rerunning every Scooby Doo episode ever made. I think he was just happy to let his eyes glaze over.

I prayed and laughed and prayed and checked the news in between Scooby Doo's adventures and prayed and went quietly out of my mind.

Somewhere along the line, I fell asleep.

# 22

THE CLOCK BESIDE THE BED SHOWED 2:14 A.M. WHEN I AWOKE to the familiar chimes of a cell phone. Andy had refused to personalize his phone, so I knew immediately it was his.

Bleary eyed, he was struggling in the dim light of the television to get his phone out. He finally got it open, glanced at it, shook his head, mumbled, "That makes no sense." He might have clicked off if I hadn't come off my bed at him.

"What is it?" I don't think I quite shouted.

"Just some dumb spam e-mail. You know, *We have your pain meds here.* Makes no sense."

"What's it say?" I demanded.

Andy handed me his cell. Like so many teenagers' phones, this one was far more than Alexander Graham Bell ever thought a phone could be. Camera, Internet port, game platform... Right now it had an e-mail displayed on the screen. I glanced at the message under the header. It said simply: *I C U Thunder Rid AT.*

"Thunder Ridge!" I whispered, astonished and profoundly

relieved. I might not be a teenager and genetically programmed with the codes, but even I could read *I'll see you at Thunder Ridge. Annie Taylor.*

My wife had somehow found a way to send me a message! And I knew where she was, more or less.

"What's all that mean, Dad?" Joy asked.

"It's a place your mom and I stopped at on our honeymoon."

"Yeah? That's a long time ago. So how come you remember it?" Andy asked. "And is it the right place? There must be thousands of Thunder Ridges. Are you sure that's what Mom means?"

"Yeah, I'm sure. It was kind of special."

My son eyed me as if it were impossible for two adults to remember anything for more than five minutes. Then his eyes got wide. "So you and Mom. . . ?" Andy croaked.

"It's none of your business, young man," I shot back, but my hormone-driven teenage son had got it right. There was no way that Annie or I would ever forget Thunder Ridge. Those two young newlyweds we once were, exploring the world and each other, had a shared moment that years later gave us a place that spoke to our hearts when almost all communication was forbidden. Now I had a way to find my wife. For the first time in days, my panic and fear gave way to a sense of purpose.

I grabbed for my own phone, dialed the FBI office, and found that except for an officer manning the phone, the task force was out. The force that was supposed to save my wife or find the drug kingpins or whatever.

"Give me the duty officer," I demanded, pleaded. I was not at all sure what my voice was doing.

"FBI," came noncommittal, but it was Agent Hunter's voice.

"I've got a message from my wife," I started.

"Yes, I know that your son is in receipt of a message," she said. "We're monitoring your incoming calls, of course. But according to the header, it appears to be spam."

"It's from my wife," I insisted. "I promise you."

"Hang on."

There was a pause. I could hear the sound of a voice in the background. I even recognized it, though I couldn't make out the words. Apparently, the computer wizard from the task force had also stayed on the night watch.

"It did come along the same path as the earlier message," Agent Hunter said. "Its last relay was the Russian server, but we don't know where it was before there." Her voice told me she was tired and frustrated.

"It's from my wife," I repeated.

There was a pause. Long enough, I guessed, for her to roll her eyes at the ceiling and say some bad words about why she'd ever thought that helping desperate people like me would be a good job.

"Assuming, for the moment, that this is from your wife, what does it tell you?"

"That she's somewhere around Thunder Ridge."

"Look, let's say that you're right, and I'm willing to concede that you may be. It still doesn't help us much. There are several hundred Thunder Ridges—everything from mountains to lakes to forests to streams—in the Pacific Northwest. We can't even begin to search them all." Her voice wasn't quite exasperated. Close, but not quite.

"How many along the coastal range?" I asked.

Again there was a pause on her side of the phone. Was she having the computer geek do a search on the coastal range?

"Why?"

"That message is from my wife, and I believe that I know which Thunder Ridge she's talking about," I added, trying to sound helpful, not desperate. "It's a forested area on the coast near Lincoln City."

"You didn't hear this from me," said Hunter in her hardest tone yet. "But everything I've got from the other side"—I heard "drug task force" there—"says we should be looking on the eastside of Oregon. That's been the pattern in the past. There's a lot of desert out there for people to disappear into. And never be found."

I wanted to shoot back, "But I'm right, and I know where to start looking." I swallowed the words with an effort. Her leads said to look east. My gut reaction to the e-mail was to look west. Who was right? Well, I knew that, but I didn't know if the authorities would believe me.

I took two deep breaths before I risked a word. "Agent Hunter, if that message is from my wife, and I'm sure it is, I have very strong reasons to believe that it's pointing us to the west. Can I talk to Special Agent-in-Charge Sanders?"

"Not tonight, Ben. We've been working twenty-four hours a day for four days. Brent sent the team home with orders to get a good night's sleep. I don't think he intended me to wake him up, even for this."

"And you won't?" I asked softly.

"No. I won't."

"When can I talk to him?"

"Nine at the earliest," came back at me.

I took another one of those deep breaths. The relaxation experts say they are supposed to do just that, relax us. Those experts have never had their wife kidnapped and found the FBI looking in all the wrong places. I let my head fall, and my chin came to rest on my chest.

And I found myself staring at the paper. I'd left it open to that gun show ad. It opened at nine.

Where did I want to be at nine tomorrow? This morning, rather.

"Thank you, Jennifer. You've been as big a help as you could," I said.

"You'll be here at nine?" she asked.

"Or maybe a bit later," I said, not exactly lying, and hung up.

"What happened, Dad?" both kids demanded. I filled them in. They weren't any happier than I was.

"What are you going to do?" Joy asked as I finished. "We've got to help Mom!"

"I'm going to think about it," I said. "There's nothing else I can do right at this moment. So let's get some sleep. Tomorrow's going to be another day," I said, repeating the invocation Annie and I had used on them since they were two. "And it looks like it's going to be a very busy one," I added.

They eyed me like they weren't buying a word I was saying, but they went back to bed when I shooed them in that direction. I settled down on my own bed, lying on my back. It was time to think.

I knew where "our" Thunder Ridge was.

But all those years ago, our Thunder Ridge was little more than a timber road that led past a clear cut with a lovely view of the ocean. Were Annie and her kidnappers hiding out in a tent there?

Not likely.

There had been some houses as we drove back into the woods. Maybe there?

Or maybe not. Maybe Annie was just trying to point us west when she knew the drug business pointed us east.

And the Pacific coast of Oregon was what, three hundred miles long?

If I went looking for Annie, I might be looking for a long, long time.

I went back to the beginning of the tangled knot of my problems and started all over again, looking for something new, some new thread to pull to get my family straightened out.

And ended up in the same place.

Twice.

Three times.

And then the light streaming through the side of the blinds woke me up. *Dear God, how could I have slept?*

*Because you were exhausted,* I answered.

"And today is going to be a busy day," I muttered to myself, glancing at the clock. Seven. Time to shower, shave, take care of things up here, and be down in Salem at the gun show the moment it opened.

I tiptoed to the bathroom, leaving Andy asleep.

Twenty minutes later he was still under the covers, his back to me. I had intended to leave instructions for the kids, but maybe it was best if I didn't wake them. Instead, I left two hundred dollars cash and a quick note: *Stay here. Don't go out except to eat. If the FBI comes by, tell them I went out and will be back. Take care and stay out of trouble. PLEASE!!!*

I slipped quietly out of the room. My next stop was the hotel's office. A woman was managing the desk. I'd learned that she was the owner. "I want to pay ahead the next couple of days," I explained.

"You don't have to. We'll settle up when you check out." She smiled, brushing a stray gray hair back toward the bun that held most of it.

"Well, I may not be all that visible. Wouldn't want you to think I'd checked out while my kids were still here."

She eyed me. "You're the fellow whose wife is missing, aren't you? You going to be spending a lot of time with the FBI or something like that?"

I was glad she offered me options. "Yeah, something like that. My kids will still be here, though."

She sighed, the sound of a fellow parent who knew the ropes. "Regretting you brought them?"

"I do wish they'd stayed home," I said. That was nothing but the heartfelt truth right now.

"Happens. When my kids were that age, there were days when I wanted to lock 'em up and feed 'em through a slot in the door. We get a lot of the FBI trade. I'll look in on them as I get the time. Maybe I'll bake some cookies. Never baked a chocolate chip cookie that couldn't keep kids distracted."

"Thank you. I appreciate it," I said, though I was not at all sure Andy or Joy could be distracted from something like this with a few cookies, home baked or not. I settled up the bill, including four more days, and left. Crossing the parking lot, I looked back at our rooms' closed and darkened blinds and said a quick prayer for my sleeping kids. God willing, I would manage to end this mess soon, maybe even before the day was out. I turned to unlock the car with the key-chain remote and found it already unlocked. I shook my head. I could have sworn I'd locked the car last night. Then again, there were a lot of things I was sure I'd done of late that I hadn't done. I knew that this situation was getting to me.

*Stress,* I reminded myself. *You're stressed, Ben. Take things carefully or you're going to end up as a statistic. Be no good if they got Annie back only in time to attend your funeral from some fool accident.*

Very carefully, I exited the motel parking lot, found my way to I-5, and motored south. Most of the traffic was headed into Portland this time of the morning; I got off easy as I headed for Salem. Still, I stayed in the slow lane. I was running ahead of my schedule. Unless I got lost finding the fairgrounds, I'd be there right on time.

Which left me time to get distracted. My mind wandered again along the problem of finding Annie...and came up with nothing better than heading for the part of the Oregon coast where we'd honeymooned and asking people if they'd seen my Annie.

Lousy plan.

"You got a better one?" I asked no one in particular.

*You could go back and talk with the FBI. There's still time,* a little voice in my mind said. There was no easy answer to that one.

Yes there was. They knew everything I knew. They hadn't shown all that much interest in listening to me. If Hunter couldn't persuade her boss to check out the Thunder Ridges along the coast, did I really have any chance of convincing him? The man had demonstrated nothing more than total contempt for me so far. In fact, judging by my experience with him, he'd probably think I was trying to lure him into hunting in the wrong place.

But, for their own reasons, I knew they actually were hunting for Annie. Hunting 'round the clock. And at least, for the moment, there were two groups hunting for my Annie: me and the FBI.

I stomped on the temptation to laugh at the image of me pitted against the Federal Bureau of Investigation. Me, a lone Human Resources honcho, right up there with our nation's finest in all their buttoned-down legions.

Actually, I'd stomped on the gas, not temptation. I let the car coast back down to sixty-five and focused.

I knew Annie. I loved Annie. And somewhere in all that confusion was God's plan for me and Annie. And I knew that had to be for our good. Like my pastor said, "Pray as if everything depended on God. Work as if everything depended on you. In the end, our Savior will bring good from all this."

It was time for me to go to work.

As I neared Salem, I concentrated on spotting the exit for the state fairgrounds. After exiting, I followed the signs to it. And then I followed the handwritten signs to the gun show.

The parking lot was a grass-covered field in front of a metal-sided pole barn. My rental car, big enough to seat six adults comfortably, was unique among pickups, vans, and a few recreational vehicles that had seen heavy use.

It looked like the lone city mouse come to visit the country cousins.

I parked, made sure to lock the car this time, and headed for the entrance. The smell of former animal occupancy and hay met me as I entered the dusky barn. The overhead lights gave enough illumination to see by, but they were nowhere close to OSHA standards for a work area. Then I frowned at the thought, a distraction at a time when I needed to focus. I guess old habits die hard—and that was how my brain worked. The scent of straw came from underfoot where it had been laid on the dirt floor over the few areas where the roof leaked.

Lines of tables had been set up. Merchants were laying out rifles, pistols, knives, and a wide assortment of wares. Several were moving their tables forward or backward, trying to avoid being stuck in the mud. There were shouts and conversations between old friends and new acquaintances and exclamations at the accommodations, most in the kind of language I hadn't used since my army days.

This early, everyone seemed to know each other to some degree, and all the vendors seemed to be looking forward to a good day together. Some of them might actually make some money, though I was none too sure how high a priority it was among them, judging by their comments to each other.

The place had the feel of a particularly well-armed gypsy camp. Just a bunch of folk having fun, but a bit careful of outsiders.

I stopped by a table with a gleaming display of knives. There were blades from our competition, but it looked to me like Carter knives took up about half his table.

"Looking for a knife?" the guy behind the table asked. Intent on setting out his stock, he didn't even glance my way.

"You just selling, or do you buy?"

"Both, but I don't buy junk."

I'd already noticed that. His Carter inventory was all old stuff. None of the new, cheap line that Jason was so proud of. I took my ten-year anniversary pocketknife out and laid it on the table. I had no intention of parting with it, but it might cut me some respect here, three thousand miles from home.

The man whistled as he looked it over, extended the big blade, then the other ones. "Nice. We don't see many of these this far west. I bought a five-year knife at a meet in Missouri once. How'd you come by this?"

"That's my name on the handle," I said, pointing to the words carved into the knife's haft. "I work there." I didn't mention what I did. Most places, being a manager was something a bit higher in the pecking order than working on the line at a plant. Here, I strongly suspected, all they'd be interested in were the folks who made the knives. I wasn't one of them.

The fellow hefted it, rolled it over in his hand. "A good knife." He eyed me. "If you really want to sell it, Ben, I suspect I could make you the best offer you'll hear today."

"Actually, I'm looking to buy a hunting rifle. I figured a good knife man like you might point me in the right direction."

The man folded up the knife and handed it back to me with a handshake. "I'm Manuel Gomez." He waved at a guy in the next booth. "Hey, Jeremy, you know anyone this fine stranger might buy a good hunting rifle off of?"

An old fellow had been leaning against the table next to us, not missing a thing. He stood to offer his hand to me. Where Manuel was short and spare, this fellow was tall and thick. His thinning hair was pulled back in a ponytail, and his jeans and flannel shirt, though worn, were clean. The fatigue jacket he wore bore the patch of the First Cav. He could have bought it, or it could be original issue. I reserved judgment.

"I'm Jeremy Metzger. What are you looking for, stranger?"

"I'm Ben Taylor," I said. "I'm looking for a hunting rifle. Scoped. Something not too hard to handle."

"What are you familiar with——.30 caliber or .22?" Jeremy asked, his eyes catching mine, locking on them, and holding them. He seemed to look past my eyeballs into some part of me I didn't usually let people into.

"I fired a 5.56 millimeter during my army days."

"Ah, so you aren't totally green, eh? What outfit?"

"Ninth, up at Fort Lewis."

"Then it was a while back," he said.

"A few years," I admitted, dropping my eyes from his to look at what he had to offer. His table held an AR-15, the civilian cousin of my M-16. It looked like a match for the one Jeb Shepherd had, the one I'd fired just a few days ago. I reached for it.

He made no move to stop me, but he did take half a step back.

The magazine was missing, the weapon on safe. I verified that the open chamber was empty, then palmed the bolt carrier release. It slid forward with ease and locked in place. So I pointed it at the dirt, flipped off the safety, and pulled the trigger. It clicked empty.

"Not very trusting, are you?" Jeremy said, a grin on his face. But Manuel was grinning too. I suspected I'd passed a test. I took aim at a dead light fixture overhead and slowly squeezed. It was neither a hair trigger, nor overly difficult to pull. I brought the weapon down. "I'll take it. What kind of scope will it take?"

"Any of these," Jeremy said, indicating five with a flip of his hand.

"I'll take the most powerful one you have," I said. "Any place we can sight my purchase in?"

"Not here," Manuel said. "Have to do it at a firing range."

I produced my credit card and my Maryland driver's license. "Do you need more ID for a check?" I asked.

Jeremy didn't reach for my ID. He reached for the gun and took it from my hands. "Mr. Taylor, why do you want to buy a weapon?"

Those eyes were back on me. His voice wasn't exactly what I'd expect to hear from the Lord God of Hosts rolling off of Mount Sinai, but movie producers had done a whole lot worse producing knockoffs.

Now it was my turn to take a step back. I frowned. "If you don't want to sell me a weapon, just say so."

"Jeremy, I've never seen you refuse a sale," Manuel said.

"I've never been party to the possible kidnapping and murder of a man's wife."

"It's not like that..." I stumbled over the words. "I need it to..." Then a thought occurred to me. "How do you know me?"

"I watch the late news. I saw you and your kids at the airport."

Ah. I had to admire his integrity, but right now, I needed a weapon. "What happened to innocent until proven guilty?" I said.

"Good starting point, until a man with a missing wife tries to buy a rifle three thousand miles from home. Again, Mr. Taylor. Why do you need a weapon?" Jeremy wasn't budging, not one inch. And he wasn't letting go of that rifle.

"Because I'm going hunting for the jerks who kidnapped my wife. That's why."

"Isn't the FBI doing that?" Manuel asked.

"Yeah, but they're looking in the wrong place, they won't listen to me, and they're not moving fast enough," I spat.

"Why don't you tell me about it?" Jeremy said, indicating a chair on the other side of the table.

He put the gun back and leaned on his table again. I weighed my options and sat down.

The man knew how to ask the right questions, and he knew how to listen. In five minutes I got a lot off my chest.

Manuel looked more and more shocked as I talked, until at the end he looked like Andy and Joy had back at the pizza parlor, when we first heard Annie was missing. Jeremy, well, he just shook his head. I got the impression he was one of those guys who don't get shocked.

"Don't sound like much has changed in the big government since Nam," he said, then added an army word that went far past snafu.

*Lord forgive me,* but I said, "Amen."

"Okay," Jeremy said, leaning toward me in his chair, "assuming you ain't buying this rifle to use on the FBI, why do you need one, Mr. Taylor?"

"I told you. My wife is being held somewhere around Thunder Ridge. The FBI doesn't believe me. So I'm going looking for the guys that took her. I don't exactly think the folks holding her for a million bucks in ransom will take kindly to me walking off with her after I ask them nicely. I figure I better go armed with something more than my good looks."

"You ever killed a man?" There were those eyes again.

"No," I said without blinking.

"Hmm," was all Jeremy said. Then he fished in his pocket and handed Manuel a twenty. "Who sells those map books?"

"You mean the *Atlas and Gazette of Oregon?*" Manuel asked, but he was out of his chair and trotting down the row of tables without waiting for an answer. He stopped at one that offered a selection of magazines and books.

He was back in a minute, handing the change to Jeremy. I had a twenty out by now, but it seemed that my money was no good here.

"You know there are plenty of Thunder Ridges in our fine state?" Manuel said.

"That's what the FBI tells me."

"Which one's your Thunder Ridge?" Jeremy asked.

It took me a while to find it, never having looked for the place on a map before. On about the third try, I was able to find our hotel, then follow the drive Annie and I had made up into the hills so many years ago.

"There," I said. "Somewhere around there."

Both men eyed the map. Then shook their heads.

"You really are a stranger to these parts," Manuel said.

I closed my eyes, ordered myself to take two deep breaths, then decided the first two were too shallow and took four more. "What do you know that I don't know?" I finally got out through gritted teeth.

"Ever heard of the spotted owl, Mr. Taylor?" Jeremy asked.

"Spotted owl?"

"It's a bird, but it's only a name we locals toss around to cover a whole lot of unhappy people. Since you took your honeymoon, there've been a lot of people marching and going to court and hanging themselves from trees. And putting nine-inch spikes in trees. You have any idea what those spikes do to saw mills?"

"No," I said.

"Or to people working in the mills when the spikes and saws come flying out in pieces? My brother-in-law stopped a chunk of one a bit back. They think he may be able to work again next year. But we're not counting on it. The doc said the same thing last year, too."

"Okay, I've heard about stuff like that back East. How does it impact me?"

"See that little dot at the junction of your road?"

I nodded.

"That means that that logging road has been closed to public traffic," Jeremy said. "There's a nice solid steel gate across the road at that point. A few pounds of C-4 might open it. A bulldozer, maybe. But not your average, everyday picnic-gear carrier. You're not getting up that road these days. No way, slick."

My stomach was back in free fall again. I blinked back the moisture in my eyes, but I felt a tear work its way down my cheek. I didn't want to wipe it off in front of these men. Maybe they wouldn't notice.

Jeremy handed me his handkerchief. It was clean. I turned my back on them and put it to good use.

"Ain't there nothing we can do, Jeremy?" Manuel was saying as I turned back to them.

"Seems like the missis went to an awful lot of effort to send you a message," Jeremy said slowly. "She wouldn't do that if it meant nothing. Our problem is figuring out what it does mean and how to use it to find her."

"Our?"

"Yeah. Our problem, Ben. Our problem," Jeremy said, extending me his hand.

Someday I hope to shake the hand of God. Until then, I'll hold on to the memory of that first handshake with Jeremy as a dim shadow of what His handshake must be like.

"Now will you sell me a rifle?" I said.

"No."

"But, Jeremy, you just said…" Manuel started speaking before I could.

Jeremy looked at us like we were a couple of not-so-smart four-year-olds. "To sell Ben here a rifle, we'd have to run a check on him, wouldn't we?"

Both of us nodded.

"How much you want to bet that the powers that be have a flag beside our Mr. Taylor's name? He tries to buy a gun, the ATF delivers a report direct to the FBI. And they come find our Mr. Taylor here. With guns drawn."

"Hmm, hadn't thought of that," Manuel and I said at the same time.

"Mannie, you're a kind soul," Jeremy pointed out. "And, Ben, I suspect you've never been waist high in this kind of sewage before."

"No. It was never part of my job description," I admitted. "Not even in the army."

"And I hope you thank God every day for the gentle way He's dealt with you."

"I do," I said. "Or I did. Just lately, things have been a mite bit hard in my life."

"I kind of took you for the churchgoing type."

"Yes, Annie and me and the kids, we show up every Sunday," I agreed.

Jeremy pursed his lips. "Never thought I'd be anyone's guardian angel, but then I'm in hock for a few good deeds. Looks like it's payback time. Let's see. You want that rifle and that scope. Consider them loaners for the time being. Now, I'll need this one," he said, picking up a rifle that Jeb would probably have drooled over and named to the third decimal place. To me, it just looked big, powerful, and very, very accurate.

"We'll need that pistol if I can dragoon George into one more charge up San Juan Hill. And we'll need ammo," Jeremy said. He slid a .45 into a shoulder holster and strapped it on, then slipped both rifles into carrying scabbards and pointed me at three different piles of ammunition.

I took a box of one hundred rounds from each stack. Jeremy shook his head. I took two.

Jeremy nodded.

And then I pulled out my credit card.

Jeremy just shook his head. "FBI know about that card?"

"Yeah." I put it away.

Manuel laughed. "Don't worry, Jeremy will make sure you pay for all this. Just later. Much later."

"Mannie, you take care of my booth today?" Jeremy asked. "Tomorrow too, maybe?"

"Sure, I'll take care of it. Maybe even sell something. You know, sell. That thing you aren't doing now."

Both men laughed.

"And if you're not back by Saturday," Mannie said, "I'll take it home. You know where to find it."

Then Jeremy was herding me out of the barn and, with a little guidance from me, toward my car.

My remote opened the car's trunk and unlocked the doors. I headed for the doors with the ammo while Jeremy headed toward the back of the car with the guns. Color me strange, but I still wanted the ammo in the backseat of the car, away from the weapons. Even at a time like this.

I finished stowing six boxes of the scary stuff in the backseat only to find Jeremy still standing beside the open car trunk. His mouth was actually hanging open. In such a cool character, that was very odd.

I started worrying even more.

Then he looked at me again.

"I know, Ben, that Maryland is bound to have some different laws from Oregon, but ain't it illegal in all fifty states to transport teenagers in a car's trunk?"

I walked around to join him. There lay Andy and Joy, wrapped up in blankets...and shivering.

# 23

"CAN WE GET OUT NOW?" JOY ASKED ME.

"What are you doing in there?" I yelled.

"You said to stay out of trouble," Andy said.

"And Andy figured the best way for us to do that was to come along," Joy added. "We figured the FBI would be after us pronto, once you didn't show up at their digs this morning."

"What part of my instructions about staying in the hotel didn't you understand?"

"But you said *please* stay out of trouble, Dad," Andy said. "You know you did. Did you want us to just sit there and wait for the FBI to come after us?"

Jeremy's chuckling finally broke into a major laugh at those words.

I looked away from my kids for a second to give him an exasperated glare.

"You know," he said, "I can't tell you how glad I was when them scientific people discovered that the human brain don't get fully growed-up until we're twenty-five. It's a relief to know that I really was brain-damaged as a teenager."

"We're not brain-damaged," Andy glowered at him. "We're just still growing."

"Can I get out now?" Joy repeated, climbing over her brother and out of the trunk without waiting for an answer.

"Why not?" I growled. "Do whatever you want. It's not like you pay any attention to what I say."

Andy started climbing out after his sister.

"You know, both of you are going right back to the hotel room," I said.

"Could we at least get in the car and turn on the heater while we discuss it?" Joy pleaded, her teeth chattering. It hadn't felt that cold to me outside. And the barn wasn't too bad, either. Maybe it had been worse on the kids in the trunk, not moving around. Maybe that would teach them a lesson.

Not likely.

I herded them into the backseat. Joy's eyes got huge, big as saucers, in fact, as she set her feet down beside all that ammunition. Andy took in the ammo, then the cloth shapes Jeremy was gently placing in the now-empty trunk.

"I told you, Joy. He's going for Mom. I told you."

"But how are we going to find her?" Joy said, repeating the question that had been hounding me since I'd seen the e-mail.

Andy settled in beside his sister, scrunched under her blankets, and said nothing until his teeth quit chattering. About the time

Jeremy took his place in the passenger seat beside me, my son said, "Dad, I have an idea."

"Let me guess. An idea that will slow me down from taking you back to the hotel," I said.

"Dad, you can't take us back," Joy put in. "That would be wasting time you could spend hunting for Mom."

Beside me, Jeremy raised an expressive eyebrow. "Girl's got a point."

"Dad, I really do have an idea about finding Mom," Andy repeated.

"What's your idea, son?"

"Okay, listen to all of it before you say no," Andy said, his nervous hands working under the blanket. "Mom sent us an e-mail. Two of them. So we, like, know she can get her hands on some kind of Net access. But it's not easy. She didn't correct her typos or spell stuff out all the way. That's not like her."

"Mom always sends perfect text," Joy pointed out.

"So she's able to sneak onto the Net, but it's a mondo risk," Andy said. "Okay?"

Jeremy and I nodded.

"Mom had to have done something to make whoever has the Internet access trust her enough for her to be able to sneak on, right?"

We didn't object. I wasn't sure I liked where he was going, though.

"I think that whoever has Mom has one of those really new

257

game systems. The one I begged Mom to get me—the Barracuda Vn. It's got wireless Internet access and everything. And Mom's helping him play some of the games I play, and she talked him into asking for the million and then managed to send a message out at two this morning," came out in one big rush.

"A video game," I said.

"Yes. One of those cool new ones you can only get in Japan. I know I can't prove it. And I know I am so jumping to all kinds of conclusions, but Dad, why else would Mom be able to send out a message but not phone us or escape?"

His sister put in, "And I had to listen to him whispering all about this for the whole drive and the entire time you were inside, but it does make sense." She paused. "If you ignore all the holes in it."

For once, Andy didn't slug his sister for dissing him. He was too busy pleading silently with me.

"You know," Jeremy started up slowly beside me. "There is a lot of leaping in faith in there. But leaps of faith can be good exercise for young souls."

I eyed him. Was this man touched in the head, or was he more touched in the soul than I was at the moment?

Maybe I needed to follow for a while, rather than try to lead somewhere that was totally dark to me. "Okay. For now let's say that Mom has made some kind of peace with someone who has a new Barracuda Vn game system with Internet potential. Where does that leave us?"

In the backseat, Joy and Andy exchanged blank looks and shrugged. I sighed. Thunder Ridge was locked down. Even if Annie was in the same room with a contraband video game, we were still up the creek without a prayer.

"You have a portable phone at your house?" Jeremy said beside me. I nodded.

"Ever walk into a room full of computers while you're talking on that portable?"

"Reception goes all to—" Andy swallowed the next word with a glance at me. "It gets all staticky, and sometimes you lose the line."

"Yep. Ben, why don't you put this car in gear and aim it for the coast? I got a buddy from Nam. He likes to play with that kind of static."

I backed out and headed for the exit, still not sure what I was doing as Jeremy kept talking.

"George was a wizard back in the war. Flew with the air force while I played jungle bunny in the mud below. You know, it's strange. He had it a whole lot easier then, but it ain't helped him all that much. He's still stuck in the country long after I found my way home." The man with the ponytail had gotten thoughtfully quiet beside me. I started to make a wrong turn, but he roused himself to point me right.

"Anyway, George has this place at the coast. He fixes TVs, computers, anything that you have to plug in for juice. But his real love still is ECM."

"What?" Andy said before I could.

"ECM. Electronic countermeasures."

"Electronic countermeasures," Andy repeated slowly.

"Maybe it's easier to think of it as creative static," Jeremy smiled.

"Now you're losing me," I said, catching the sign that pointed us to a turnoff for the coastal beaches.

Jeremy pointed at Andy. "That cell phone on your belt. It's got an FCC approval stamp on it, right?"

"Yes."

"Your computer, it also has an FCC approval number, and your monitor and your video game box. Ever wonder why all those things have to go through the Federal Communications Commission?"

"Mom said I couldn't have that new Barracuda game platform until it had been approved by the FCC, but I thought it was just some adult thing to keep me from getting my hands on something cool until after final exams."

"Which may be as right as anything else," Jeremy said. "But she was also telling the truth. All of those electronic gizmos have to be checked and blessed by the FCC to make sure they don't have too much static leaking from them. Static that would mess up the things you put them next to. It's like, when somebody back in the old days—before cable and the FCC rules—ran a vacuum cleaner during a playoff game. It left you with nothing by gray fuzz on the TV screen. Men used to get all riled up and yell at their wives. Too much static at the wrong time can make for some seriously unhappy people. And it isn't just a domestic problem. George tells me that back in the Big One, World War II to you young uns, the Germans knew our B-17s were coming over to bomb them that day long before our planes showed up on radar."

"But I thought radar was the big thing in that war," Joy said. The French Revolution wasn't the only history she was interested in. "How could they know before our planes were on their radar scopes?"

"Missy, they knew we were coming before we even got off the ground," Jeremy said to sounds of disbelief from the backseat. "As George tells it, when the bomber crews got in their planes, the first thing they did was turn on the radios to warm them up for when they'd want to use them. The radios made all kinds of static on a certain frequency. The Germans listened for racket on that frequency and knew we were on the way. It took us some time to figure out why the German fighters were always there, waiting for us. Then, once we learned, we kept the radios off until we were over the channel. That surprised the Jerries."

"And if everything gives off some kind of static," Andy said slowly, "do you think your friend could, maybe, locate the static given off by a Barracuda Vn game system?"

"Son, if anyone can, George is the man to do it."

Assuming, I thought, that he knew what kind of noise you could expect from the Vn set. And could rig something to listen for that noise. But the backseat sounded excited and hopeful for the first time in days.

My stomach stayed in a knot. I'd seen better plans in a Rube

Goldberg cartoon. But for right now at least, it was the only plan we had.

We drove into Lincoln City not quite two hours later. I followed Jeremy's directions to a small shop two streets back from 101, the main beach road. The home had a white-painted picket fence and a roughly done addition in front that served as a shop. The sign outside was small but promised "George will fix it if you broke it…or it's no charge."

"Optimist," I said as the kids piled out.

"Folks around here will tell you that he's just telling it like it is."

Inside, the shop smelled of musty ocean and wood, ozone and fresh plastic—a strange blend. The man bending over the innards of a television set was spare where Jeremy was round. His gray hair was cut close to his scalp, but his eyes had the same distant look I saw in Jeremy's.

George turned in response to his friend's warm greetings.

"What brings you to my coast, you old swamp rat?" sounded friendly enough. "Trudy, you got any coffee?" he shouted. "We got company, not customers."

"Coffee coming up. How many cups?" called a woman's voice from through the open door at the back of the shop.

"Three old coots," George answered. "And two cookie grabbers, if I'm any judge of the next generation. And one for you, if you wanna kibitz."

In no time at all, there were two colas, three coffees, and a tall stack of cookies on the low table in front of a beat-up old couch.

Apparently, Trudy had more important things to do than listen to "old coots." But she waited to make sure we were comfortable. The kids and I settled on the couch. George relaxed into an overstuffed chair beside us. Jeremy rolled an equally beat-up metal chair away from the workbench.

We sampled the coffee, as well as the cookies, and sang our praises to the baker before she retreated back to her domain. Somewhere in the back of the house a television set was tuned to a home-improvement channel.

Jeremy leaned forward. "George, I got some friends here with a problem."

"The one complaint I got against you, Jeremy, is that you never seem to darken my door except you got a friend with a problem."

"But I think you'll like this one. Young man, let my good buddy here in on your problem and what you think might solve it."

So Andy told George our story. The man frowned as he learned of Annie's plight, then leaned back into his chair as my son presented his thoughts on how his mom had gotten her message out and what that could mean.

"Lot of ifs there," George finally said, his hands steepled in front of him. "Lots of ifs, and as the song goes, I don't believe in ifs anymore," he went on, Andy's face falling. "You know, you're just a kid…"

Andy looked shocked, then angry.

Then George turned his full attention on Jeremy. "But what's that you're always saying? 'And a child shall lead them.'"

"It's been known to happen."

"And you'd say it wasn't just a chance that I was talking with a Japanese buddy of mine this morning who had a customer walk in with a problem with one of those new Vn systems, but a gift from your God."

"Like as not," Jeremy said with a confident smile.

George screwed up his mouth in clear doubt.

"What kind of problem?" my son asked.

"Young guy, living at home with his folks, and his hot new Barracuda Vn was wrecking their television reception."

"Static," Andy and Jeremy said at once.

"Something like it. Japanese like to get their latest stuff out to their local markets 'cause they are as like as not to talk to a repairman like my buddy rather than look for the nearest lawyer. Anyway, by the time they've done some local beta testing and passed our FCC, they can usually expect to have all the bugs worked out before they dump a couple of million copies on our not-quite-so-generous consumers."

"Did you fix it? Is it the kind of thing we can look for?" my son shot at George.

"Yes, we fixed it, but no, I don't think we can count on your mom's 'friend' to have the same kind of squawker. We concluded that this particular unit slipped past quality control checks. But…" George pulled himself out of his chair with obvious effort and took his cup of coffee over to a computer to sit down in another banged-up rolling chair.

The computer's case had seen better days. A whole lot of them. But the speed with which the screen filled with data in response to George's clicking on this and that icon proved that the innards were nowhere near as old as the box they were in.

"Yep, I got it. Here's the test data on the Vn." He pointed at a small window that opened on his huge computer screen. From the size of it, it must have been one of the first nineteen-inch monitors ever made. We'd gotten one for the research lab at Carter, but it had been a problem from the start, and we replaced it in a year. Something told me George didn't allow his machines to be problems.

"This ought to be interesting," George said softly. My son was now hovering over his shoulder. "My guess is this noisemaker down in the E-Band will not pass our FCC. They'll have to make some changes."

"Can you make something that might catch a box with that?" my son asked.

"Can Moses walk on water?" George asked with a grin for Jeremy.

"Moses parted the water, George. Jesus walked on the stuff."

"I get confused," George said, sharing a conspiratorial grin with my son. "But, yes, boy, we can put together something to listen for that buzz."

George reached for his phone and, without looking at it, speed-dialed the second number on it.

"Henry, George here. I need some stuff," He said, then rattled

265

off names for things I had never heard of. In less than a minute, he hung up and swiveled his chair around to face me.

"Henry at the local Radio Shack keeps a few things handy for me, but they may be a bit pricey. You don't mind, do you?"

"Anything that might help get Annie back is fine with me."

"I figured as much. Jeremy, you know where the store is? Can you take your friend there to get the stuff?"

"We're on the way already," Jeremy said.

"If you don't mind leaving the kids here, I might be able to put their young eyes and fingers to work," George said, pushing his chair over to an empty place on his workbench and reaching for a couple of tools the likes of which I'd never seen before. "My fingers are getting a touch of that rheumatism stuff."

I glanced at Andy and Joy. I was leaving them with a total stranger. No, with a man Jeremy vouched for. Part of me was pointing out that Jeremy wasn't all that far from being a stranger, but another part was too busy thanking God for these pilgrims helping me along the way.

"You feel okay?" I asked my kids.

Joy nodded. "We can help, Dad," Andy said.

A minute later Jeremy had me turning right, back onto 101.

"George looks like a good man," I said.

"He is, most days."

"And other days?"

"George did three tours in Nam. Easy ones, the likes of me

would have said. He just flew high over the trail, listening to bugs we dropped, then calling in bombers to stop the flow of supplies from the North going south. Just another day at the office, complete with clean sheets at night and a cold one at the O club after every mission."

"Then what?" I asked, for there was clearly more to the story.

"Then his plane went down," Jeremy said softly.

"Bad?"

"Bad enough. George was the only survivor. The air force has a bit of advice for their plane crews. Don't bail out over the people you just bombed. George broke that rule. He landed right in the middle of the road. For once, he couldn't call out for pizza. It took him a week to walk far enough from the trail for the Jolly Green to risk picking him up."

"But he made it out," I said, thinking that was all there was to it.

"Yes, he made it out. But think about it. For five, six days he's in the middle of the road, dodging the air strikes he used to call in. His buddies from back at the BOQ are still calling them in. He got to see firsthand what he'd been doing all those months. You know, they don't put a road in just for its good looks. People were walking it, driving it, maintaining it. He had to dodge those people if he wanted to stay alive. It's easy to hate folks, bomb folks when they're little and far away. But when you're living up close to them, seeing them eat, laugh, go about their day, you get to see that they're humans. And what your nice, clean job had been doing to them."

I tried to imagine what that might have felt like. "It wasn't pretty."

"Nope. Trudy tells me she doesn't dare burn a roast. The smell of burnt meat will put him in bed for most of a week."

"He was just doing his job," I said and tasted how weak those words were against what George had been through. What Jeremy had been through to be able to talk with his friend the way the two of them did.

"Here's your store," Jeremy said, ending that conversation.

A smiling fellow, about my age, already had a box half filled for us. He added a robot and a remote-controlled pickup truck with huge wheels. "This what George ordered?" I asked, not able to keep the doubt from my voice...or my face.

"I got no idea what George is up to today, but this is what he asked for," the salesman said and rang up a significant bill.

I glanced at Jeremy. He shrugged as if to say, "Don't ask me, I'm just the poor bloody infantry."

I gave the clerk my credit card and tucked the receipt in my wallet. If George saved my wife, he was entitled to a few toys. More than a few.

But I might just strangle a man who'd used time and my search for Annie as an excuse to Christmas shop.

The drive back to George's was silent.

## 24

JEREMY OPENED THE DOOR FOR ME TO LUG MY LOAD OF TOYS into George's shop. Joy and Andy, screwdrivers in hand, were bent over the workbench with George, each taking something apart.

"Dad, this is just so spectacular, like so very spectacular," was the highest praise Andy gave anything. He used it now. He turned to me. "This guy is more cool than Mr. Hanson."

Mr. Hanson ran the electronics shop at school. It had taken all the pull that both Andy's school counselor and I had to keep him from taking that elective a third time.

"Well, here's what Mr. So Cool ordered," I said, trying to keep my voice even and my doubts out of it. After looking at what I'd purchased, I was beginning to believe I'd been sent on a fool's errand. I must admit, even Andy seemed a bit surprised at what I laid out on the floor beside them.

"Andy, you take the head off that robot," George said. "Ben, you and your girl open up that red pickup, and let's see what it has inside. I hope they haven't changed their design since last year."

Maybe he knew something I didn't. I looked for a screwdriver of my own and attacked the truck. And got into trouble. Me and screwdrivers just don't work all that well together. Do you turn the screw to the right or to the left? Or maybe it's just me and tiny screwdrivers. Or maybe it was the way they put these fancy new toys together.

For once, this wasn't just a laughing matter. Joy took over. "Dad, you should have taken an electronics lab," Andy said for nowhere near the first time in his young life.

"But a herd of dinosaurs stampeded through my high-school campus the summer before my sophomore year, and the cave men hadn't gotten the lab back up and running." If you're going to be accused of being as old as the dinosaurs, you might as well admit it.

"Dad, there weren't cave men when there were dinosaurs," my daughter corrected me.

So much for my attempt at humor. Not my best talent under stress, I supposed.

"What are they teaching children in school?" George sighed. "No respect for their decrepit elders. None at all. Somebody bring me that magnifying lamp."

Both my kids jumped to help him. What had he done while I was gone? Whatever it was, it had certainly gained him their respect. The lamp was a large magnifying glass surrounded by lights so that what he wanted to see was both easy to see and well lit. Still, reading glasses came out of his pocket as George went to work extracting something from the head of that robot.

And it struck me. "Eye of newt. Leg of toad," I said, turning to where Jeremy had settled into a chair and was reading a small book of Psalms that had come out of one pocket of his fatigue jacket. "This looks more like magic than science."

"Or close enough to it," Jeremy said without looking up.

"It's not magic, Dad," my son corrected. "If you'd just taken electronics lab, you'd know what he's doing."

"And you know?" I shot back.

"Well, not what he's doing, but how he is, and"—he wilted as George leaned back and stared at the boy over his glasses—"well, I know something like what he's doing."

"Took twenty years of my life to know how to do this. And twenty more to know when and why to do it. We'll save your mom, son, but make no mistake. If Jeremy hadn't brought you here, you'd still be praying for a miracle." George leaned back to look at his work, then added, "Rather than making a miracle happen."

"My stomach says it's lunchtime." George said, returning to his work. "Jeremy, you want to take these kids off and feed them? Bring me and Trudy back a hamburger and fries."

"That is something I can do," Jeremy said, putting away his book of Psalms. The kids trailed out after Jeremy with my car keys, a couple of twenties from my wallet, and our lunch orders. Then I went to sit beside George.

He kept on adding tiny pieces of electronics to a box that was taking shape under his skilled hands and a parabolic antenna that was growing an interesting horn. I watched until he grunted and said, without looking at me, "How's Jeremy taking this?"

"Fine," I said, frowning in puzzlement.

"He didn't take a drink while you were out?"

"No. Does he drink?" Had I just sent my children out with a potential drunk driver?

"Not recently. Never 'on duty,' even when he was drinkin'." George stopped to look my way. "Your kids are safe. I just worry about Jeremy. And us going gunning for the cruds that have your wife. He's gonna start doing flashbacks. He has some nasty memories to stoke 'em with. We gotta be quick about this. Before he remembers too much the hard way. Before your wife gets too many memories of her own. Between your God and my gear," he said, waving his screwdriver at his collection of gadgets, "with luck, we'll have her out before Jeremy can start flashing back."

I didn't want to think about what my wife was going through. I might break down myself. So I concentrated on Jeremy.

"He have it bad in Vietnam?"

"He was First Cav up country. Finest man you'd want to have beside you, or so I'm told. I met him in a VA group. We were both tryin' to figure out why we were drinking so hard. He wasn't too bad a man to have in the chair next to you there, either."

The aging airman fixed me with eyes that saw past me by decades. I'd led infantrymen; I tried not to squirm. "I'm glad my buddy is helping you find your wife. I think, with him—and me—

you got a chance to find your woman. I just want you to know it ain't gonna come cheap for him.

"Or for you, love," said his wife, suddenly standing in the doorway that led into the shop. Her hands twisted at the small towel she held. I don't think it was water she was trying to get out of it.

"Tru, this ain't nothing like what I did over the trail. Nothing. Don't you worry about me."

The wife blinked back the moisture in her eyes. She wasn't buying his protest.

"Maybe it's wrong of me to be asking this of you, of Jeremy, but I am so grateful. Forgive my asking, but I can't help but think that God has led me to Jeremy and now to you so that I can get my Annie home safe."

George snorted at that. "I keep telling your God that I've had enough of Him. I don't need or want Him in my life. You hear?" he said, eying the ceiling.

The rafters gave back no answer. Neither did his wife. But it was clear she didn't agree with him on that point, either.

The door opened and the commotion of my kids returning overflowed the quiet building between us. Trudy took her lunch, gave me a look that told me to watch out for her man, and headed back to the kitchen. Andy saw that the bags were emptied and everyone got what they ordered. As the chow vanished into mouths, Jeremy took me aside.

"What'd George tell you? I could tell we interrupted something when I walked in the door."

"He said that you were going to pay a price for going gunning for my wife's captors." I glanced at the now empty door into the shop. "And I suspect he'll be paying a debt for me and Annie, too."

"Not like it's something that can be avoided. But this time," Jeremy said, eyes taking that long focus I'd seen on some highly decorated sergeants in my time, "this time, God willing, everything goes in the win column."

"Amen."

An hour later I was back in the car, driving the rental at the speed limit on U.S. 101. Jeremy was seated beside me, the weapons still in the trunk, and now the ammo was too.

George sat in the center of the rear seat, Andy on his right, pointing that parabolic antenna out his window. Joy was behind me, the black box with gauges in her lap. As the person with the best eyesight in the car, she'd been elected to watch the gauges.

"We ought to get something soon," George said.

"At the Teddy Bear Factory," I said. It was ahead on my right.

"No," George said, his voice crinkling with a hint of laughter. "From the Arnolds' place two blocks behind it. Hold the antenna level, son."

"I got something," Joy half shouted.

"I thought you would. Kelly should be home from school by now and on that box. Your top readout, that shows you the frequency. That's about where the Barracuda game systems leak a bit. Vn's should be just a bit higher than Kelly's system. And a bit louder on your second gauge. Think you can tell the difference?"

"I don't know," Joy said. I could almost hear her gnawing at her lower lip.

"You can do it, Baby Ducks," I assured her.

"Dad!" came right back at me.

"Yes, Joy of my life."

"Ugh!" she said. But at least she smiled.

"See what you get in the next block," George said.

I switched to the right lane and slowed a bit. Only silence came from the backseat. "Nothing," Joy finally said, three blocks farther south.

"Phaedra must be staying late at school to work on some project."

"There's something," Joy said.

I took my foot off the gas.

"It's a Barracuda IV," George said. "Must be a rental kid. Don't know anyone on this block."

"Rentals?" I said.

"I know most of the game-addicted local kids. Sooner or later they come by the shop to get something fixed. Kids visiting the area for a weekend I don't often learn about, and I can't claim to know every rental house on the strip, either."

I didn't like the sound of that. Were we still looking for a needle in a sandy haystack? The sighs from the back said I wasn't the only one worried.

"But the Vn looks different from the IV, doesn't it?" Jeremy said.

"Should. According to the lab report, anyway. Slightly higher frequency. And much stronger squawk," George said. "You can keep driving the strip, but if I kidnapped someone, I wouldn't keep them in town where, if they could just get out to the neighbors, I'd be in all kinds of hot water. I'd want them a lot more isolated."

"Where would you hold someone?" I asked.

"There're a lot of places up and down the coast, off the road a bit, or a tad inland. I think this black box of mine is good for six, maybe eight hundred meters off the road. Why don't you find the hotel you stayed in back when, then you can drive us out to Thunder Ridge. Let's go hunting."

So we did. I found the hotel. It had a new name, but it was definitely the place.

I drove the route Annie and I had followed so long ago, back when we were young and so new to the world of married life. I ended up facing a big metal gate, a very solid thing that didn't look like anyone had messed with it in decades, or would want to. Andy had the antenna pointed out the window, both going and coming back, as we rode along the trail of my memories.

According to the backseat crowd, there was no noise at all from any of the houses along the way.

I pulled back into the old hotel parking lot, and we pored over the road maps. "Annie wouldn't have said Thunder Ridge and meant nothing by it," I muttered.

"But she didn't mean exactly the same thing." Jeremy said.

"If her kidnappers had her blindfolded or stuffed in a trunk, she might not be all that sure where she is," George said, rubbing his chin.

"But she had to mean something!" Joy said.

"So what could she mean?" I said and thought about it. "Head for the coast, not the desert," I started with.

"Maybe 'I can hear the waves,'" my son put in.

"Or it took about as long to drive here as it did back then," Jeremy said slowly. "That might not be a real good judgment. I doubt she was keeping a stopwatch on you for that drive. And I know she wasn't using a watch for this drive."

I slumped in my seat. Everything we had, and it was pitifully little, was based on a hunch, a bunch of my teenager's what-ifs, and a desperate belief that we could do something to find my wife.

"Let's take another tack," George said. "Let's think like the kidnappers. If I had a woman in my house that could get me a death penalty if she got loose, I sure would want her well away from anyone that might see her or help her if she escaped."

There was muttered agreement to that.

"Now then, the coast is pretty popular, but there's farming and other roads that drive back up in the mountains. They smell of trees, like that drive up to Thunder Ridge. And the houses along them don't have a lot of close neighbors." He pulled out a pen and circled the likely roads on the map. One led to Portland and Salem; we'd just driven it. The others, like the road to Thunder Ridge, went up into the hills to a dead end.

"Which one do we start with?" I asked.

"I'd save the road to Portland for last," George said. "The houses may be far apart, but the roads are hardly deserted. What with the Indian casinos, those roads get plenty of traffic. If she got loose, she could thumb a ride real quick."

That left two country roads farther south and one between the Thunder Ridge road and the main drag inland.

"The logical thing to do would be to take the southernmost one, drive it, then the next, then the next, and drive the Portland one last," I said. I glanced at the backseat. Joy's eyes were closed, her lips moving in prayer. Andy's fingers wiggled as if he wanted them to point the way, but dared not. Beside me, Jeremy prayed silently, his eyes also closed.

"When the rest of you finish praying and make a decision," George drawled, "I'll tell you what I think of the idea."

"There are times I wish God would whap someone I know good up beside the head," Jeremy muttered. "Your call, Ben."

I put the car in gear. "We go south, start at the bottom, and work our way up. Andy, keep the rig working while we drive. George, are we at risk of our batteries running out?"

"Nah. I brought plenty of spares. We'll change 'em out before we head up each road."

We drove to the beginning of the first road, checked it up and back. Like the last road we'd followed into the hills, it had one of those solid gates where it ended, so there was no question of going farther. The second road turned to gravel. I drove it for a mile. When it turned to dirt, and muddy dirt at that, I stopped.

I turned to the locals. "Well, guys, do we go on?"

Jeremy got out of the car to walk the muddy road. He wiped his feet off carefully before getting back into the car.

"I don't see any evidence that it's been driven on since the rain last night. Before that, I couldn't say."

"Mom could be up there already," Joy pointed out.

"I know. But I'm not sure the car can make it much farther. Let's try the third road," I said. "If we have to, we can come back and search on foot."

The drive through town to our new target gave us several noticeable reports, but George could attach a name to most of them, and they all fell into the range of the Barracuda IV, not the newer Vn model. I headed up the third road, fourth if you counted Thunder Ridge. The backseat was very quiet. I was starting to wonder if I shouldn't have driven farther down that second muddy road.

"Stop, I have something!" Joy shouted.

I didn't stop. That didn't sound like a good idea to me—I kept driving. I did slow down. "George, what's it look like to you?"

"Andy, did you see that house back there in the trees?" George said.

"No, but I saw the driveway going back up there."

"Keep the antenna pointed back there."

I kept my mouth shut when all I wanted to do was shout, "Is my wife in there?!"

"Is it? It is." Joy whispered.

"It is," George said. "Right where it should be on the gauges. There's a Vn system operating in that house."

"Let's not get all unwound," Jeremy said. "Could be someone local got his hands on one without doing anything wrong. Could be some nice Japanese teenager on a holiday, even."

"Could be," I agreed as I drove about a mile farther up the road before I found a place to turn around. I pulled over, weighing my options. I didn't really want to drive by that house a second time. Someone might get suspicious. I set the parking break and turned to the backseat.

"Could be a good reason they have a Barracuda Vn, but I for one would sure like to know what that reason is. I think it's time for a little reconnoiter."

We got out. I popped the trunk open. We stood around like hunters did regularly, I imagine, checking our guns, loading our magazines, and then loading the guns. Jeremy and I checked each other's weapons. "Locked and loaded," he said. As expected, George slipped on the .45's shoulder holster. "Just like old times," he said, settling the weapon in place.

"You aren't going to, you know, knock on their front door and ask if they have Mom, are you," Andy asked. At his elbow, it looked like Joy was worried about us, too.

"Nope," Jeremy said. "We're going to settle up in the trees and do some looking around. That's all. They'll never know we were there unless they look to be up to no good." He glanced my way. The kids were mine to dispose of.

What I wanted to do was give Andy the keys and tell him to drive back to George's place. Get them someplace safe.

But if my son's hunch played out, if my wife was in that house, I might need that car in a hurry. The car had to stay here, so that meant the kids had to stay here as well. *God, that's not the choice I want to make. But I could at least give the kids the chance to be mobile if they needed to move in a hurry.* I handed my son the car keys. He took them with a serious look in his eyes.

"Dad, we'll stay with the car. I'll keep my cell phone on. If you need us, you can call. Turn off your cell, though. Don't want it ringing at a bad time." Andy was being logical and also checking his phone as he spoke. His precautions turned out to be of little use. "Oh," he said. "No signal. I guess we just wait for you to, uh, come back." He'd almost said, "bring Mom back," before he swallowed.

Since Andy had voiced what I was just about to ask of him, I simply nodded. "You will stay in the car," I said. "You will be careful."

"We'll stay in the car," both kids said dutifully. But Joy was worrying her lower lip. "You be careful too. We can't afford to lose another parent," she said tearfully.

Andy cleared his throat, then jumped, like an idea had just bit him. "Dad, if they don't have cell phone coverage here, how did Mom get her e-mail out?"

That wasn't something I wanted to think about. "In the mountains, wireless stuff is unpredictable," Jeremy said. "Who knows what kind of reception we'll get closer to the house? Up here, you can have clear coverage one place and be in a dead spot five feet away. We won't know what gives until we're inside that house. Which we don't plan to have happen for a long while yet. We'll cross that one when it's close enough to fall over. Meantime, look at it this way. Is your cell phone coverage all that regular?" he asked. We shook our heads. "Well, it's even trickier up here. Don't think about it."

"So let's walk in from here," George said. "It will give us more of a chance to look the area over and check the phone coverage closer to the house," the old air force fellow continued, then frowned. "Even if it will be a bit of a walk back with your wife," George said.

I liked his optimism. So did the kids. *With my wife,* he said. Not, *If we find your wife.* I prayed with my whole heart that he was right, and we weren't just spinning our wheels out here.

"If we think we've found the right hooch, we can send Ben back to move the car up closer," Jeremy said.

George nodded at that and pulled a sack from the trunk, a sack that his wife had handed him at the last moment before we left. With it slung over his shoulder, he looked ready to start walking.

I gave the car keys in my son's hand a glance. He looked at them too for a moment, then passed them along to Joy. "We won't do anything without the both of us agreeing, Dad. And you know what a scaredy cat Baby Ducks is.

"We'll be very, very careful," Joy said, pocketing the keys.

"Stay here," I said. "Stay down. Don't do anything risky. It's bad enough what I'm doing," I said, half to myself, as I picked up my rifle. What did I think I was doing, a middle-aged man, running around through the woods with a loaded rifle and a couple of ancient vets? Did I really think I had a chance to save my wife?

At that instant I knew I should have gone by the FBI's office this morning and sat in a corner while they hunted for Annie. Only they wouldn't be standing out here, getting ready to go into this place. They'd be off in the eastern desert, stirring up dust as they looked for drugs. And Annie, if she happened to be handy. *Lord, if You did lead me to just the right men to put this all together, to have us here, where we could move in and save Annie, thank You! Please, God, keep us all in the palm of Your hands.*

I let out a deep sigh, hugged my kids, said good-bye as though I did this every day, and joined Jeremy and George. The old soldiers waited while I watched the kids lock themselves in the car, then we started walking on the shoulder back toward the house. The house that a box cobbled together out of fragments of electronic toys said was emitting noises it had no right to be making.

I had to believe that a gracious God was looking after us and had led us there to find my wife safe and alive.

*Dear God, please give me the grace to believe that.*

# 25

WE HADN'T WALKED FAR DOWN THE ROAD BEFORE JEREMY handed me George's electronic marvel and relieved his old friend of the sack from the trunk. "Doubt if a wing wiper like you has the gear a boonie rat needs."

"How much you gonna bet me?"

We kept walking while Jeremy took a look in the sack. "Hmm, not bad for a fly-fly guy."

"Who's done a bit of hunting in these hills over the last couple of years. Course, the stuff I been hunting lately don't shoot back. You know, I kind of like it that way."

"God's been gracious to both of us old coots."

"And kind enough to stay out of my way," George added.

"Now don't tell me you honestly think you've stayed alive this far on your own tab. Neither one of us had the sense to come in out of the rain when we were kids."

George didn't answer that.

After that, we walked along in the silence, listening to the sounds of the wind in the trees, the insects, and the occasional animal. Not a lot today. I picked up a hint of wood smoke. It might be from the house we were headed for or from any of the several other homes I'd spotted on the other side of the road well back in the woods. Hard to tell. You could see pretty far back into the trees. The woods were a mix of evergreen and hard woods that were just starting to bud in the chilled air of early spring in the mountains, their bare black branches in stark contrast to the green of the firs and spruces. How easy would it be to spot someone in the thin cover provided by this landscape? How much of my field craft did I remember from my army days? Did I want to crawl on my belly through half a mile of this stuff?

Could I still do it?

"You gonna ask him?" George said finally. "Or you want me to?"

Jeremy frowned. "I think it best if I do the askin'."

"Ask me what?" I said.

"Ask you if you're going to kill these people. Assuming they have your wife."

"Kill them?" I said. I mouthed the words and was surprised at how good they tasted.

"Yeah," George went on. "Do we kill them and set your wife free, or do we try to set your wife free and leave these cruds for the cops and the courts?"

"Do we have a choice?" I asked.

"We always have choices," Jeremy said.

George nodded.

"I want to save my wife," I said.

"So do we. That's what we're here for," George agreed. "But, if we get lucky, and we find her, we can go at this one of several different ways. If we play our cards right, we can fix it so we just *have* to kill those guys, self-defense and all that. Even Jeremy here could swear it was self-defense in a court of law."

"Yeah. That can be arranged," Jeremy said, a small frown on his face, as if he was remembering something uncomfortable from his past.

"Or we can see if there's any way to do what we need to do without killing them. But still get your wife out safe."

"We can do that?" I said.

"Don't rightly know," Jeremy sighed. "Don't know if it's possible, but the type of fools that will let your wife e-mail out not once but twice don't exactly strike me as the do-or-die squad. 'Vengeance is mine, says the Lord,' son, but today you get to decide that for yourself."

I fingered the rifle slung down the front of me. The urge to blow away the men who had caused me and my kids all this pain was palpable. The need to kill the men who had put my wife through God only knew what kind of hurt was overwhelming. Killing them was something I would deeply enjoy doing.

"Thinking about it feels good, don't it?" Jeremy said. "But think some more about living with it. I got faces I see every night. Some are my buddies that never made it home. Some are strangers I only met long enough to kill. What do you see at night?"

I swallowed on that thought. "I see my wife's face before I turn out the lights," I said.

"Nice way to go to sleep," George agreed. "Be nice to keep your memories like that."

"But I want her home safe. Are you asking me to dull our knives as we're going into—"

"A fight," George finished for me.

"Don't intend to do nothing of the kind," Jeremy said. "But I need to know. Have you hardened your heart to be a killer today, or are we keeping an open mind about who lives, who dies?"

Hardened my heart. Even the words were painful to my ears. It was so easy to think of these men dead for what they'd done to me, to Annie, to the kids. But to think of me as their killer—did I want that?

I took a deep breath. "We don't know that the men we want are in this house. We sure don't want to hurt the wrong people."

That got a nod from the two old vets.

I took a deep breath, then said, "Let's take things one step at a time as we look for Annie. Not burn any bridges before we cross them."

"Pretty good advice from someone who hasn't been in a fight, I'd say," Jeremy said.

"Good advice all around," George agreed.

The smoke smell was getting stronger. "What say we get off this road and duck into the woods?" Jeremy said. We nodded. "I'll take point. You two bring your clumsy feet along twenty, fifty yards behind me."

And with that he turned off the road. I can't say he disappeared. There wasn't enough foliage for that. But he did hunker down a bit, and I noticed that he moved from small evergreen to small evergreen smoothly and paused behind each tree to observe. When George offered me the next move, I followed Jeremy, moving from cover to cover, following in his footsteps. A moment later George was doing the same behind me.

It seemed like it took forever as I moved from tree to tree to tree as we approached the house, but when I glanced at my wristwatch, only ten minutes had passed before Jeremy made a curt wave toward a tree fall.

Two of the larger trees in this second-growth tree lot had been blown down, forming something of a deadfall with leaves and other debris collected behind them. The house was some one or two hundred yards beyond our vantage point as I collapsed beside Jeremy. George was only a moment behind me.

"Nice place you got here," the flier said to Jeremy.

"Needs a bit of cleaning up, but I do like the lived-in feel." Jeremy wasn't looking at us, though. A raccoon was waddling away from us as he spoke. It climbed a bare tree and proceeded to read us the riot act from a low limb. Jeremy frowned.

"I hope the folks in the house are city folks," he said. "Me, if I heard that, I'd wonder what kind of beast was in my yard."

It was too late to do much about it. I ignored the raccoon's chatter and studied the house. There was a detached barn or work-shop or garage closer to us on my left in the clearing that held the house. From the lessons I'd learned in my long-ago battle training, I expected those structures would draw the eye of anyone in the house, making it harder for them to look deeper into the woods. I hoped Jeremy hadn't forgotten any of his training. It didn't look like he had. He seemed to be right at home in our pile of logs and leaves. From the sack, he'd drawn out a pair of binoculars and now he used them to study the house.

At this distance, all I could see was a wooden two-story struc-ture in desperate need of paint. There was a low porch along the front. The wooden cover looked long past keeping the rain off of it. The chimney belched a big glob of smoke; someone must have just refilled the wood stove. Someone was definitely in there. I hoped that it was the right someone. From our hiding place, we had a good view of the front and left side of the place. There were several windows I would've loved to peek in.

"That's interesting," Jeremy said and handed me the binocu-lars. I focused them quickly, studying the windows.

"Very interesting," I agreed. All the downstairs windows were closed and the blinds pulled. I checked the upstairs windows. The ones along the front had flowered sheets over the windows. "For a house with a great view of the woods, they don't seem to be much interested in looking at it," I said, handing the glasses to George.

"Yeah. Strange. Most folks come to the coast to see that view.

Even if they can't see all the way to the ocean, it's nice to see Momma Nature up close."

"But not these folks," Jeremy said.

I pulled out my cell phone. Again, no signal. I showed it to the two friends. If my wife was using some kind of wireless platform to send her messages, we could be at the wrong house.

"Could mean something," Jeremy said.

"Or nothing," George said. "No guarantees the dead spot is the same between here and there. Could be a lucky signal that's reaching only the upstairs."

"Or God's providence," Jeremy added.

George looked at him, seemed to have a comeback on the tip of his tongue, then swallowed it. "Let me have my gear," he finally said.

I handed him his antenna and black box. He took them, held his hand steady on the log, and ran a scan on the house.

"Big honking TV is playing in the living room," he said half to himself. "I make it one of those plasma screens. Easy to carry in. Strange for a place this broken down. But I'm not pickin' up a cable or satellite box. Yep, there's the DVD player. Microwave in the kitchen. New one, I'd say. Not a very big one. I don't think any of these folks is much of a cook," he told Jeremy.

"A Barracuda Vn?" I asked.

"Coming to that. It's upstairs, behind one of those two central windows. Can't tell which window for sure. I'd tend to bet on the one to my left, if I had to bet."

"Anything else upstairs?"

291

"Hold your horses, Ben. I know it's tough," he whispered. "I'm not getting anything where batteries should be. Let me check. Yep, there's a power supply that's hotter than, well, you know what, Jeremy."

"Plenty hot, huh."

"Yep, ain't been turned off for a while. If he wants it to last, he really should give it a rest."

"How long?" I snapped. I was out of horses to hold.

George looked at me and shook his head. "It might not last through the night."

How would the guy upstairs behave if his pacifier went pop? I didn't want to think about that.

"Can that box of yours pick up wristwatches, pacemakers, PDAs, anything to tell us how many people are in there?"

"Nope." George shook his head. "We're on our own there. I hear tell they got stuff so sensitive that it can pick up the electrical pulses between your brain and your heart. But I'm not budgeted for that kind of stuff."

Would the FBI have brought that kind of stuff? Should I be doing this at all? *Lord, any advice?*

"Mind loaning me your phone?" George asked.

"You need to make a call? No signal, remember?"

"I feel a need to wander around to the other side of this place. See what kind of signals I get from there."

"Do you think it's safe?" I asked Jeremy.

"People who close up their windows like that don't usually spend a lot of time looking out them. You be careful, George."

George pocketed my phone. Hefted his antenna. "Hey, anybody asks, I'm out looking for Big Foot."

"And we hear your .45, we're going to come running...and shooting," Jeremy said. No question then about killing anyone.

"Just be careful you don't go shooting me. Your eyes aren't what they were back in your Nam days."

"None of us are what we were."

But Jeremy was talking to George's backside as the ex-flier took off, moving slow and low.

"Well, let's see what Trudy sent along for us," Jeremy said, not taking his eyes from George, but opening the sack. A quick glance inside brought a small smile to his face. "God's just way too nice to that man, giving him a woman like her," he said.

I took over watching George and the house while Jeremy pulled plastic ground cloth out of the sack, just the thing to have between you and the damp ground. He spread it, before producing three sleeping bags, the new kind with that wonderful insulation.

"I guess he's gone hunting a few times," I said.

There was also a thermos bottle. "We'll save that for later. We also don't need to be making the woods smell all full of coffee until we know a bit more about who's in that house. You see that little house out there? Think they got to come out here to do their business?"

"I don't know," was the best I could manage.

"Well, let's settle in, do some watching, see if we can remove a few of those 'I don't knows' from our conversation."

So we sat and watched as nothing happened. For about an hour.

Then I spotted George working his way back. I nudged Jeremy, who might have been asleep for all the action I'd seen from him of late. "Yep, I noticed him about five minutes ago. He's getting pretty good."

And I couldn't even tell when a man was asleep and when he was keeping watch anymore. It had been a long time since I'd been in this mind-set.

George was very careful coming back. Too careful, it seemed to me. Had he seen something? I waited, gnawing my lower lip.

Finally, he slid into our deadfall, his teeth chattering. Jeremy slapped a sleeping bag around him.

"Give me some of that hot tea," George said.

"Tea?"

"Yeah. You think Tru would want us smelling the woods up like coffee when we're going hunting for bear? And bear with guns to shoot back at the man she loves for some reason that defies me?"

"Very smart woman," Jeremy said as I cracked the thermos and poured some of the contents into the cap and handed it off to George. He wrapped his hands around it and slowly warmed up.

"I got a signal on your phone," he finally said. "Had to hold it up on a stick, but I'd say that the upstairs of this dump has a signal. Weak, but a signal."

"So Annie could have sent something out," I said.

"She could have."

"See anything else?" Jeremy asked.

"Not a thing. Windows covered all the way around. Garage was all closed up, so I don't know what's in there. Didn't see that many footprints in the field, except those from the garage to the house. You see anything while I was gone?"

Jeremy shook his head.

George took in a deep breath off the steaming cup, risked a sip, smiled happily as it went down and shook his head. "This could be the place. Then again, it might not be the place. Opinions?"

"You say there's a Barracuda Vn in there," I said.

"More likely than not," the electronic wizard said. "Looks like it to me."

"But no guarantees," I said.

"Life don't come with them, son."

I glanced at Jeremy; he just shook his head softly. Life must be tough without the love of God around you. Then again, God wasn't promising me that I was going to get Annie back safely, only that He loved me. *Dear God, please take care of my Annie,* I prayed.

I took a deep breath and wished fervently for a direct message from God. As usual, the heavens neither opened nor did I hear any voice. But I felt a small bloom of peace in my heart. *Into Your hands I commit myself, oh Lord.*

"I vote we stay here, keep watch for a while," I said. "See if anything develops." There, I'd committed myself. And Annie, wherever she was. I hoped and prayed she was in that house.

"I agree," Jeremy said.

"Me too." George pursed his lips. "You know, I've been thinkin' about today. I think it's a safe bet your God wants us here. If not, He's sure done a good job of leading us wrong."

That was not something I wanted to believe.

We settled in, watching the house. Watching nothing happen. A whole lot of nothing. About an hour before dark, I asked for my cell phone back and glanced at its screen. If I was figuring on calling the kids, it wasn't going to be on that phone. No signal.

"I think I better walk back to the car and see how the kids are doing, reassure them that we've found the house and that there is a Barracuda Vn system inside. A teenager's promise is, well, about as good as a teenager can make it."

They agreed. Hunkered down, I started the long way back.

The walk back wasn't a problem. I found the road and followed it to the car with no trouble. Both kids were huddled up in their blankets, fast asleep. I found that hard to believe, but sleep was one way for teenagers to handle both terror and boredom. During finals week at school, it was almost impossible to get them out of bed. They came awake quickly when I rapped on the car door.

They came awake quickly and scared.

"Oh, it's just you, Dad," Andy said unlocking the doors.

"Just me. You have any problems?" I said, slipping into the car, filching the keys from Joy and turning the car and its heater on.

"Not much traffic. We stayed down, and no one stopped."

"A lot of folks must park here and go hunting and fishing," I said, wondering how often that happened in the spring. Wasn't hunting and fishing season in the fall? Shows you what I know. "You two okay?"

"No problem, Dad." Joy said, and there was nothing hidden in the face she turned to me. "Have you found Mom?"

I sighed. "I don't know, kitten. I think maybe." I filled them in on the house we had under watch.

"They've got that game. And you got a signal," Andy said, hopping on the response George got when he lifted the phone up to the second-story height.

"George got a signal," I repeated.

"It could be her," Joy said.

"Could be, but nothing definite."

"Dear God, please don't let Dad shoot up the wrong house," Joy said, and she clearly meant it.

"I'm not going in shooting," I said, only deciding that as I said it.

"What are you going to do?" Andy asked.

I thought for a moment. "Looks to me like we keep watch on the place until the time is right, then we try a little housebreaking. See what's inside, hopefully while everybody in there is fast asleep. But not for a long time yet. I think it's going to be a long night."

"You're going in for Mom," Joy said.

"Early tomorrow morning, if nothing changes our mind about the place."

"So we just sit here and wait," Andy said, pulling his blanket close around him.

"Afraid so, kids."

"Better to wait than, you know," Joy said, not able to work her young mind around all the things that could go wrong.

"Better to wait," I said. "You kids have any problem with waiting here?"

"It's been a while since lunch," Andy said. Teenager, thy king is thy belly.

"But we aren't going to leave here," Joy put in real fast. Then she frowned. "But I do need to go potty."

"I told you, that's what trees were made for," Andy said.

Joy growled at her big brother, then looked expectantly at me. "Sorry, kitten, that's what folks did before they invented bathrooms." I spotted a couple of evergreens that made for a decent screen and nodded toward them.

"You won't look," she said to her brother. "Dad, you make sure Andy doesn't look."

"I will, kitten."

Five minutes later Joy was back in the car. Andy had spent the time studying the other side of the road. And I'd kept enough of an eye on my daughter to know she was safe. I was warm for the first time that afternoon. It was spring in these woods, but spring along the Oregon coast was a chilly, wet affair, not at all like my Maryland. At least it hadn't rained.

Satisfied that my kids were safe and were likely to stay safe, I kissed them good-bye, left the warm car, and headed back to our observation post. Andy immediately turned the car off and handed the keys to Joy even before I turned away.

*They are such good kids.*

The trek back to our hidey-hole was into a setting sun. A cloud-bank off the coast is usually what the sun sets into in Oregon, and today was no exception. It was going to get dark sooner than I'd expected. I turned into the woods about where I figured I should and tried to stay low.

In about five minutes I had no idea where I was.

I could smell the smoke from the house, so I knew I wasn't going the wrong way, but I was very lost. I turned to my right and found the road just about the time I was starting to panic.

In the dim light I could still make out the car. Afraid of stumbling into the field around the house, I'd never gotten anywhere close to it.

Getting a bit mad at myself, I stalked down the road until I could make out the turn off onto the dirt road that led to the house. Then I backtracked and headed back in.

*Mighty hunter, ex-lieutenant of infantry, rescuer of a fair damsel in distress,* I ranted to myself...and got lost again.

Now it really was getting dark in those woods. Dark and cold. I could see my breath in front of me. "Where are you guys?" I muttered to myself as I considered going back to the road and trying again.

"Right behind you," Jeremy whispered.

I jumped near out of my skin.

"You don't do much hunting, do you?"

"Never been hunting," I admitted.

"And you don't have any of those fancy doodads I bet the army issued you back when."

"They weren't nearly as fancy then as they are now," I pointed out. "But, yeah, I sure could have used something to set my trail. Even some white paint or cloth."

"Sorry we didn't think of that," Jeremy said, turning around. I followed him back to the deadfall.

He said nothing to George, and George said nothing to me, except, "I think it's my turn to go pay dog's honor to a tree," and he slipped out of his sleeping bag and disappeared into the gloom. A moment later Jeremy broke one of those chem light sticks that glow in the dark and put it behind us, easy to see from the direction George had headed off to but invisible to the house.

"Save me from having to go chase after him," Jeremy said.

I got into my sleeping bag, pulled it up to my chin for warmth, and sat, facing the house. The lights were on, showing through the drawn blinds. "Anything change?"

"Nope. Those guys got no idea of security. Unless they think just burying their heads in the sand is gonna keep them from being noticed."

"Looks like an okay plan to me. If we hadn't had George's gizmo to point us at them, they'd pretty well be out of sight and out of mind."

"Glad to see you appreciate my handiwork," George said, re-joining us.

"Just wish you could have slapped together a gizmo that said 'Kidnappers, this many of them, right here,'" Jeremy said.

"That's just like the fighter jocks," George said. "You'd complain even if you were being hung with a new rope."

"Certainly," Jeremy agreed, smiling in the pale green light of our chem stick.

The hours went by. The house lights never dimmed. Once or twice I thought I smelled popcorn. The second time, George turned his gizmo on the house. "Yep, microwave is on. Nice to know what they're eating. Wish I had some."

Midnight came and the house stayed the same. I found myself wondering if these guys ever slept. It was cold out here. How long were we going to wait? Still, Jeremy and George seemed prepared to wait forever. So we waited.

And I prayed.

## 26

GEORGE MUST FINALLY HAVE BEEN GETTING TIRED OF WAITing. At 12:30 he checked the house again. Nothing had changed.

But come 1:00 a.m., George frowned into the still-glowing green light. "That DVD player ain't on full power. I think it ran to the end of the movie and no one's turned it off. Plasma screen has kind of powered down, too."

"Like they'd fallen asleep in front of the TV?" I asked.

"Kind of like that. No real way to tell."

"What about the Barracuda?"

"It's still going strong."

So we settled in for another half hour. "Still there. Boy, is that power supply hot."

At two o'clock that had changed. "The game ain't on. Its power supply is cooling down," George said.

I eyed the house. Every window still showed a light. "You've been awfully quiet, Jeremy. You got an opinion?"

"Weren't quiet. Was catching my beauty rest," the old boonie rat said with a yawn.

"Who's that saint of hopeless cases?" George asked.

"Don't know," Jeremy said, "but I pray he or she is down here with a whole posse of angels tonight."

"Saint Jude," I said. "I'm praying as hard as I can. I hope the Lord and all His angels hear me."

"Wouldn't mind the company," George muttered. "Especially if they brought some heat with them."

"How long should we wait?" I said, eager to go.

"Give them thirty minutes to get sound asleep," Jeremy said.

"We go in the front or the back?" I asked.

So for the next thirty minutes we talked quietly, drawing up a plan of attack that I, for one, had been thinking about since we found the place this afternoon.

A half hour later, in the dying glow of the chem light, we did a weapons check, then moved out. We approached the house, using the cover of the garage. While Jeremy and I headed for the back door, George broke off to check out the garage and its contents.

The back door had just a small stoop. Jeremy went to work picking the lock, a skill he'd mentioned he learned during his misspent youth, while I provided cover.

The door slid open just as George rejoined us. We looked at the half-open door for a moment, then I slid the safety off my rifle with an audible click. Jeremy brought his rifle up to the ready, a click telling me he, too, was loaded for bear. George pulled his .45 from his shoulder holster and, holding it at high port, clicked off the last civilized checkpoint between us and possible murder.

"I'll take point," Jeremy whispered, reaffirming what we'd agreed upon. In one big step, he went from the mud beside the stoop to inside the back door. The floor creaked under his weight.

We paused to listen for a reaction.

Nothing.

Just silence and the sound of our breathing.

Jeremy moved inside and I followed, cringing at every creak that our footsteps made on the wood floor. An old house is not a silent place to move through. There was a reason why I trained my infantrymen to toss a hand grenade in first as their calling card when entering. Like I told them back then, if there was anyone left who wished you ill after one of *those* went off, well, their ears were in no shape to listen for you by the time you arrived.

But we weren't troops in a combat zone. No, tonight, whether we liked it or not, we were doing the job of cops, and cops have a whole lot harder life than soldiers.

The kitchen opened off to the right of the passage, a bedroom to the left. The kitchen was a mess, and the bedroom looked no better. The bed was strewn with open luggage, dirty clothes tossed about, frozen pizza boxes and Ramen noodle packages mixed in with the wreckage on the floor.

Pigs lived here. But pigs weren't necessarily kidnappers, I reminded myself.

Jeremy was at the end of the hall. I followed him. He'd stopped where the living room began. The room filled the front of the house. Yep, George had it right. There was a large plasma screen television. Across from it, crashed out on a beaten-up couch, snored two men, one tall, one short, both in need of shaves, baths, and self-respect.

No Annie.

I motioned up. Jeremy nodded in agreement. As we backed out of the living room, George stepped forward, his automatic at the ready. Jeremy gave a silent hand signal for him to watch those two. George nodded.

Back at the stairs, I cringed. If the floor downstairs creaked with each step we took, the stairs were likely to shriek. If there was a book answer to this one, I'd forgotten it long ago. I took the stairs two at a time. Slowly at first, then biting my lip at the groaning steps, faster. Jeremy kept right behind me.

At the top of the stairs, a hallway led to four doors. Three were closed. The fourth was open. It was the door to the room George thought might hold the Barracuda Vn.

There was a human-sized lump in the hallway between me and the open door.

As silently as the house would let me, I edged down the hall, looking over the sights of my rifle at the lump. It took my brain a moment to separate all the parts before me, then it snapped into focus.

A man slept on the floor near the open doorway, curled up in a sleeping bag. The empty junk-food wrappers surrounding him formed a collage of crackly filth. I made a mental note not to step on any of it. I stood still as a statue, my hand raised to halt Jeremy.

In the silence around us, I could make out the breathing coming from the sleeping bag.

It sounded like this one was a light sleeper or had just fallen asleep or…could he still be awake?

I waited.

He rolled over, and a small snore issued from him.

I sighed with relief, slipping closer to him until I could see into the open doorway. With the agony of a tooth being slowly pulled, part of the room came into view.

I saw nothing at first.

A linoleum floor, a dresser against one wall. Then another wall with the window I'd stared at for the last forever hours. I could see the flowers on the bed sheet pinned over that window.

Now I had reached the sleeping man and a mess of garbage on the floor around him. I prayed like I had never prayed before and gingerly stepped into the space in the hallway beside him.

He didn't even slow his snoring.

I took another step down the hall. Behind me was a smelly bathroom. My eyes jumped between the man sleeping at my feet and the room with the open door. Nothing, nothing.

An inch farther.

A bed came into view. Hands were tied to the metal bed frame.

Those were the hands I knew so well.

My wife.

We'd found her.

Thank God.

I almost keeled over from the sheer relief of it. Our long shot had paid off. As relief flooded me, a second thought slammed me. Was my Annie okay?

I fought the urge to rush into the room, to pound my foot into the sleeping man's skull. I wanted to act…act…act. I willed my feet to stay in place. I forced my breath to come slowly. Steadily.

Out of the corner of my eye I could see Jeremy. His mouth formed a wordless "What?"

I signaled him that we'd found her. Even in the dark I could see the glow of his teeth as he smiled at me. I lowered my rifle and gently clicked the safety back on. With my free right hand, I signaled Jeremy to keep his rifle on the sleeper. He nodded. Then I motioned that I was going into the room. Again he nodded.

I took a deep breath, tensed every muscle in my body, and edged forward, still careful of the junk-food wrappers in my way. I braced my hands, one on each side of the doorjamb, and took a big step over the man's mess.

It was agony to keep my eyes from looking back at the sleeping man. But I knew I had to stay focused just for a moment more. It would be so easy to make a misstep, to start a slaughter. Was that what I wanted? Not now.

I had to see Annie.

I brought my foot down inside the room and turned to face the dearest desire of my heart. Annie lay stretched out on the bed, her ankles and wrists tied to the frame. Her hair was a rat's nest.

Her blouse and slacks were filthy. My Annie was lovely to look upon. No bride, be she Solomon's or any other man's, ever looked so beautiful to her husband.

Leaving the sleeping man to Jeremy, I crossed the room to the bed. Kneeling beside it, I put one hand gently over my wife's mouth, then softly kissed her forehead.

Her eyes came open in terror, then widened in shock, then softened as she took me in. She opened her mouth to say something. I clamped my hand down a bit more firmly to remind her that we had to keep silent.

She nodded.

I fished in my pocket for my knife from the plant, then I opened it and sawed through the ties at her wrists. She surrounded me in a hug. I could feel her tears on my neck.

I let myself sink into her arms for a second. Then the creaking of the bedsprings reminded both of us that now was not the time for this. She released me so I could cut her feet free.

"Can you walk?" I barely whispered.

Annie shook her head.

I picked her up. She was light as a feather. I turned to the door.

As I stepped off the distance, Jeremy lowered his rifle barrel to point-blank range. If the sleeper so much as twitched, there'd be a burning hole in the back of his skull.

"Don't shoot him," my wife whispered softly. "He was nice to me. I think I owe him my life."

Once more I prepared to step carefully through the strewn wrappers. If I could make it out with none of the sleepers any the wiser, I would for my Annie.

But we weren't out yet. This time, I had no hands on the doorway to steady me as I stepped over the sleeper. This time, I stepped on a wrapper. I paused, one foot in the room, one foot on a crinkling bag, and waited to see what my Father intended to be the ending of this day.

The sleeper snorted, rolled a bit, but kept on snoring.

Thank God.

After a pause that seemed to last forever, Jeremy raised his rifle and offered me a hand to pull myself over. We cleared the sleeping kidnapper and headed straight for the stairs. They creaked and groaned as I went down them, holding Annie close to my heart. My rifle was caught between us. It pressed against her, against me.

At the bottom of the stairs, I went straight out the door. Once outside, I turned left and headed around the house. Jeremy was right behind me. George was last; he closed the door behind himself, let it click shut, then hurried to catch up with us.

"Let me try and walk," Annie whispered.

"Okay," I said, letting her slide to the ground. I kept one arm around her. Her legs buckled under her, but she managed half a step. George came up, slipped one arm around her, and pulled one of her arms over his shoulder.

Between the two of us, we half carried, half ran with my wife. "Not the forest," I said. "Too slow, too dark."

George nodded and we made for the muddy dirt track that led back to the main road.

I glanced over my shoulder as we reached the dirt road. Way behind us, Jeremy was walking slowly backward, his eyes on the house, his rifle at the ready. *A good man to cover your back,* I thought. *One in a thousand.*

We hurried down the muddy path. Soon the trees hid us from their view. Only then did Jeremy turn and sprint to catch up.

"Where are we going?" Annie said, breathless, but running as best she could, making maybe one step for every three George and I took.

"To the car. To the kids. They will be so glad to see you."

"God, I want to see my children again," my wife breathed. She put an effort into her running, maybe making half the steps we did.

Then I could feel her stiffen beside me. "What are Andy and Joy doing here?"

"If *I'm* ever kidnapped, *you* try and leave those kids back at the house," I said, overwhelmed by love for her.

"Oh, Benjamin. My Benjamin," she cried and laughed for joy. "You run that plant of yours, you could command an army, but you never could make me or the kids do what we don't want to do."

"Sounds like a normal husband to me," George said beside us.

Annie was recovering her composure as we jogged. She turned to George, "I don't know who you are. But thank you. Dear God, thank you."

"I suspect He will," George agreed.

At the road, we paused for breath. "Will they be coming after us?" I asked Jeremy.

"Didn't see no pursuit."

"And they'll never catch us now," George added, pulling four valve stems from his pocket. "I let the air out of their rig. They ain't going nowhere except on foot, and they don't look like the hiking kind of folk to me."

"They aren't," Annie agreed. "Where are my babies?"

I couldn't remember the last time she'd referred to those over-tall offspring of ours as babies. "The car's this way."

She took off in that direction but stumbled on her second step. George and I got her between us again and hurried down the road in our four-, five-, now six-legged race. I don't know how we did it, but we covered the distance in record time.

Before I knew it, we were at the car. Annie was crying happy tears, and I was pounding on the window to wake the kids inside. Andy came awake and was trying to open the door while I was still pounding on it from the outside. Andy and I got our act together just in time for Annie to fall into the backseat while Joy was climbing over the front seat to fall on both of them. In only a moment, the backseat was full of happy, dirty people trying to hug and kiss each other. There wasn't a dry eye in the place.

"Anybody got some car keys?" Jeremy asked. "I think we need to be someplace else."

"Andy?" I asked.

"Joy?" he asked.

Somehow my daughter managed to produce keys from her pocket without taking her arms from around her mother. I passed them to Jeremy who passed them to George. "You know where the police station is in this one-horse town?"

"Yep. Go there every year to donate toys," he said.

"Folks, I don't mean to interrupt the love fest," Jeremy went on as George got the motor started, "but we got loaded weapons here, and I'd sure hate to have something go wrong this late in the proceedings."

The man had a point.

I slid my rifle off my shoulder, pulled out the magazine and opened the chamber with the same ease I had years ago in the army. *How fast it comes back,* I thought.

Jeremy took my weapon, satisfied himself it was safe, and laid it in the trunk. I noticed that George kept his automatic, and Jeremy still had his rifle when he settled into the passenger seat, ready to ride shotgun for his friend. Both men had their weapons on safety, though.

"Doors closed and locked," George called. We verified everybody was in the car, then tried to belt four people into a backseat with only three seat belts. Andy and Joy obeyed when ordered to belt up, then demanded that Mom and me do the same. I ended up with one around me, and me holding on to Annie like my life depended upon it.

If I'd ever had doubts about that, I didn't now.

Amazingly soon we pulled into the municipal center lot and George parked us in the sheriff's own parking spot. "Let Grant ticket me over this. I dare him."

Jeremy and George were out and doing a weapons check at the trunk while the four of us were still struggling to untangle ourselves from the backseat. Then we were finally all together in the light.

It was a great moment when we strode into the nearly empty sheriff's office.

"George what kind of trouble are you in, bringing a mob in here at this hour of the morning?" a round woman half shouted from her place behind a desk full of radios and communication gear.

"Betty, I got a woman I want you to meet. Betty, this young lady, looking a might bit the worse for wear right now, is Annie Taylor."

"Annie Taylor," the woman said, puzzlement on her face. Then her eyes got wide. "The kidnap victim. That Annie Taylor?"

"Yes." She looked at me with love in her eyes. "I hope you didn't pay the ransom," Annie said, deadpanning the line we used so often when we were overlong at the office. Then she turned her attention back to the dispatcher. "I seem to have escaped with a little help from my friends…and my very wonderful husband here," she said, giving me another hug and kiss.

"I knew he didn't do it," Betty said. "I told them your hubby didn't look like the type to do anything mean to anyone."

I hugged Annie back, fighting tears at being so loved, so clearly a man of peace. "I was plenty close to doing something mean tonight. You need to get the people who did this. There're three men at a cabin just outside of town. George or Jeremy here can give you the details. They came very close to ending up dead tonight," I breathed to my wife, my kids. That got me another strong hug.

"Betty," George said, "You might want to let your boss know that those three cruds are very much in need of collecting. Course, if you don't want to disturb his sleep, you could call the FBI in Portland instead. I'm sure they'd love to charge out here and do the honors themselves."

"Grant would have my head on a platter if I did any such thing," she said, reaching for her phone and dialing. "Grant, boy," she said a moment later, "guess who's in our office?" There was a pause. "Yes, Grant, I know what time it is. Okay, Grant," she said, letting a truly evil grin take possession of her face. "You just go back to sleep, and I'll call the FBI to come and pick up the kidnappers in our jurisdiction." We could hear the expletives shoot from the phone line from where we stood.

Betty was beaming from ear to ear.

"Now is that any way to talk to a lady?" she said. "And in front of Mrs. Taylor, who's been through so much, and her husband, who rescued her." More noise from the phone. If possible, her grin got bigger.

"Yeah, boss, that Mrs. Taylor. Didn't I tell you her husband wouldn't hurt her no way, no how?"

Betty held the phone at arm's length, then stuck her tongue out at it. "He hung up on me. I don't know why I work for that man," she said, but she was speed-dialing another number on her phone. "George, you be a good boy and run down to the Safeway and see if they got any donuts cooked yet." Betty spoke into the phone, "Ah, yes, Judge Randall, it looks like we're gonna need a warrant right now…"

While she talked, Jeremy was already making himself right at home, putting on a new pot of coffee to add to the half-empty one on the top burner. I suspected Lincoln City's finest would need the caffeine this morning.

While the official folk and locals rushed around on their errands, I settled my family in a circle in the middle of the waiting room. We held hands, all together at last. Then we bowed our heads to pray.

"Dear God, we thank You for our deliverance from this captivity, like the Children of Israel of old." Never before had I been so happy to offer a prayer of thanksgiving. Andy followed me in thanking God, and Joy after him. It was Annie who finished, bringing us all back to tears.

"Dear God, I never thought to see my husband and children again. I called on You for strength to survive my ordeal. Now I want to thank You for giving my family back to me, and me back to them. I know it's not possible, oh Lord, but if You could somehow make it so, I never want to leave them for a moment again. Not even a second."

And then we let our tears and hugs be our prayers, saying in our outpouring of emotion things we could never hope to find words for.

We looked up when the sheriff charged into his office. "You the Taylor woman?" he demanded of Annie.

"She's the Taylor woman," Betty said, handing him a picture off the Internet that looked a whole lot better than Annie looked at the moment.

"Yes, I'm Mrs. Ann Taylor," my wife said.

"And you the husband?"

"Yes," I said. "And these are our kids."

He whistled. "What happened to me asking the questions first and people answering them then?"

"Well, boss, these folks are clearly self-starters. They did kind of like rescue themselves, now, didn't they?" Betty pointed out the obvious.

He shook his head. "Kidnapped people are not supposed to come walking into my office uninvited and at all hours of the night," he said, catching some of Betty's attitude.

"I'm not going back," Annie said. She frowned at me. "Even though I think I could sneak back in without them missing me."

"Over my dead body," I said. At this hour of the morning, my sense of humor could only stretch so far.

"Can't agree with you more," the sheriff said.

At that point, George arrived with fresh donuts, followed by two deputies to eat them.

"Where's Ches?" the sheriff asked.

"Visiting his sick mom," Betty supplied. "It looks like all you got is those three...and me." She brightened at the prospect.

"George, you good for anything besides Christmas presents?" the sheriff asked.

"He went in beside me," I said.

"What about that shifty-eyed stranger?" the sheriff went on, looking Jeremy's way.

"They ain't shifty eyes," George protested. "He's just having trouble keeping them eyes open."

Jeremy threw a wadded-up coffee envelope at him.

"What I'm getting at," the sheriff said to stop this incipient riot, "is are either of you two interested in wearing a badge for a short spell?"

"Thought you'd never ask," George said.

"Will you need me and my wife to go back with you?" I asked as George and Jeremy stepped forward to volunteer for another trip up that valley.

"Afraid you two are going to have to sit this part out. Something about tainting the scene of the crime or some other stuff they're teaching kids in cop school these days. Not that you haven't done your share of that already. If I was one of those FBI pukes, it'd probably bother me some, but I have better sense than that. You don't mind, do you?"

"Not at all. But there's one of them, Oz," Annie said. "Short, pudgy fellow. The one you'll find asleep upstairs cuddled up next to his game system. He was kind to me when he didn't have to be. He protected me from the others. I'd hate to see bad returned for his good."

"Good?" the sheriff asked, his eyebrow raised.

"Well, he wasn't as bad as he could have been. And he didn't let the others be as bad as they might have been," my wife finished.

"Can't make no promises, ma'am. But if they ain't no more trouble than they were when you walked out, I suspect I'll have them all back here real soon.

And the posse headed out.

Three hours later I listened in as the sheriff called to announce that the situation was taken care of. He cleared Betty to phone higher authorities. Like the FBI. That woman did enjoy making that call.

An hour later the local posse was back, with all three kidnappers in handcuffs. The tall and the short one they led in, right past Annie. I wondered what they would say to her. They didn't look at her. She might as well not have been there.

The short one, Oz, came last, Jeremy and George holding his elbows. He spotted Annie immediately, and a smile crossed his face. "I'm so glad you're all right, ma'am. I was so scared when I woke up and you weren't there. Then these two guys told me you was safe, and I figured everything was going to be all right for you."

"Oz, why do you follow those two? They're nothing but trouble. And they've led you so wrong," Annie said.

"They're my buddies. Who else could I hang with?"

"Jesus would love to hang with you, Oz. He'd never lead you into trouble. And He'd love you like you've never been loved."

Oz looked after his friends, then at Annie. "Can I have my Barracuda back?"

"I doubt it," George said. "It's evidence now."

"But I can get you something to read, if you don't mind reading the Bible," Jeremy said.

"I never read that book. I guess if I don't have my game, I might as well read it."

"And I'll drop by to see you, see how things are going. Maybe we can talk," Jeremy said.

"That would be nice," Oz muttered.

And Annie and I sent our prayers with Oz as he went to be booked and locked up and, God willing, to find a book more worthy of his time than wicked friends and video games.


Three hours later the FBI rolled into town at the lead of a long caravan of cars with whirling lights on top. Special Agent-in-Charge Brent Sanders was first in the sheriff's office, issuing orders and being ignored.

Jennifer Hunter was not far behind him, but while he and several other federal, state, and local officers debated their jurisdictions and prerogatives, Hunter quickly came to stand with my family.

"Mrs. Taylor, I am so happy to see you safe and surrounded by your loved ones."

"Not nearly as happy as I am to *be* safe and surrounded by them," Annie said.

"Do you know why you were kidnapped?"

Annie just shook her head. "I have no idea why. I heard them often enough say that the guy in charge wanted me out of circulation, but never why." Annie paused. "I overheard enough to know that their absent leader went by the name of Bill. There's a Bill Parton at my new office who wasn't too happy about my promotion, but it's a bit much to leap to any conclusions about who Bill is right now..." Her voice trailed off.

"We'll keep that bit of information in mind." Agent Hunter nodded slowly, as if it meshed with something she already knew. "Mrs. Taylor, you look in need of a bath, a hairbrush, and some fresh clothes."

"Oh yes," my wife said, but she eyed the agent as if she suspected an ulterior motive.

"The news folks aren't far behind us. If you looked relatively fresh and cared for, and said that you had no idea why you had been taken, it might have some interesting repercussions."

"This Sanders's idea?" I asked.

"No, this is one of my own," she said.

"What do you think, Benjamin?"

"Love, yesterday wasn't the first time I wanted to take a rifle to a bunch of people. But even when I had strong doubts that the FBI was on our side, I was pretty sure Agent Hunter was with us. You want me to buy you some clothes? There's an outlet mall just down the road a ways. I imagine we can get what we need there once they open up."

"Not necessary. I brought shampoo and soap," Hunter said. "And a spare clean shirt, just in case. I'm sure there's someplace for a woman to get cleaned up around here."

So an hour later, when the news crews did roll into town to interview—separately—all the police agencies involved in this arrest, Annie looked very much like the professional woman she was, not the victim she'd been for the past few days.

She fielded the questions posed to her a whole lot better than most of the people I've watched on the evening news, but then I've always known that she was something special. I watched her as she looked straight at the camera, batted her long eyelashes, and said, "No, I have no idea why I was kidnapped. The three men who held me said their boss wanted me out of the way, but they never dropped any hint as to why."

Hunter smiled at that, satisfied. Me, I wondered what kind of trap we'd set, and who'd be caught in it.

The reporters asked the usual inane questions of Annie. Some of them turned their attention on me. I did my best to give the usual answers. Of course I was glad to have Annie safe and home again. What was I supposed to say to a question like that? I guess I shouldn't blame the media all that much. They were conditioned to view law enforcement as the big heroes. While the various police agencies talked about how they'd apprehended the kidnappers, none of them ever got around to mentioning that the kidnapped hadn't been with her kidnappers.

I just smiled and kept quiet. I could imagine how the news folk would love telling a story of a husband who tiptoed into the den of thugs and spirited away his bride without so much as interrupting the beauty snores of said thugs. *People* magazine, the *Today* show, *Oprah*. Nope, I wouldn't say a word.

And if my staying quiet would make sure that Annie and I were out of whatever game the people were playing here, I was all for it. *We were finished and done with this chapter of our lives, thank you very much.*

*Right, Lord? Please!*

## 27

THE THING ABOUT GETTING BACK TO NORMAL AFTER A MAJOR
disaster is, well, it takes an effort. Once the bright lights are cut off,
and the reporters have raced out to meet their deadlines, and the
cops are busy filing their reports, the subjects of all that pain and
anguish are left alone to pick up the pieces of their lives. I've never
read a book about what you do next. Someone really should write
it. Maybe Amazon could even guarantee speedy delivery to the
folks who really, *really* need it.

*Dear God, an angel delivery service would make You a mint in
that niche market. You listening?*

I guess that didn't qualify as a prayer.

I rounded up my herd and got them moving for the car, then
offered Jeremy a ride back to Portland.

"Think I'll pass, though I'll trouble you for my trading goods
in your trunk. Trudy's coming down to pick up George. I think I'll
hang with him for a while. I'm none too sure, and I gave up on the
good Lord delivering miracles by my schedule a long time ago, but
I noticed that George ain't invited God out of his life in the last

couple of hours. Usually, he feels the need to remind God on an hourly basis, the Almighty being so forgetful, you know. Anyway, maybe the Holy Spirit finally planted a seed there He might want me to water. It would be a nice outcome for all this.

"And I did promise to look in on Oz. See what God does in his life. Anyway, I'd enjoy a ride with George back to Portland, no matter what the Lord intends from it." Then he grinned. "Besides, you and your family don't need an extra set of ears in the car. I imagine you got plenty to say to each other. You take care of them, you hear?"

"God willing, that's all I intend to do for the rest of my life. And I'll thank you and Jeremy for what you've done for us for the rest of my life."

But the drive back wasn't exactly what I'd expected. The kids shanghaied their mom into the backseat and seemed content just to rest against her, making sure she was real, not some apparition that might vanish if they lost touch with her for a split second. Andy didn't make a single try to get the car keys from me, so I drove the whole way, my eyes on the road...and the rearview mirror aimed not at the traffic behind me but at my smiling family.

I was a lucky man.

It had been a long day and night and morning. Once we got back to the hotel, it seemed all I wanted to do was sleep. Annie, too. I told Andy to use the spare bed in Joy's room, and neither of them objected. But sometime that evening when I roused myself for a moment, I noticed that Joy was sleeping under the covers of the bed next to us.

And Andy had dragged his blanket in from the next room and was sleeping on top of the covers of that bed. I settled back in, close to Annie's back, my arm over her shoulder. She roused enough to pull my arm close to her breast but slept on.

I sighed softly. My whole family was here, safe and sound. *Thank you, oh Lord. I will give You thanks forever for Your wonderful gifts.*

Morning came slow and easy. I awoke before the rest of my kin and just lay there, watching Annie breath and marveling at the miracle of her. She finally came awake with a smile for me.

With that morning gift, I slipped next door into Joy's bathroom to shower and shave. Annie joined me in the shower and begged me to help scrub her down. "I feel so dirty. I want all of that dirt off me. All of it."

As I did, I gained a new understanding for the early Christians' use of water in baptism. Bathing truly did help wash away your past. I did my best to help Annie do the same, even while I was wondering just what she was trying to forget.

But I said nothing.

Bathed and dressed, we were ready to face the day. Or at least do something to quiet the rumblings in our stomachs. The kids still looked to be asleep.

Looked that way...

After the way they played me the day they slipped into the car trunk—what was that—only day before yesterday? But today I wasn't going off on any knight errant quest. Just to breakfast.

I left a note saying we'd be at the restaurant across the way, and we slipped out.

Annie took one look at the menu and muttered, "I want one of everything."

"Was it that bad?" I said, offering her an opening.

"I'm starving. Those guys could not cook. Not at all. Even when they microwaved a TV dinner or pizza, it was a disaster. They got them too hot or too cold. I couldn't understand it. I'm sure they didn't like their own food. All they had to do was read the instructions."

I prayed that was the worst they did to my wife was to feed her poorly.

Annie looked across the table at me and seemed to read my mind. She reached for my hands, and I surrendered them to her, steeling my heart for whatever she said next.

"And apart from scaring me half to death and keeping me tied up and far away from the people I loved, they didn't do anything to me, Benjamin. I think there was one time when it could have gotten worse, but that game-addict Oz blocked the door for me. Thank God for Oz and his addiction and for Andy talking my ears off about his game." She paused, her eyes getting distant. "Who would have ever thought that my son being hooked on those computer games would save me?" She chuckled softly. "I've got to get him a Barracuda Vn game system just as soon as I can."

"Legal or illegal?" I asked.

"Whatever it takes," she said. "As long as I get it fast."

I started to pull my hands back, but Annie held on to them as if her life depended on them. "Benjamin, I'm ready to go home. Go home, stay home. Quit my job if you want me to. Tell me what you want, and I will do it for you, 'until death do us part.'"

I turned my wife's hands over in mine, then caressed her palms with my fingers. She shivered at the touch. There, I was reclaiming more of her.

"Just before we found out you'd been taken, I took the kids to Belgato's for pizza, and we talked about how much we missed you and how being separated just wasn't working for any of us."

Annie nodded along with my words.

"We agreed that waiting to move until summer break wasn't really that important. I was about to call you and tell you to get the moving company headed our way"—Annie's eyes were wide in surprise—"when the FBI called to ask if we knew where you were."

"You were ready to move out here!"

"Yep."

"Oh, my...," my wife muttered and looked away. "Didn't O. Henry write a story about that? Two people who loved each other very much wanting to give each other the perfect present?"

"I think so. I don't remember the name of it. I bet Joy would."

Annie nodded happily. "She would. Or Andy."

My wife smiled easily at me. "So, what do we do?"

I took a deep breath. "I don't think God wants us to crawl into a hole and cover it up behind us. That doesn't sound like life and life to the full to me."

Annie nodded.

"I've also been struck about how much of my life lately is just a rerun of the last year or the year before. Before that phone call came, I was pretty sure that it was time for me to open myself to something new from the Lord."

"Like rescuing your wife?"

"That wasn't what I was thinking, but I guess that's what I ended up doing."

"Have I thanked you for that? In the last five minutes, I mean?"

"You're very welcome. Anytime," I said.

"Dear God, please, never again."

"Amen," I said heartily.

"But what would you do out here?" Now my wife flipped my hands over and played her fingers on my palms. Most of her long fingernails were broken off cruelly short. The bandages on her wrists were hidden under her sleeves. Just a few short hours ago she was in mortal peril. Still, I trembled at how good she made me feel.

"You might think I wasn't noticing just how much trouble you were having job-hunting," Annie went on, "but I was. I just didn't know what to do about it. I wanted this promotion. I wanted you here. It just didn't look like a good match for you, and I didn't want to see that, God forgive me."

"Maybe I was just insisting on looking for too much of the same old same old."

That got a puzzled look from Annie.

I went on. "I like teaching Sunday school, don't I?" Annie nodded. "I enjoy teaching pay administration to the supervisors who do the wage survey. I'm regularly getting up in front of the plant foremen and teaching them about this new law or that way of handling a problem, am I not?"

"You are. I've said you ought to be a teacher," Annie said, her eyes lighting up.

"There're a lot of colleges in the Portland and Salem area. I could get a PhD to go with my MBA and teach business. I bet you I'd be good at it."

"I'm not going to bet against you."

"Of course, you'd have to pay all the bills while I'm a college student."

"Déjà vu, huh? I can see you surrounded by all those pretty girls," Annie sighed. "But then you didn't complain while I was a college student surrounded by all the hunky young men."

"Just part of the risk we take when we love someone enough to let them grow," I said.

"And I've been growing while I was asking you to stand still. Except for running out and rescuing a fair damsel in distress. That was a rifle you had slung over your manly chest when you cut me free, wasn't it?"

"You know me—I like to be prepared. Even though I know how you feel about guns. I didn't feel like I could walk in there and say, 'Please, let my wife go.' It turned out, I could have."

Annie sighed. "I can't tell you how glad I was to see those rifles on you and your friends. Maybe I've got to do some growing too."

I frowned. But not at Annie. Joy and Andy had just rushed into the place. While Joy trotted toward us, Andy was talking to the receptionist. Like most restaurants, this one had a bank of televisions on so people could watch sports, news, whatever. Like in most places I eat, I'd been ignoring the sets.

Joy reached our table and stammered, "M-Mom, Dad, you need to see this. Agent Hunter asked me to get you to watch. It's about drugs and…"

The set nearest us switched channels. "We are still waiting for the police to identify the headless body pulled from the Willamette this morning," a female reporter said into her handheld microphone. "There are early reports that this death may be drug or gang related. If it is, it's a new and ugly escalation of the battle between gangs struggling for control of the drug market here in Portland. We expect to have more in the next fifteen minutes, but now back to you in the studio."

The camera panned to a body lying beside the river. Now it was covered by a tarp, but there was no disguising that it was a head shorter than a body ought to be.

"Ewww, that's nothing to watch while eating breakfast," some customer said. "Change that channel."

Andy shrugged my way. I waved at him, and he said something to the woman beside him. The channel did change.

"Do you think that's about, you know, all those people in the FBI office who were working with those looking for Mom?" Joy asked. "That drug task force."

"Yes." I sighed. "I think Agent Hunter went fishing and now it looks to me like she caught something."

"Jennifer wouldn't kill anyone," Joy insisted. "Not unless she had to."

"No, that lovely young woman didn't kill that man," my wife said, hugging her daughter close. "But she set some things in motion based on what I said," Annie explained, then swallowed hard. "And that man got what evil men thought he deserved. 'Oh Lord, grant us not justice, for who can stand before Your justice.'"

"God rest his soul," I said about the man I strongly suspected had caused all this pain to my wife and my family. *Oh God, You will have to take care of that poor man, because I'm not sure, left on my own, that I wouldn't have done exactly what his associates did.*

Andy joined us. "Was I right to think you'd want to see that?"

"Yes, although I wish we didn't have to see it. Now I think we need to get over to the FBI office and see if they'll tell us anything more. I know they want us to come in today and help them fill in all their forms."

"You going to eat that?" Andy asked me, looking at my breakfast that had arrived during the news report. I shook my head. I was no longer hungry.

So our teenagers ate our breakfasts. Nothing, it seems, can put a teenager off his or her feed.

Later, after the check was paid, I eyed the streets of Portland as we got ready to head back to our room. "We going to walk?" Andy asked, turning for the bridge that crossed the Willamette.

I glanced around and shook my head. I wanted my clan in a big car with locking doors. Quickly we crossed the street and piled into the rental car. Annie hit the button to lock the doors even before she went for her seat belt. Maybe I wasn't the only one looking for a fortress.

I drove carefully across the bridge and turned into the underground garage at the FBI office.

"Only authorized cars," the gate guard said waving me to a stop.

I pulled out my Maryland driver's license. "I'm Ben Taylor. This is my wife, Ann Taylor. We have an appointment with Agent Hunter, and I really don't want to park on the street."

"I can understand why," the guard said, then pulled out a clipboard. "You are on my authorized list. Let me get your car license number." He did, then glanced in the back. "Who are they?"

"Breakfast bandits," I said, "but they usually go by the name of our kids. They on your list?"

"No, just you and the wife." The guard eyed our teenagers. "Let me see your hands. Any of you got a gun?"

Was he serious?

"Dad won't let us have guns," Andy said.

"Except when we go to the shooting range with Uncle Jeb," Joy added.

"Shooting range?" Annie said beside me.

"I'll explain later," I said to her. "Officer, I'm not leaving my kids outside on the street. Not after what we've been through."

"Just a second," he said and retreated back to his guardhouse to reach for a phone.

"Call Agent Jennifer Hunter," Joy called.

"So now you're on a first-name basis with that young woman," my wife purred.

"You should have seen her in that sweater," Andy put in. "Joy wants a sweater like that one."

I sighed. "You had your trials and tribulations, wife. I had mine."

"Mine weren't nearly so attractive," she said primly.

"Nor nearly so easy to run away from," I agreed.

"You're cleared," the guard said, putting an end to that conversation. Whatever happened to stories ending happily ever after? *I could sure use some happily ever after, Lord.*

A little voice inside me, not anything like the booming Jehovah you'd expect, reminded me that happily ever after was not in *His* book. At least not this side of heaven.

The guard handed me four passes for my family and pointed us toward the visitors' parking. A few minutes later the secretary at the FBI office was greeting us with a smile and, "I'm so glad to see you again, and with your wife this time."

I returned her smile, as Agent Hunter came out to meet us. She deftly separated the grownups from the not-there-yet and got the kids settled in the waiting area before maneuvering Annie and me into her office. As she closed the door she said, "I take it you have seen this morning's news."

"Yeah. Thanks to you, the kids made us watch the bit about Shortie." I said.

"Was that why you had me say what I said?" Annie blurted out.

"Be it upon my head," the agent said, holding her hands out palms up. "I was expecting something to break in the night. But even I didn't think it would be this drastic. That corpse has even me surprised," she said, taking her seat behind her desk and waving us to chairs.

I helped Annie sit, but I refused to sit down myself. "What were you expecting?" I said.

"I was hoping the perp would run to us. Turn state's evidence and sing like a nightingale. I wanted to get his bosses." She shrugged. "If he ran for us, he did so too late or too slowly."

"They cut off his head," my wife said.

"No, my love. Who cut off his head is the question we want

answered," I said. "Hunter, my wife is trying to decide if it will ever be safe for her to go back to work. For the last couple of days I've felt like a Ping-Pong ball in a game no one would tell me anything about. We're not leaving this room until we know whether we're safe or whether we're being set up again as a stalking-horse in the FBI or DEA's latest game."

Hunter locked eyes with me. I stared right back at her. I could see her weighing how much to tell us. How much would upset her boss, whether it would damage her career if she gave us everything.

*It's my wife's life.* I glared back at her. *That trumps anything you've got. And you wouldn't have anything at all if I hadn't taken the situation into my own hands.*

Finally Hunter nodded and looked at Annie. Only then did I take a chair beside my wife, take her hand in mine. "We suspect that your firm is being used by a major crime syndicate. Your co-worker Bill, now deceased, had a contract to ship heroin, hidden in your company goods, in from the Orient for the main gang in the Pacific Northwest. We also suspect he's been shorting the 'Boss,' and siphoning off parts of the shipments and passing them along to a competitor that is trying to move in here."

"Stealing from drug lords," I muttered. *What was he thinking? How long did he expect to get away with it? And when had he decided to involve my wife?* But I didn't say anything out loud. My anger toward the man might not sound so good to the FBI.

"That's Bill from my office under the tarp?" Annie said.

"Yes. We think so. Naturally, it isn't certain yet. Facial and dental identification isn't working this morning, for obvious reasons. No-body seems to have a set of his fingerprints for comparison. We're toss-ing his home, collecting prints, fiber, hairbrushes, and other things."

"And how does my wife fit into all this?"

"She doesn't. She's an innocent bystander. Except that Bill wanted the promotion she got. I suspect Triton Imports would have become Heroin-R-Us if he had gotten your job. When you arrived, word on the street is that he apparently took the opportunity to steal an entire shipment. I don't know if he figured he could con-vince his partners in crime to blame you for that or what. I'm not sure he thought this through as well as he might have. Or as well as he wished he had before his eventual fate caught up to him," she said. "One thing I am sure of—he got what was coming to him."

My wife shivered. She didn't even like it when I pointed at cows as we drove along and said, "Look at all the steaks." The thought of a slaughtered cow had always been too much for her. Now she was involved in events that had resulted in the slaughtering of a human being. Albeit as a passive victim.

Hunter folded her hands on the desk in front of her and leaned toward my wife. "Mrs. Taylor, have you ever thought of getting a permit to carry a concealed gun? They are allowed in Oregon."

"No!"

"I can help you fill out the permit request."

"You don't understand me. I will not carry a gun."

"Mrs. Taylor, you've just been kidnapped."

"And I never saw them coming. One minute I was walking,

same as any other day. Next moment, they were beside me, just like so many people are when you walk the streets. Then they shoved me into their truck and had me."

"That's how it happens," the FBI agent agreed.

"Even if I'd had a gun, I wouldn't have had time to use it unless it was in my hand and ready to shoot at that very moment. I'd have to be ready to kill all the time, living as a victim. Every minute of every day. No, Jennifer, I will not become a killer. What if some children are playing tag and one of those kids bumps into me? Should I shoot them for that?" My wife shook her head. "That is not living. I will not exist that way."

"Mr. Taylor, can't you explain things to your wife?" Hunter began.

"What things?" I asked.

Hunter looked at me. And I looked back at her. It looked like the two of us had run out of words.

"Let's try a different tack," I said. "Bill wanted to turn Triton into a one-stop heroin shopping agency. I take it the government would frown on his entrepreneurial spirit?"

"Yes," Hunter said.

"So now that Bill isn't around, what're the business prospects for Heroin-R-Us at Triton?"

"I really can't say."

"Okay, agreed, you can't say anything about that. But I'd like you to tell my wife what she needs to know about going back to work."

Hunter just looked at me.

"Or I go to the local paper and tell them how Annie really got free. Not so great a story for your side as the one playing today, maybe, but certainly a bit different from the one they heard on the news. Maybe the media will think the difference in the two versions of the story makes for quite a story."

Hunter called me a bad name.

"Oh, dear," my wife chuckled, "and here I thought you might have become his girlfriend while I was...indisposed."

Jennifer barked a laugh at that. "Him! Mrs. Taylor, I have never met any man so married to his wife as your husband is to you. He wouldn't even meet my eyes."

Annie squeezed my hand. "Nice to hear. Now, can I go to work tomorrow? Or the next day? Will I need to drive a tank or carry an arsenal?"

Hunter shook her head. "You two are quite a pair. Okay, you're not hearing this from me, but yes, I strongly suspect you can. We've intercepted two shipments in the pipeline, and the folks in Bang—uh, I didn't say that either—have picked up other people of interest. Heroin-R-Us is closed for business. We are pleased with that outcome." She paused, then smiled.

"There *is* the matter of the shipment that started this whole situation. I suspect a lot of people want to know where it is."

"Do you know?" I asked.

"Yes. But there is no reason why you should know. No reason to tell you. We will be letting a few of the city's less reputable citizens know of its whereabouts shortly. You're safer not knowing."

"I think we can agree on that," my wife said.

"So, Mrs. Taylor, are you planning on going to work tomorrow?"

"No, I'm flying home to help my family arrange their move out here. I'm also calling my boss and telling him I want a full audit of my office's books going back for two years. I'm going to advise him that the auditors he hires might want to wear sidearms. Big sidearms. Then, when Triton Imports has control of its local office back, if he wants me to run it, I'll run it. Like a good, profitable...legal...import office. Nothing that you and anyone like you or the people that you hunt would be interested in."

"And I have no doubt you will make sure of that," Agent Hunter agreed. She stood to show us the way out of her office. Meeting adjourned.

The kids immediately joined us. Agent Hunter went to talk to her boss. And my cell phone rang.

"Ben, Pastor Evans here. I see from the news that the FBI solved the problem faster than we could raise the money."

"More or less," I agreed. "Annie is back at my elbow, and I'm sorry I didn't call you sooner. I hope I didn't cause you too much trouble."

"I do God's work. If not for you, my efforts will bear fruit for someone else."

"Well, we're about to get tickets for home."

"You coming back?"

"At least long enough to pack up the house. We're moving west, all of us, to join my wife."

"Then I'll see you in church Sunday. I can't wait to hear what the Lord has done in your life."

"And we can't wait to tell you about it," I agreed.

Even as I clicked off, Andy was on his cell phone, cruising the Internet for plane tickets. "We can leave at five. It'll get us home late."

"So you can make school tomorrow," I said.

"Dad," came in two-part harmony.

"He's just kidding, children. Aren't you, Benjamin?"

"A bit. Jay at the plant wants me to cut a position out of my shop. It will be interesting to hear his reaction when I tell him he can have my job for his cutting. Real interesting."

"Benjamin," Annie said. "I think you are developing a nasty streak."

"Didn't I say something about growing, doing new things?"

"Yes, I remember something about that."

"And don't I know these really great guys who have invited all of us out to the firing range? Jeb on one coast, Jeremy on the other."

"Firing range," Annie said with a decided scowl.

"Firing range, my bride. You may not be carrying a weapon, and I haven't decided if we're going to have a weapon in that beautiful house you bought for us, but I do think you need to know how to shoot if you ever should want to."

"Me! Want to!"

"You can never tell what life and the good Lord may bring your way."

Annie sighed as she leaned against me in the elevator. "I have noticed that lately."

And so we hurried to catch a plane. It was time to find our place in the new life we would have together.

I knew, between our hard work and the good Lord's love, that we would patch together some happily ever after for us all.